Harlem on Lock

Harlem on Lock

A novel by

KAREN WILLIAMS

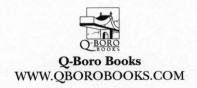

Q-Boro Books
WWW.QBOROBOOKS.COM

An Urban Entertainment Company

Published by Q-Boro Books
Copyright © 2008 by Karen Williams

ISBN-13: 978-1-933967-34-9
ISBN-10: 1-933967-34-X
LCCN: 2007923274

First Printing January 2008
Printed in the United States of America

10   9   8   7   6   5

Cover Copyright © 2006 by Q-BORO BOOKS, all rights reserved.
Cover layout/design by Candace K. Cottrell
Cover photo by Ted Mebane
Editors: Andrea Blackstone, Brian Sandy, Candace K. Cottrell

Q-BORO BOOKS
Jamaica, Queens NY 11434
WWW.QBOROBOOKS.COM

Dedication

This book is dedicated to:

My daughter for being my daily inspiration;
My sister for being there every step of the way;
My mom for just being my crazy mom;
And to **my friend Ronisha**, a true angel who always
pushed me to live—not sweat the small stuff.
Rest in peace.

Acknowledgments

Wow. This had been an incredible journey for me. A journey I don't think I would have been able to get through if I didn't believe in Him and all the blessings He had in store for me. Thanks, hugs, and kisses go out my family. My mom for showing me my book had a fighting chance by walking out of my house shaking, after I read a couple pages to her and for plain out being her crazy self. My sister for being there with me every step of the way, reading as I wrote, keep in mind, having someone like you in their life gives one a significant source of love and support. When it comes to you I can't say enough, just know that I feel extremely blessed to have a sister such as you. To my daughter, you have made this experience of being a mother so easy and joyous and I love you more than I love myself. To all my cousins and nieces, Donnie, Devin, Jabrez, Mu-Mu, Mikayla, Madison, who kept my energy up by chasing you guys around the house between breaks from writing. To my god daughter Lanaya for watching television while your god mom slaved away on her computer. Hey Amari! Hey Faye! Thanks to my uncle Noonie, aunt Tammy, my cousin Ray, Shauntae, and Michael for believing in me.

To my friends, Lenzie, now you didn't exactly help me with the story but you made me laugh when I needed to laugh and I figured if I didn't mention you I would get cursed out. Linda, I'm so glad we reconnected, Ronisha R.I.P, Sewiaa, Cheryl, Misty, Valerie Hoyt, you've helped me so much over the years, Markeiba, Valerie Sweet, Phillopo, Shannon, Brooklyn, Christina, for your third eye, Africa, Maxine, Jennifer, Barbara, Sandra, Lydia, Lexus, I always appreciated your wisdom, Kevin you're a part of the family and Vanilla, who I know your Christian ears burned when you heard about the story. Roxie and Carla, you were one of the first to read *Harlem on Lock* and give me your feedback. In fact, *Carlita*, you read all my books! Thanks for the support and I treasure our friendships. Thanks for always lending me an ear, Pearl. Hey Victor!

Special thanks to Chanin Paige, The Evans Family, Yolanda Perdomo, and the Perdomo family for helping me make my daughter everything she is today. Keith Lily, Mrs. Bonner, Adara's and my favorite teacher! Shout out to Candis, Nashawn, Ricky, and Shana, from the Westside English Crew. Hey to Leyla, Carlos, Angelina, Maggie, Anthony, and Jason, didn't forget about you guys, keep striving. Special thanks to the teens of Carmelitos Boys and Girls Club; no matter how much time goes by I'll always reserve a spot in my heart for you guys. Hey Duncan! Hey Stone!

Thanks to all my professors who inspired and pushed me, starting with Long Beach City College. Mr. Lastra, they need more people like you. Mr. Dominguez, you showed me I had something I didn't know I had. And Mr. Gaspar, you showed me how to let my voice come out, it's been out ever since. Thanks to California State University Dominguez Hills professors Mr. Brueckner, you got me writing again, Dr. Turner, you kept me optimistic, Dr. Sherman, taking your class was an experience I'll never forget, and like Dr. Feuer, you really pushed me to give all I could and I still do. Dr. Becker, Dr. Oesterd, you both inspired me to write with passion and expression. And of course my favorite high school literature teacher, Mr. Conard.

Thanks to the staff of Oakwood Academy. Special thanks to Ms. Antoinette and Ms. Green for believing this day would come.

Tremendous thanks to the "veteran and new staff" of GSHU at Los Padrinos Juvenile Hall. Your encouragement and support is greatly appreciated!

Thanks to authors Victoria Christopher Murray, Mary Monroe, and Darlene Johnson, for all your help.

Thanks Fara Kearnes for your help and insight. You went far and beyond what an editor does and I appreciate everything you did for *Harlem On Lock*!

A million thanks to Candace Cottrell and Mark Anthony for believing in my vision. You gave me my start. I cannot say thanks enough; just know I strived to give you the absolute best writing that I could!

Thanks to Andrea Blackstone.

Thanks to the writers and artists that have inspired me over time, Jack Gilbert, James Baldwin, Darnella Ford, Pablo Neruda, Scotney St. James, Linda Lael Miller, Eric Jerome Dickey, Diane Mckinney-Whetstone, Mary Monroe, Jay'Z, and Tupac.

To Terrock, I love you. I believe in you. Thanks for being proud of me, loving me, making me feel like I'm important to you, listening to me whine and hugging me when I needed to be hugged.

Thanks to anyone else I didn't mention who supported me. Charge it to my mind not my heart.

In the words of Tupac: "If you believe, you can achieve just look at me."

Prologue

I was tasting my own blood. It was dripping from my lip, my right cheek, and the gash on my head where he had fucked me up. But the worst wasn't over. My life was ending tonight. He had convinced me of it, after yelling it each time he attacked me. As piss ran down my legs, I was hoping God would be merciful and not let me shit myself. But then God hadn't been too merciful to me. Otherwise, why would I be in this fucked-up situation?

"Bitch, you got the muthafuckin' game twisted," Chief said.

He punched me in my stomach, and I slid to the ground. All of his crew stood around and watched, some laughing at me getting my ass kicked, others shaking their heads in shame.

"Before the night is over I'm gonna kill you, Harlem. And you can yell as loud as you want to. Ain't no cops going to come save you. They on my payroll. And even if they wasn't, they wouldn't give a fuck about a ho from the projects who's kin to two dope fiends anyway. So if I wanna cut your slutty ass up in little pieces, I will. Or if I choose to set your ass on fire, bitch, I can."

I believed every word he said. I scooted as close as possible to the corner by the bar. I was so scared, I couldn't stop pissing myself nor stop my teeth from chattering.

Chapter 1

Now before I start venting, let me tell you who I am. My name is Harlem. And I'll bet you're wondering if I'm from New York. Well, sort of. I mean I was born there, but I couldn't begin to tell you shit about the town. The only damn thing I knew about New York was what I'd learned watching TV. I knew Jay-Z and Notorious B.I.G. were from New York. I'd heard they made the best pizza there, and that niggas and females from New York sometimes carried razors in their mouths. Yep, that's about all I knew about the NY.

My mama Aja pushed me out, and three days later her and my daddy, Earl, hopped in their hooptie and set out for "killa Cali." And I knew she missed Harlem—the life, the club. She longed for it; it was in her eyes.

When I was little she would sit me on the beat-up couch, get dressed in one of her old get-ups, and sing for me. Hell, by the time I was six I knew all the songs of Billie Holiday, Ella Fitzgerald, and Nina Simone by heart and would sing right alongside her.

See, her leaving was all part of the plan, my mama's plan, that is. She wanted to do right by me and be the best mother she could be. I guess she figured if she removed herself from the environment she could get rid of her drug habit. And I'm not talking about Tylenol, Mylanta, or Orajel. I'm talking about that heavy shit—"smack"— the shit that talked to you, pleaded with you, could bring you up, bring you down, could make you shit, could make you come. It had its claws in my parents, especially my mama, and I ask myself time and time again, How did she get there?

Now, if you thought Beyoncé was fine, I wish you could have seen my mama back in the day. She had that exotic look that drove men wild—mahogany skin in the purest form, oval-shaped face, high cheekbones, chinky eyes, and long curly hair that hung down to her round ass. Delicate features. Not only did she have the ass and hips, she had big ol' titties, fat, juicy legs, and a high, small waist. My mama was a bad bitch, and she could get anything she wanted out of a man. My daddy used to say she stopped all movements even on her worst day,

I found out many things I never knew about my mama's life. A jazz singer before she had me, she used to work in a bar called Aces, a spot for high rollers. For starters the so-called club really was a cover for some big-time dope slingers. While drinks were served, people shot pool, danced, and listened to the entertainment, in the back room, which they called the "chop shop," they manufactured pure heroin. Still, when the dealers were done handling their business, they rolled up joints, got their drank on, and let my mother's sultry voice unwind them. And they let their eyes be blessed with the sight of her beauty. For the runners—Stuckey, Chisom, and Ramsey—Mama was like a little sister, and they kept her out of the chop shop. But my mama was a free spirit, a wild child who threw caution to the damn wind for a night of fun.

And so that's what heroin was to her—a night of fun one day after the club closed. A friend had introduced it to her like you would a family member or a friend. Only it wasn't like, "Hi, this is my friend, Heroin" but more like "Man, you got to try this shit. It will give you a triple orgasm."

But, hell, that night just never ended for mama. And after she became one of Stuckey's, Chisom's, and Ramsey's biggest customers, all they could do was shake their heads and say, "Damn, Aja on that shit too? What a fucking waste. She's too talented, too fine, too sexy, too smart, and got too much potential to be doing that."

And she knew it too, what they were thinking. Soon she was too gone, too hooked, to ever come back. So she never did. It was never part of the plan. So I came to understand.

Mama had her choice of men, but she chose my daddy. Crazy part was, he was no high roller. My daddy was an auto mechanic and she was hoping that he could save her. Only, she got him caught up in the shit. She said it was his mysterious, seductive eyes, the same eyes attached to my face. The rest, I'm told, came straight from my Mama, as I am the spitting image of her, except while her hair was jet black, mine is a combination of browns. I have my daddy's full lips, a beauty mark in the corner of my mouth, and my skin is a copper-brown complexion.

They settled outside of Los Angeles, the city of low riders, Chucks, and Roscoe's House of Chicken 'n Waffles, but not the nice part. We stayed in the projects, a place I hated. We lived there since I was a baby but didn't nothing about the projects make me feel at home or that we had a better life. I always felt separate from the rest of LA, being in the projects, which was a closed-in community of violence and despair.

The place to be was Baldwin Hills, the black Beverly Hills, where wealthy black people lived in these big-ass houses that sat high up on the hills. In the projects you could live up high too, but it wasn't on no damn hill.

The apartments were so close to each other you could hear your neighbor's TV and radio through the paper-thin walls, or you knew when they were taking a shower or even a shit. In fact every Thursday I knew my neighbor Tiny got some, 'cause her headboard beat up against my wall and their screaming and moaning kept me up the whole damn night.

You shared the same yard with your neighbor and belonged to a building with six little apartments, and twelve feet away was another identical building with six more apartments. You either had to hear people stomping upstairs, or somebody was complaining 'cause you were stomping. There was a road dividing one side of the buildings from the other and a big-ass tree to every building. On a nightly basis you would see teen boys and even grown-ass men sneaking up trees, hiding from the cops. Sometimes they'd fall and bust their ass and get caught.

They did have parks for the kids, but other shit beside little kids playing went down there. People my age smoked weed there, drug dealers slanged their shit there, and dopeys found corners and bathrooms to get high in, despite the kids playing on the swings, in the sand, or on see-saws. If you were poor, which we all were, you were pretty much confined to going to the park or sitting on your stoop to entertain yourself. Most of the time I hung out on my stoop. You saw all kinds of shit there, weekly shootouts that had me running for dear life in my house, fights among the different type of gangs that wanted to run the projects, or you would see "chicken heads," young and old, out in the streets, the park, their small yard, or other people's yard fighting over a damn man. Sometimes you even saw mother and daughter fighting over a man. It was a damn shame.

When I needed an escape from the projects, I hooked up with one of my friends from school and saw how other people lived. They'd scoop me in their ride, and we'd hang out on Crenshaw, which was the spot, or Broadway. Teens and grown folks kicked it there. You just parked your car and sat in it, or stood on the street mingling with people. They had car shows, where you saw fly-ass low riders, Impalas, or Caprices, on chromed-out twenty-twos. The motorcycle clubs even came out to stunt. I had fun hanging there 'cause I didn't need no damn money.

Or we went to Baldwin Hills Plaza, or the Slauson Swap Meet, or Magic Johnson Theatre to watch movies. Most of the time I passed, when it came to hanging out at places like these, because you needed money. While my friends were buying clothes and shit, I didn't even have enough to buy me some damn French fries, so I'd sometimes take my bus fare and just ride the bus as far as it would take me before I had to get off. The bus always passed Baldwin Hills. I always wondered what it felt like to live in one of those big-ass houses with the manicured lawns and roll in the Escalade or Lexus parked out front. But after the bus ride it was back to the fucking projects.

As bad as it was, I knew why my mama and daddy came here. They came out here hoping California would give their cravings the relief they needed. It didn't. The projects was just a different place with the same old shit—addiction, sobriety, relapses, anger, frustration, fights, tears, blood—but that was our life.

Chapter 2

I don't know how it got this bad.

I sighed loudly as I watched my mama walking up and down the ho stroll located down the street from our house, or shall I say shack, 'cause that's what the fuck we lived in. It was just me and my parents, but we had visitors who didn't take their ass home—roaches. And I ain't talking about them baby ones. I'm talking about the muthafuckas that could fly and bite the shit out of you. Them bastards were so slick. If they caught you looking at them, they ass would play dead. Not to mention the fucking rats that would give birth in the cabinets and drawers. Shit, you open one up to get a spoon or a shirt and you see the little babies with their eyes closed and crying in a squeaky-ass voice, thinking I was gonna pick they ass up. Hell no. If it's one thang I can't stand it's a fucking rat. I don't care if it's a possum, hamster, squirrel, ferret, mouse, gerbil, or guinea pig. If you had whiskers and a pointed-ass nose, then you best stay the fuck away from me. And both of them took up unlimited residency in our home among the water bugs and "daddy long leg" spiders. In the fall the rats and mice would bite through the wood in the walls, trying to ease their way into our house. They also loved to drink water out of the toilet. I always had the end of the broomstick ready to beat they ass.

We had a beat-up old couch. Our carpet was damn near black and run-down. Mama was no Martha Stewart and never made an attempt to clean it. And our walls had so many bullet holes and cracks in them, they made a pattern. Because the gas was turned off, we didn't have hot water, so I took cold showers and baths. At first it was hard as hell to get used to. I was always catching a cold or flu, but after a while my body adjusted to the temperature and cold water and hot water felt no different to me.

I usually cooked the little food we had on the electric skillet. It was the one thing besides the couch, refrigerator, and my mom's wedding ring we had left. The TV and stereo were long gone. My only entertainment was my homework, library books, my cheap little Walkman, and my thumbs that I twiddled when I got bored with my other limited fucking options.

In my room was a blow-up mattress that I slept on, and the blankets were so old, they were almost as thin as the sheets. I had nothing on my walls except sketches and various art work like plaster and metal frames, and papermache that I had made in art class at school and whatnot.

It wasn't the best living. Some would call it a horrible living, but it was the best my parents could do for being what they were. Junkies. And junkie or no junkie, they were my parents and they loved me. It's just that they had a problem, plain and simple, like anybody else. So who was I to beat them up? After all, I was their child, their flesh and blood. And things could've been worse. They could have thrown me in a dumpster, like some of the other dumb-ass people do to their kids, or I could've been in the system. But at least I had a roof over my head. And, hell, something, no matter how small, was better than nothing.

The block was small. On one side was the slingers, which consisted of the little hoppers, runners, lookouts, and the leader. They all worked together to make sure they got the money from the junkies, the junkies got their product, and that all of this was done without the leader touching any of the money or the product, and no cops seeing a damn thing. The action was always quick. First, the "hoppas" got the money from the "cluckheads," the runners passed the dope to them, and the lookouts made sure there were no cops coming. The leader watched the whole thing, making sure the shit went smoothly.

Then farther down the street the hoes paced the stroll for men. The traffic in this area was crazy as fuck from all the nasty-ass men that came from the east to get some cheap pussy from the hoes, half of whom would trot right up the block to get dope from the slingers with the money they just got from selling their pussy. And my mama was there, wearing some hot pink stretch pants, a faded red top with a hole in the front, along with some dirty, busted flip-flops, and a flimsy scarf covering her uncombed hair. And I knew my ass should have been embarrassed—any other teenager would have been—but I didn't give a damn. Shit, this was my mama, and I loved her. Her pain was my pain.

I know it killed my mama to have to lower herself to this, to go from having men flock to you to throwing your pussy at them for a few dollars that seemed to never be enough 'cause fifteen minutes later you back on the track, to needing something so bad you'd die to get it 'cause no matter how much of it you got in your system it never stopped calling you. I could never understand her addiction. I always wondered why and how it got my mama, but I was too scared to ask her.

The first time I caught her on the track I was ten. Back then cars flocked to her. At first I thought she was just taking rides from strangers, but eventually I learned it was more than that. I overheard my neighbor Netty, who had a son a little older than me named Bo Bo, say to the neighbor across from her, not giving a damn that I was on my stoop all up in their mouth, "You know Aja around the corner out there on that track now, girl. It's bad enough that pretty woman putting poison in her body, but now she having sex with them dirty, disgusting men."

I ran down the street and out of the projects, and sure enough I saw her. She was wearing a sexy dress and hopping into a long black Cadillac. My eyes scanned the driver, a fat, greasy-looking, white man.

"Mama!" I shouted.

She froze, and her eyes passed over me. Her face flushed instantly. "Harlem, go home!" she said.

"Mama, where you going?"

But she didn't answer. She just slid in the car and slammed the door, and they drove away.

We never discussed it, what my mama was doing in that man's car.

That night she just came in my room and curled up on my mattress with me. "Mama won't leave again," she said.

And, yeah, over the years Mama promised me she would stop, but hell I'm seventeen now, and if she ain't stopped yet, she never would.

Poor thang. Time had passed, and so had her looks. She was no longer the beauty queen that she used to be when she was in Aces. She practically chased cars down, but none of them stopped for her ass. And I couldn't blame them. Yeah, I loved my mom, but if I was the ugliest man on the fucking earth I wouldn't fuck my mama for free. That "dope overtime" had murdered her looks. She was gone, and she looked bad. But I would never tell her that though. It would hurt her feelings.

Mama slapped her beat-up purse against the fifth car that sped past her and stopped at another hoe.

I ran up to her and grabbed her thin arm before she could raise it to hit another car. "Mama, what in the world are you doing out here? Where's Daddy?"

"Oh Lord!" She gripped my face in both of her hands. "Harlem, they got Earl, baby. You know they always fuckin' with him. There's no telling how long they going to keep him in that hellhole."

I made sure my mama didn't see me roll my eyes. Daddy was always getting locked up for trying to find illegal means to feed the ugly-ass drug habit that both of them had. He was known around the projects for jacking people. It was ridiculous how many times he got his ass whipped for doing that, but he never stopped.

"Mama, don't worry. You know they'll probably release him tomorrow, and if not, they probably won't keep him no more than a week."

Cops didn't give a damn about no dopey. There were too many of them running around for them to continue to detain them. And whether you detained them for a week or a year, the minute they got out, they were going right back to the block to buy drugs to get high.

Her hands dropped from my face, and her eyes started to water. "Why the hell did he have to take his ass out and get into some more shit?" she asked, her back to me. She turned around and faced me with a desperate look in her eyes. "Harlem, baby, you know I can't wait that long."

I stared down at the concrete. When I looked up at my mother again, she was coughing and holding her belly. Then her hands was acting like they had a mind of their own. Like she was covered in flea bites, Mama kept on scratching all over her body, making my ass itch too. I knew her withdrawal was kicking in. I started getting flashbacks of the last time this happened. Then she was throwing up and shit, pissing on herself like a baby, shivering like her body temperature had dropped, and constantly screaming.

Her voice interrupted my thoughts. "Just your hands, baby. You know that's all you need. And I promise you, baby, this will be the last time. Last time, Harlem, I promise."

I placed my hand around her shoulders and mumbled, "Come on, Mama, you know I got you."

We walked back to our house. Even though she promised this would be the last time, in the back of my mind I didn't believe her.

Once I escorted my mama to the house, I told her to lie down till I got back. I pulled my loose tee-shirt in a firm grip and tied it behind my back in a knot so it showed the shapeliness of my 30C cup breasts and my taut stomach. I pulled the rubber band out of my hair so it fell loose and cascaded down my back. I fluffed it out a little. I then took a deep breath and walked to the Property Manager's office. Once there, I knocked on the door softly and was told I could come in.

I turned the doorknob and stepped inside the office. I stood in the center of his office on his Persian rug.

"Hello, Harlem." His eyes snaked down the length of my body and froze at my breasts.

My eyes scanned the office. I did this every time I stepped foot inside, telling myself it would be the last time and mama would just have to deal with it, but I always came back. Although the projects were run-down, his office wasn't. I looked at the shine in the cherry-wood walls before my eyes passed over his degree and certificates, his employee-of-the-month plaque. A big picture of African queens and kings always had my attention. The framed photos on his desk were of a lady that sure as hell wasn't his woman. She was far too cute to piss on Mr. Barry if his monkey ass was on fire, so I know it to be a damn lie.

Front all you want, homie. Your ass is not fooling me.

Now I'm not saying Mr. Barry didn't have no woman, but the bitch was probably as butt-fucking ugly as he was. Maybe even worse. There was also a picture of his mother, who looked just as fucked up as him. Yeah, Mr. Barry didn't have a chance. And he had an 8 X 10 photo of the damn dog too sitting with his tongue slobbering, like he was his damn twin, to complete his little family.

I inhaled, and as usual, the room smelled like cinnamon potpourri, which was strange for a man. But, hell, he wasn't considered a man to most. Most considered him to be a chump. I agreed, but to me he was a dirty one. Supposedly a Christian, he was always playing gospel music. Shit, I wondered if the members of the congregation knew of this nigga's extracurricular activities, getting off on young girls and slanging "yay" on the side.

I forced myself to stare at his ugly-ass face, hiding my disgust. A short, pudgy muthafucka, his teeth were as yellow as the sun and bigger than Mr. Ed's. In fact, you could see their imprint in his cheeks before he even opened his mouth. They were so fucking big, it looked like he was always smiling. But that wasn't the worse thing about him. On the right side of his neck, the nigga had a lump the size of an apple, like someone shot him with a harpoon. And on top of all of this, the nigga had one regular arm and one stump.

I bit my bottom lip. "Hi, Mr. Barry. How you doing?"

He leaned back in his chair. "Good. What can I do for you today, Harlem?"

I forced a smile to my lips then leaned over in his face and whispered, "I need a couple caps."

He arched his right brow then nodded at me.

I watched him rise from behind his desk, his belly bumping into the edge. He walked briskly to his windows, closed the blinds, then locked his office door. He walked over to me and smacked my ass with his good hand, chuckling when it jiggled.

I bit the inside of my mouth to ward off any smart comment about this sleazy pervert touching me.

He relaxed back on his couch across from me. "Get undressed, Harlem."

As I pulled my shirt over my head, I could hear him unbuckling his belt, then pants, then zipper. What the fuck his big ass had on a belt for, I didn't know, since the nigga's belly was so big, it looked like a big-ass kid was in there trying to find his way out.

Before I could even get my pants down I heard him moan, "Oh yeah." He jerked his little dick and threw his head back, them buck-ass teeth poking out.

I posed in my bra and underwear, shaking inside, as he worked his dick like a machine.

"Goddammit!"

I held in my laugh when he tried to stroke it with his stump arm. His other hand must have gotten tired.

"Harlem, come and finish me off, baby."

I strolled over to him and curled up on the couch. *Mama, I must really love you to be doing this*, I thought.

My hand gripped his sweaty dick, and I stroked it up and down,

He howled, "Awwwww shit." His hand smacked my ass. "Moan, baby, moan!"

"Ahhhhhh."

He slapped my ass again. "My dick big, ain't it?"

Does he really want me to answer that shit?

"Aint it?" he said louder.

"Big as King Kong, Mr. Berry." I stroked his shit faster.

Suddenly his breathing quickened and became ragged, and his voice hoarse. He gripped one of my butt cheeks as his legs started slapping against the bottom of the couch like he was choking. He howled again. "Awwww!" Then his big-ass teeth clashed into each other.

Right before his tip filled with the milky substance and it shot out, I snatched my hands away and looked in the opposite direction. When I looked his way again, it was leaking onto his pants as it hung sideways.

"Aw shit!" He leapt up from the couch and went into the small bathroom located in his office.

I took the opportunity to quickly put my clothes on.

See, Mr. Berry was a big-time joke in the projects. Word was, one time a tenant couldn't pay her rent, which was crazy 'cause rent in the projects wasn't all that much. But when people got their county and GR checks they usually fucked them off on weed or heavier dope, clothes, shoes, boost minutes for their chirps, or they drank. Or they got so far behind that the rent piled up on them. So, instead of her rent money, she offered Mr. Berry some pussy instead.

After some sucking and rubbing, the lady sat down on his dick, which went limp the moment it entered her pussy. He didn't get in one single stroke. And every woman he got with in the projects said the same damn thing. The nigga couldn't stay hard.

Whenever he would come to our doorstep if my mama was late on the rent, she always cursed him out. "Fuck you, you fat, pudgy, cripple-ass muthafucka. You'll get the rent when you get *the . . . rent.* Worry more about trying to stay hard than when you gonna get your hands on my greens."

He would never argue with her though. He was too embarrassed. He would just sigh and repeat himself, "You need to pay your rent," then walk away.

And I'd be in the corner laughing hysterically.

He never fixed his dick problem, so the nigga had no choice but to be contented with being jacked off or sucked. Mr. Berry got smart though, once he realized the women were passing on the info to each other on how to get away without paying rent. I guess he figured, if he didn't stop fucking with them like that, he'd have no damn rent to collect and it might get back to his supervisor.

So he only fucked with us minors because, for one, we wouldn't expect as much as an older woman—just a twenty or a forty—and most of all we kept our mouths shut. Plus, I also think he had a thing for young girls, probably 'cause he was a pervert and he knew deep down money was his only means of getting us to be in the same room with him. Only, my mouth wasn't going anywhere near his shit. But I'd jerk the shit out of his meat, if it meant stopping my mama from crying or getting sick again.

When Mr. Berry came back out, I was fully dressed and my hair thrown back in a ponytail.

He slid me three thin plastic packets filled with the shit my mama and daddy craved and would break every law known to mankind to get. He handed me an extra twenty on top of that and said, "Maybe next time you could use that lush mouth of yours, Harlem." He licked his lips suggestively, spit all in the corners of his mouth, disgusting the shit out of me.

I tossed the twenty on his desk and rushed out without answering. It was funny how men were willing to pay for a pretty face.

This would have to be the last time I did that shit. If things got really bad again a friend of mine from school named Roslyn told me she had a way to make extra money quick. "And it don't involve sex, girl," she assured me.

I was glad about that, but I knew it had to be something risky, but still I hoped Mama was telling the truth when she said this was the last time I'd have to do this shit. I was hoping they'd get they shit together.

It was Christmas Eve and I made the best out of what we had. I wasn't too worried myself, since it was on and crackin' at school.

My homeroom class had a Christmas party, and I ate so much of that free food that my belly hurt. Students in my class brought tamales, enchiladas, fried chicken, orange chicken, boxes of pizza, chips, dip, salsa, apple cider, cakes, pies, Christmas cookies, and even eggnog. I guess I stuffed myself because I knew, once I went home, it wouldn't be much of a Christmas. And all my broke ass was able to bring was a $1.07 gallon of ghetto punch that had an acid feeling when it slid down your throat. But nobody tripped.

Now had it been a party in the projects, I would have been the laughingstock of the damn thang. It was bad enough that bitches in the projects teased me since I was a kid, 'cause while my mama took her county check and bought drugs, their parents took theirs and bought them nice clothes and shoes.

My mom said it didn't have shit to do with what I was wearing. "Come on, Harlem," she said, "think on this. You are a pretty girl. Yeah, they got clothes and shit, but they look like they belong on a chain. The little bitches look like dogs."

But the reason I think she gave such a passionate speech about how pretty I was was because she once again shot up her check in her veins and the first day of school was the following day and she couldn't afford to buy me any school clothes.

It didn't matter I didn't have the same shit they did, and it didn't matter if those females still didn't like me, because when I was in class none of that shit mattered. My brain made me popular. I was placed in a class for gifted kids, and even the work there was no challenge for me. Hell, I always finished fast and sometimes helped the other students. My intelligence took the attention away from my tacky clothes and even tackier parents. I just always made sure I did my hair in a nice style, like those twisties in the front, made sure my outfits were clean and crisp, and scrubbed my shoes till they were white.

When I got home from school and came in the house, I noticed Daddy was gone and Mama was sick, and it was only three-thirty. I found a piece of salt pork in the freezer and cooked it with some kidney beans. Shit, hopefully it would be enough to last us for Christmas Day, so we would at least have something to put on the damn table.

My friend Stacey invited me over to her house for the holidays, and just hearing her talk about turkey stuffing, sweet potato pie and making Christmas cookies had me salivating. But I couldn't leave my mama on the holidays for nobody.

Besides, Stacey said her family always did a gift exchange, and I had no money to buy her a gift. And that would be too embarrassing. I knew Stacey came from money. She was always fly—G-Unit, Ecko, True Religion—while I was wearing the same shoes I wore in the ninth grade.

I wanted to get a job somewhere to make my own money. Shit, I would have flipped burgers, cleaned up, done laundry, whatever. But my daddy wouldn't let me. And the occasional side hustles went toward feeding my mama's habit. All the same, something told me 2006 would be far better than 2005 and the years before that.

I pressed the taped-together earphones to my head and struggled with the tuner on the cheap Walkman, the one that my extra quarters bought me from the dollar store, while I stirred the beans in the pot and listened to Keyshia Cole. She knew what I was going through. As the beans began to boil, I sang "Love," as if the song was about my life.

I peered out my window and caught sight of Savior's fine ass. He looked through the blinds and nodded at me, and I nodded back.

"Get out that window looking at them niggas!"

I jumped and glanced my father's way as he slammed the living room door. "Sorry, Daddy," I said, putting my attention back on the food.

"Eddie, you got my shit?"

I shook my head. My mama didn't have no shame anymore. Wasn't any need to try to hide it from me. I knew what was going on.

He tapped his right pocket and looked back my way. "Finish them beans. Your mama and I will be back in here in ten minutes."

I nodded and continued stirring the beans as they boiled in the pot.

But they never came out of the bedroom as I sat at the table alone, listening to music with my headphones on.

After about twenty minutes, I put the beans in the fridge, cleaned up, and went to bed.

The next morning I woke up bright and early.

"Ma! Daddy! Merry Christmas, y'all!" I jogged out of my room, went past the living room, and burst in their room to find it empty. I rushed downstairs, wondering if they were outside, but they weren't there either.

Although it was still early, the sun was shining brightly. That's Cali for you. Wasn't no "Winter Wonderland" out here. Right now it felt like it was mid-spring or the beginning of summer. You could never play it safe out here. The weather was too unpredictable. It could be a heat wave in the winter or a heavy downpour of rain smack dab in the summer. But today, even though the weather was just right, everything else felt all wrong, because I was here alone.

I sat on our stoop for a while twiddling my thumbs. Then I braided my hair in some plaits, sang every song I knew, and still my mama and daddy were MIA. Kids started running outside to play with their new toys. One kid, Toby, was happily riding past me on his bike. I smiled and gave him a thumbs-up. "Nice bike, little man."

As he sped past, he yelled out, "Whatchu get, Harlem?"

"A lot of stuff."

He turned around and raced back over to me. He jumped off the curb in front of me, startling me. "Like what?"

"Boy, why you all up in my business? I said I got a lot of stuff."

He shook his head and took off.

I soon felt a pair of eyes on me and swung mine in that

direction. It was Savior. Embarrassed, I looked down at my bare feet and tapped the pavement.

I had a mad crush on Savior. He wasn't much older than I was. I think he was twenty-two or twenty-three. He was buff, tall, and dark chocolate, the way I liked them. Pearly white teeth and jet black eyes, his hair was thick and braided in cornrows. Now, I don't know if Savior was feelin' me, but he was always lookin' out for me.

He stopped in the section of the projects I lived in to visit my nasty-ass neighbor Bo Bo, who I had to slap once or twice for slapping me on my ass. Other than that, Bo Bo's crush was harmless. Bo Bo and Savior were also dealers for some dude named Chief, who had the whole projects on lock. Which was crazy as hell, because you never saw him traveling through the projects. Yet, the nigga had a whole lot of pull. Word around the way was he'd just killed somebody for stealing a five-dollar weed sack. I ain't never seen his ass before, but I ain't never heard about no nigga standing up to him neither. And with the pull he had in the projects, I knew he was making major dough.

Savior strolled over and blocked my view. He was wearing a white tee, some black jeans, a pair of clean black-and-white chucks, and a do-rag over his braids. "Why you go off on little shorty? He just wanted to know what you got for Christmas."

"He don't need to be all up in my business." I rolled my eyes.

He chuckled and bit his bottom lip. "What about me?"

"Who you?"

"Girl, you know who I am."

Yeah, I did. I wondered if he was going to bring up how I knew him.

Shit, I remember one time when my parents went on

one of their binges. They'd been gone for three days, and like a damn fool, I went looking for them at the last place somebody told me they'd seen them, Keefee's house. Boy, was that a mistake.

I stepped slowly into the house, not knowing what I was walking into. The living room was dark as fuck and quiet, except for the flicker of a cigarette lighter and a constant fizzle sound, and there was a weird foul-ass odor in the room. I walked into a bedroom and found a woman bobbing up and down on a man's dick. As I rushed away, I saw a man in the bathroom sucking on a pipe like it was a woman's titty. Alarm hit me. I knew where the fuck I was— I was up in a crack house.

I turned on my heels quick and rushed past the bathroom and the bedroom. Only, two dudes were now standing in the way of my damn exit and shining a light from a cell phone on me. I took a step back.

One of them said, "Damn! What's up, shorty? You lost?"

With the little bit of light in the room from the flicker of another lighter I saw he was tall and slender, and the one laughing was short and stocky. As both dudes approached me, I shook my head nervously. "No. I mean, yeah, I was looking for somebody."

"You find them?" The short one took another step toward me.

I backed up. "No, they ain't here." When I tried to step around them, they wouldn't let me. I cleared my throat. "Excuse me."

They continued to block my path. The tall one said in a husky voice, "Shorty, you ain't gotta lie. You want some yay, then shit, you want some yay. Just say it. Only"—He flickered his cell phone down my body then held it up to my face—"what are you prepared to give us? 'Cause you damn sure lookin' right."

"Yep, yep. Ain't nothing in here fo' free," the short one said.

I hid my nervousness and glared at them both angrily. I knew these niggas were not going to rape me in a damn crack house in front of all these junkies. I placed my hand in the tall one's face and glared at the short one. "Check this out—I don't want shit from y'all niggas, and I'm not giving y'all shit, so step the fuck off, you ugly mutha-fuckas!"

"Girl, what the fuck you doing here? Man, I should kick your ass."

I bit my lips fearfully when they closed in and cornered me.

Before I could respond, an unfamiliar face snatched me up. He had a tight grip on my arm. He yelled, "Come on! Damn!" and we brushed past the two dudes.

Now I didn't know whether or not to trust him either, but he made me feel a hell of a lot safer than the two grimy-ass niggas in that crack house. I kept my mouth shut and followed his lead.

"Damn, Savior," the tall one said. "You never told us about her. Nigga, you came in the nick of time. It was going to go down."

As we swept past them, Savior turned and looked at them. "Nigga, wasn't nothin' goin' down with my fuckin' cousin. Y'all fuck with her again an' I'll shoot your fuckin' dicks off and feed 'em to my guppies."

I took a deep breath as the dude I now knew as Savior gave me a lashing about how stupid it was for me to run up in a drug house if I wasn't a cluckhead, a ho, or a drug dealer.

I snatched my arm away from him. "Well, I didn't know it was a fucking crack house! I was just looking for my parents. Shit!"

His face softened, and he stared down at me. "I don't mean to be harsh, shorty, but your parents are grown. If they want to stop shooting that shit in their veins they will. You can't stop 'em though. You comin' round here is just going get you caught up in some shit. Trust me, I know." Then he added, "And I know you don't want to hear this, but your parents are junkies in the worst way. And right now they just might not be ready. One day, maybe they will, but from the looks of them, they ain't checkin' in rehab no time soon."

I unpoked my lips. "You know my parents?"

He chuckled. "Aja and Earl? I've seen 'em around. Seen you too." He looked away when he talked about seeing me. "I seen you coming home from school and shit, chillin' on your stoop. You never hang out like I see a lot of females your age do, which ain't bad, by the way."

"Oh." I knew he was right about my parents, so I didn't argue with him. And it was kind of him to save my ass.

"Come on. It's kind of late. I'll walk you on back to your house."

And as we walked I was nervous. Not nervous in a way where I felt he was going to do something to me, but nervous because I thought I would do something stupid in front of him, like trip over my own feet or say something silly, and he would think I was just a dumb little girl.

When we got to my stoop I told him, "Thank you."

"What's your name anyway, girl?"

"Harlem."

He nodded. "All right. I'll be checkin' for you in a few years."

I just laughed and went inside my house, but truth be told, I wouldn't have minded that one bit.

When I walked in the house I discovered my parents still weren't home. I went into the kitchen to watch Savior from the window as he left. Then once his tall frame vanished, I grabbed a dishrag and attacked the dishes in the sink.

Fifteen minutes later as I was sweeping up the kitchen floor, my head shot up when the living room door opened and my parents came flying in the house. Before I could ask what was going on, my mom raced to the kitchen and clung to me like she was the daughter and I was the mom. My dad, meanwhile, tried his best to close back the living room door, but some dude was still able to bust through. My dad backed away, but dude grabbed him before he could get away.

The next thing I knew, my daddy was lying flat on his back and receiving a barrage of punches from the dude, but he didn't fight back. My mom and I screamed, and she pulled away from me.

"Stay back!" my dad yelled.

"Bitch, you betta. Else, I'll fire a load in your junkie ass 'cause I gives a fuck about a dope fiend." The man paused the ass whipping to raise his shirt and show my mama and me his gat.

I grabbed her before she could rush the guy because I knew in a hot second she would.

"Get out of my house, you bastard," she yelled at the top of her lungs, jumping up and down. "And get the hell off of my husband!"

There was nothing we could do besides watch. We couldn't call 911. We didn't have a damn phone.

Just as quickly as the beating came, it stopped. But that didn't mean my daddy wasn't hurt. He was lying on the sofa groaning in a low voice.

"Nigga, going to jail don't excuse your debt. You betta get us that money—two hundred, fool."

The man's eyes passed over my mom like she was a piece of shit laying on the carpet. Then he turned his eyes to me. His lips twisted to one side in a smile. He nodded. "Yeah, nigga, you best get that money or she'll be on the ho stroll." He pointed at me. He continued, "Chief don't play when it comes to his dough. He done killed niggas for a five-dolla weed sack. What makes you think you exempt?" He swung his foot at my daddy's head.

I tensed up as it connected with his face, and my mom covered her mouth with her hands and let out a muffled cry.

Then he bowed sarcastically, tossed me a wink, and walked out, leaving our door open.

Mama rushed over to my daddy and helped him to his feet. "Oh Lord, how we gonna get that money?" She turned to me. "Harlem, I'm gonna take him to the hospital."

I sighed, knowing I would once again have to try to save the fucking day. And I hoped I could earn a little more than the two hundred to pay Daddy's debt 'cause if she was taking him to the hospital that was another damn bill. 'Cause in Cali if your ass had no private benefits, you might as well be a piece of shit lying on one of them hospital chairs in the lobby. Hell, out here, being sick didn't mean shit. People done died in lobbies and waiting rooms, and by the time they saw Daddy it would be a new day.

When I saw my friend Roslyn in the hall at school the next day, I asked her, "You still know about that little hook-up?"

She smiled and nodded, looking fly in her red Ecko jumper skirt and matching Jordans that just came out.

I stared down at them hungrily like they were a fat, juicy steak.

Roslyn was taller than me and light-skinned with some

skinny braids. She had small breasts, broad hips, and a big, wide ass she loved to wiggle.

"How you think I got this tight-ass outfit, girl?" She spun around for me slowly.

I laughed and shook my head. "Naw, I just need to do it once."

"That's what I said the first time I did it, but now, girl, I'm hooked." She tore a piece of paper out of her note-book and scribbled something down on it. "Meet me at my house tomorrow morning around ten."

"But tomorrow is school."

She gave me a sharp look. "So you wanna make this money or what, girl?"

I sighed and took the paper from her. "I'll be there. What do I need to bring?"

"Nothin'. I'll hook you up, since you my girl and all."

I met Roslyn at her crib, and we left her house pretend-ing we were both going to school. Instead, we waited at the bus stop a few blocks away.

After about forty-five minutes of waiting, some older girl named Cocoa arrived. She swooped down on us at the bus stop, music blasting in her little Honda Civic.

"Come on, Harlem," Roslyn said.

I followed her lead and hopped in the back seat.

As soon as we were buckled in, Roslyn turned to me. "Harlem, Cocoa." Then she turned to Cocoa. "Cocoa, Harlem."

The brown-skinned lady wore blue contact lenses and had a blonde weave that went down to her waist. Her face was caked with makeup, but still under all of that was a pretty lady. She punched the gas pedal and nodded at me. "What's up, girl?"

I could see her tongue was pierced, and she had a piercing above her mouth.

"Check you out, girl. You pretty. That's a good thang too. You gonna make a lot of money."

Roslyn looked back at me and laughed. Then she turned back to Cocoa. "She said she only wanna do this once. I'm trying to school her on this shit. This money is addictive. Ain't no such thing as doing it only once."

I forced a smile, not knowing what to expect.

We ended up on 109th Street and Broadway in LA in the cut at a lounge place that was used for an after-hours club Cocoa said she frequented.

"By the way, Harlem," Cocoa said as we pulled into a parking space, "this ain't a legal stripping spot, so don't be telling other bitches about it. It's by invite only."

I nodded. Shit, I figured if I can jerk Mr. Berry off without throwing up, I can do a little striptease this one time to bail my daddy out of his mess.

We got dressed in the bathroom. I had on a short-ass leopard print dress with a matching bra and thong Roslyn had given me. It was more like a shirt than anything. She said it was brand-new, and I would owe her a pair of thongs. Roslyn had on a leather cat suit, and Cocoa wore a red see-through lace get-up. You could see her nipples and shaved pussy through it.

It was still early, but by eleven the music was already bumping in the place. While we put on makeup, Cocoa was puffing on a blunt. She passed it to Roslyn, who tried to hand it to me after taking a few puffs.

I shook my head. "I'm cool."

She shrugged and gave it back to Cocoa then went back to doing her makeup.

As Roslyn lined her lips with a dark brown lip liner I

said to her, "Ain't it kind of early for niggas to be comin' to a strip club?"

She gave me a look like I was silly. "Harlem, hustlas don't work a nine-to-five. Trust me, they'll be here, and with them come the *dollas*."

At the word "dollas," Cocoa let out a scream and bent over so her ass was in the air and wiggled so her booty, which was huge as hell, could rattle. Roslyn joined her and popped her butt. Then they high-fived each other and started laughing.

When they noticed my ass looking at them like they were crazy, Roslyn said, "The first time I did this shit I was scared too, girl. Just don't try to do too much. Relax and shake your ass like there's no damn tomorrow. Get freaky with it 'cause niggas love a nasty bitch. Be nice to all the niggas, even the ugly ones, 'cause an ugly muthafucka knows he's ugly and has more to prove. He'll give you way more money than a cute nigga."

I gave a nervous-ass laugh as my stomach twisted in knots. At least when I posed for Mr. Berry it was private, only me and him, and I only had to take off my shirt and pants to get him off. I couldn't imagine showing my half-naked ass to dozens of men, but I had no choice. *Maybe it would only be a few*, I thought, trying to comfort myself.

Cocoa added, "Oh, and another thang, don't show your pussy. Your titties and ass are enough for these niggas. We don't want them going crazy. We don't have them same rules regular ho clubs got 'cause we at an underground spot, and we damn sure ain't got no damn bouncer. So be aware, anything can go down."

"We just gotta look out for each other," Roslyn said.

"And we each give up fifty of whatever we make to the owner. That's how much he charges me to let us use the place. Now let's get these niggas' money, ladies," Cocoa chimed in.

I followed them and took a deep breath.

We exited the bathroom and walked down the long-ass hollow hallway to an area that looked like an empty dining area, except for about four round tables and chairs, a bar area, a DJ stand, and a couple of leopard-print couches.

When we stepped inside the room, the new song I had heard before on the radio from Too $hort, "Bounce That Ass," was blasting in the room. There were about fifteen niggas in the room, four at one table, six at another, and five at another.

Cocoa went to one table, leapt on top of it, and instantly started wiggling hard and fast as hell. Then Roslyn went to the other table.

I watched them both for a moment before taking my spot. My legs were wobbly in a pair of clear heels, so I didn't bother climbing up on the table. I also didn't bother looking in the niggas' eyes. In fact, I kept my head down and proceeded to move my body like Cocoa and Roslyn. The song chanted, *"Bounce that ass way down to the floor."* So I shook it way down to the floor and felt a few dollars slapping me gently in my face and on my back.

Then came the words, *"Shake that shit till you can't no more."* I wiggled my hips, quickly making my breasts and ass bounce like a damn basketball. I squeezed my eyes shut and worked my body so far into the groove of the song, I felt like I was somewhere else.

The men kept howling.

I squinted my eyes a little and saw both Cocoa and Roslyn down to their bras and thongs and men slapping dollars on their asses. When I pulled my dress over my head, the yelling and whistling got louder from the group of niggas near me. But all their shouts were doing was making me more nervous. As I squeezed my eyes shut and wiggled my booty, more dollars tickled my body.

One nigga yelled, "Shake it, bitch."

I ignored him but worked my body a little harder, hoping the pile would have the two hundred dollars I needed.

Then 50 Cent's "Candy Shop" came on. I squinted at Roslyn and Cocoa again. Now their titties were out, and all they were wearing were their heels and thong. Cocoa flickered her tongue over one of her nipples, and Roslyn was making her butt cheeks clap together like a set of hands.

I squeezed my eyes shut again and tried to unsnap my bra. I had it halfway off when I opened my eyes again and almost jumped out of my skin when I saw a dude smack dead in my damn face, making my heart pound faster. As much as I would have liked, he wasn't no stranger either. It was Savior.

Before I could say anything or cover up, he yanked his jacket over me and, like he did at the crack house, snatched me out of there with the quickness.

One angry nigga said, "Savior, where the fuck you taking that ho?"

Without looking, Savior tossed a hand at him, and led me back down the long hallway I had walked down earlier with Roslyn and Cocoa.

I was damn near naked, and his jacket was falling off of me. It wasn't very long anyway, so you could see the thin strip of material in the crack of my ass, not to mention my butt cheeks. I'm sure a nipple was hanging out, but he kept his eyes on my face, never dropping them any lower.

"Where your clothes at, Harlem?"

"Um . . . they in the bathroom," I said in a shaky voice.

"Go put them back on."

Now I know he wasn't my daddy, or my man for that matter, but something about his tone made me run in that bathroom and put my shit back on. As I stood down at the end of the hall looking like a dumb ass, Savior signaled for me to come over by jerking his head my way, then in the opposite direction.

Once I closed the distance between us, his hand went back to my arm, and he pulled me out of the warehouse. He was walking so fast, I had to jog to keep up with him.

I glanced back at Cocoa and Roslyn, who, unfazed by my departure, were still doing their thang. The men I was dancing for had split up and joined their two tables. I glanced back at the dollars resting in a pile on the floor, wishing I could go back and snatch them up.

Once we moved a few feet from the warehouse, Savior let me have it again. "Harlem, what the fuck you doin' in there?" He pointed back at the lounge.

"Makin' quick money," I fired defensively. I wanted to ask, "What were *you* doing in there?" but kept the comment to myself. For some reason I felt jealous.

"And just what do you know about quick money?"

I shrugged. I didn't know shit about it. I knew this was just my way of getting it quick.

"Girl, there were fifteen niggas in there. You know what they could have done to you?"

"Roslyn said it was safe."

"Man, who cares what she said. Let me tell you something, Harlem—You need to stop selling yourself short. Your young ass need to be at school and not with them hoes. Listen, some bitches don't want much. They impressed with money, clothes, cars, and shit. You better than this. I barely know you, and I can tell that about you. You don't need to be caught in no shit like this. Don't listen to them. All that material shit is just that. Shit. It don't have no real value. And you don't need it, if means selling a part of your soul and complicating your life."

"I didn't come here to shake my ass for some clothes."

He raised his eyebrows. "Then why you here doin' this shit?"

I crossed my arms. "To pay off a debt my daddy owes."

"Debt? What debt?"

"Some dude came to our house and beat my daddy's ass. He said my daddy owed him two hundred dollars and if he didn't get it to him I would end up on the ho stroll."

His jaw line twitched. "You know what he looked like?"

As I described him, Savior nodded as if he knew the guy. "I'll straighten it out. Come on, let me take you back home." He opened the passenger door to his Yukon for me. "Don't you ever bring your ass in here again," he barked and slammed the door.

And he did straighten things out, because the dude never bothered us again. Occasionally, when he wasn't too busy doing his hustle or hanging out with his friends, Savior would walk with me to school and home, just say what's up, or share friendly advice with me and shit. And, if I ever needed anything, he said I could always come to him. But every time his mouth moved, I was too focused on his sexy-ass lips. But that was as far as I would go. I never had a boyfriend or even kissed a dude. I just fantasized about him being my boyfriend and kissing him and sharing a tub of popcorn with him at the movies. But, hell, I was too chicken to tell him how I really felt.

Watching Savior tug his bottom lip with his teeth made my tummy quiver.

"You ain't nothing special," I told him.

He laughed. "Man, you just full of attitude today. Santa didn't put nothin' under the tree for you?"

"We don't have a fucking tree."

His smile faded, and he nodded. "Sorry to hear that. What did you have your heart set on?"

I didn't mean to snap at him, but shit, it was Christmas and I was spending it alone, just like Thanksgiving, so my parents could get dough to get high. And all I really wanted was a pair of nice sneakers. I was sick of putting white paint on my shoes so they looked halfway decent.

"Go throw some shit on and come with me."

Chapter 3

At Savior's invitation, I didn't hesitate. I dashed upstairs and threw on some jeans, a T-shirt, and my raggedy-ass tennis shoes.

We went to the Slauson Swap Meet, which was the place you went when you needed anything from a new pair of kicks, a new outfit, sounds for your ride, a tattoo, your nails done, or to even grab something to eat. I went there from time to time with friends, even though I never had money to buy shit. It was cool to look around.

Savior and I knew they'd be open because them store vendors didn't give a fuck about Christmas. Once Savior and I entered, I was like a kid in a toy store. I saw all that shit and went crazy, my eyes scanning everything.

"Since I hurt your feelings and all, I'ma buy you an outfit and a pair of sneakers."

I clapped my hands together and tried on at least ten different shoes before I settled on a pair of pink-and-white Nikes that were fly as hell. Then I chose a matching Rocawear outfit that had a jacket and skirt, the same one my friend Stacey had.

"Thank you." With tears in my eyes, I leaped on Savior and gave him a bear hug, but when I felt him stiffen, I pulled away and wiped off my face.

"No problem. You hungry?"

He knew I was. My stomach was grumbling. "Naw, I'm good."

He laughed. "Then come watch me eat this burger, girl."

We walked over to a little hut inside the Swap Meet.

He ordered two milk shakes, chicken strips, onion rings, French fries, a cheeseburger, and two hot dogs. "Girl, you better help me eat all of this."

I laughed and helped myself to the fries.

"Savior, were you born in California?"

He bit into his burger. "No. I moved out here from Jersey."

I grabbed a shake and closed my eyes as I slurped, which made him laugh. If he only knew . . . the last time I had a shake I was in pigtails.

"Why you leave Jersey for busted-ass California?"

He chewed, swallowed, and said, "Wasn't nothing in Jersey for me, 'cept my dumb-ass mama and her dude. I got sick of whipping his ass for whipping hers. Every time I turned around she was taking him back. He whipped my mama so bad one day, I couldn't take it no more. He was on that PCP and flung my mom out the kitchen window and fractured her ribs. I used to play baseball. I took my bat and broke it on his ass, and when I got through with him, I ended up breaking his arm and leg."

"Then what happened?"

"He pressed charges on me. Got charged with assault,

lost my scholarship. A friend of my moms said he had a job for me." Savior stuffed an onion ring in his mouth. "But that was bullshit. And I couldn't find a job, with my record. And you see what I do, so hell, here I am." He took a sip of his shake.

"My dad ain't much better."

"Yeah, that fucker is mean as hell. Can't believe y'all came from the same family tree."

I laughed. "What he do to you?"

"He curses me out every chance he gets. I guess he don't like me too much."

"Why wouldn't he like you if he don't even know you?"

Savior's eyes locked with mine. "'Cause I won't sell to him. Kind of don't feel right selling to *your* folks."

I pulled my lips in and looked down. I didn't know why, but it felt good to know Savior wasn't the one supplying my parents with drugs. "Do you miss your mom?"

"Yeah, but it's better this way. She ain't going to leave that fool, and you can only whip on a dude for so long. If I had stayed, one of us would have ended up dead at the rate we were going."

I grabbed one of his onion rings and munched on it. And I thought my life was screwed up. Yeah, I knew what he did, but I was in no position to judge him. Both my parents were addicts, after all, and were probably getting high at that very moment, so I didn't reply. I just kept eating up all his damn food.

He shoved his half-eaten burger away and wiped his face with a napkin. "Whatchu want, Harlem? You know yet?"

"Yeah—to get the hell out of California. This may sound crazy, but I always dreamed about going to Rome or some place like that, live in a villa, smash grapes with my feet, like I saw on those *I Love Lucy* re-runs, and make wine I can sip at night and stare at some bomb-ass view. Maybe, be a social worker—That's what I want, Savior. What do you want?"

"You," he said without hesitation.

I blushed like I was a little girl, scratched my hair, and looked down. *Me? His fine ass wanted me?*

"I wanna get out this life. Slangin' ain't for me. Neither is this player shit. I wanna leave Cali too. Now, I don't know if I wanna go as far as Rome though."

I laughed.

"I'm getting out of here real soon. Maybe somewhere quiet, like Colorado. Build a life out there. How about it, Harlem? Would you leave with me?"

I looked him squarely in his eyes. "Yes."

Now it was his turn to blush. He wiped his face with a napkin, looked down at the floor, slapped his hands together, and laughed before looking at me again.

I guess he wasn't expecting that, but I never took my eyes off of him. I was serious as hell. "My mama been with one man her whole life: my daddy. I don't want no different for myself."

"And what man is that?"

"His name is Savior. He hangs around the projects. He's tall, dark as hell, and sometimes he look like he's got Down syndrome—Awww, I'm playing."

We both started laughing.

A chuckle still on his lips, he asked, "About which part, Harlem?"

I turned serious. "About Savior having Down syndrome. I'll be eighteen next year. You think you could wait for me?"

Out of nowhere, Savior leaned over the table and

brought his lips to mine, giving me my first kiss. After the quick peck he pulled away and smiled. "Yeah, I'll wait for you, Harlem."

We continued the conversation as he walked me back to my house from his truck.

When we reached my apartment, I said, "Thanks, Savior," and lifted my free hand to wave at him as he stood still for a moment, watching me.

Suddenly the door swung open, and my daddy came out with a look of rage. He grabbed me by my shirt collar and yanked me inside. "Where the fuck you been, girl?"

"Slauson—"

"With that muthafucka?" He looked at the two bags in my hand. "Give me this shit." He grabbed them from me and ran outside. "Muthafucka, stay the hell away from my child!"

I watched from the living room window and saw him fling the outfit and shoes in the street. I winced as they hit the filthy ground.

Savior held up his hands in surrender and backed away slowly.

My daddy rushed back inside and came after me as I backed into a corner. Within an instant I was tasting my own blood, which trickled from my top lip, after he slapped the shit out of me. Then he threw me into the wall. "Keep your fast ass in this house, or you gonna get some more of this!"

I started crying loudly.

"Don't blame her 'cause we ain't got no more shit!" My mom staggered into the room, clearly loaded.

"Bitch, shut the fuck up!"

"Bitch?" She lunged at him and started pounding him in his back.

He easily threw her off of him and smacked her in the mouth too.

"Mama!" Forgetting my own pain, I rushed over to her as she hit the floor.

"You bastard!" she yelled. "We lowered ourselves to this? Now you hitting me in front of our child!"

As she struggled to stand up, I helped her by grabbing one of her arms and letting her lean on me.

He ignored us both and marched towards the door. "Like I said, Harlem, you go near that nigga again, I'ma snap your fuckin' head off," he said, an evil look in his eyes.

I looked down and nodded. "Yes, Daddy."

He slammed the door so hard, he left a crack in it.

Chapter 4

"You all right, Mama?"

She looked at me and laughed. "Girl, you always worrying about me. Shit, you took a harder punch than I did. You okay?"

"Yeah, Mama." I shrugged and went into the bathroom to grab the alcohol. There was none, so I took some tissue paper, poured some cold water on it, and held it to my lip to stop the bleeding.

Even though my cheek and lip were stinging and I wanted to cry some more, I didn't. I forced a smile on my face, grabbed another tissue, wet it, and went back in the living room so Mama could clean her face as well. "Here you go, Mama."

She took the tissue and looked towards the wall. "Damn, I bet you hate me."

I shook my head. "You my mama. I couldn't ever hate you."

"Well, you should. Hell, I hate myself."

She had that look of regret in her eyes again, all the

things she should have done as a mom but didn't, and all the things she shouldn't have done as a mom that she did. As much as I wanted to take that pain away from her, I knew I couldn't. It was all mental, and I couldn't fuck with mental. I was no Dr. Phil, but still I tried.

"Don't worry. You did the best you could, Mama, the best you knew how." I winced at the pain in my mouth and blabbered out before I could stop myself, "I hate Daddy."

"You shouldn't. He does the best he can. He takes care of both of us. He really has tried to keep us together and with a roof over our heads."

Right. From where I'm looking he ain't done much. We struggle day in and day out. How does he take care of us? I don't see it.

I watched her run a hand through her patchy, thinning hair. It was so matted in the back, it looked like it was growing dreads at the nape again. Sadly, her eyes passed over my own thick, rich mane, which hung in a braid down my back. Mama had lost seven teeth, three in the back and four in the front. Her skin was sunken in, and there were blotches all over her face. And her eyes were always bloodshot red and tired looking. Her banging body was long gone and replaced with sagging skin and bones. No ass, nothing. The beauty I remembered when I was ten had long faded. The only beauty she had left was the beauty of her soul, which she'd share with me whenever she could. For once or twice, in moments like this, when she remembered I was next to her breathing and living, she put me before her drug, even if it was for a little while.

And yeah, Mama still could sing.

I buried my head in her lap, and her smoky voice filled my ears as she sang Nina Simone's "Angel of the Morning," my all-time favorite song.

She sang: *"Just call me angel of the morning. Just touch my cheek before you leave me, baby."*

Like a little kid I allowed her voice to comfort me and lull my body to sleep. I had my escape, and before the night was over, I knew she'd have hers.

I heard the shuffling of mice in the kitchen as they ransacked the cabinets for food. I ignored the sound since I was so used to it. They wasn't gonna find shit no way. My body was banged up and cramped, and I was cold on the floor. I winced and twisted my body so I could lie flat on my back, my mom's head angled at my feet.

"Ma, get up before the roaches get you." I rolled on my knees and scooted toward her head. I shook her body slightly. "Mama, wake up."

She didn't move.

I shook her body one more time, but she still didn't respond. I grabbed her arm and, for the first time, saw the syringe in it. My heart started beating rapidly. I screamed, yanked it out, threw it away, and kept shaking her. "Mama! Mama! Wake up. Daddy! Daddy!" I looked around frantically for him as I yelled at the top of my lungs.

Her whole body was cold, and there was no air going in or out. With shaking hands, I placed my hand over her heart muscle. It wasn't beating. I jumped to my feet and ran to the door. I unlocked it quickly and ran outside, screaming at the top of my lungs, "Somebody, help me! Please, oh God! Help me!"

Bo Bo and Savior were outside. When Savior saw my face, he ran over to me. "What is it, Harlem?"

"Call the police." I dashed back in the house, not wanting to leave my mother. I crouched to my knees, pulled her upper body to me, and rocked her back and forth.

Savior came busting through the door. He took one look at me and then at my mother. He peeled my fingers from her body. "Harlem, she gone. She gone, girl."

I slapped him in the face. "Shut up!"

"Calm down, your mom—"

"I'm not listening to you!" I placed my hands over my ears and sang loudly, "*Just call me angel of the morning*"—I sobbed—"*Just call me angel of the morning...*"

He shook me gently. "Harlem, stop. Your mom—"

"Don't say that shit again!"

I threw punches at his head until he grabbed both my hands to restrain me. Then he tried to hug me. Only, I didn't want no hug. I struggled and butted him in his mouth, so he had no choice but to release me and nurse his bottom lip.

Like a zombie, I walked past him out the house and into the street. The words of the song still on my lips. "*Just call me angel of the morning...*"

I kept on singing, hoping my mama would come back. Hoping that that moment she sang to me would be frozen in time. I yelled the lyrics over and over again. Then I collapsed on the ground and beat the pavement with my fist until pain was pumping through me. And I didn't stop until my skin opened up and blood gushed out, until I passed out.

Chapter 5

Ihid at the playground, sitting on a swing, while I watched through hooded eyes as they rolled my mother out of our home on a stretcher. Part of me wanted to run up and curse them out, drag my mama back in the house, and keep her body with me forever. But that other part of me knew. Man, I knew my mama was gone.

We didn't have no damn funeral. To tell the truth, I don't know what they did with my mama's body. In a way it made me mad as hell that I couldn't say goodbye to my mama properly but was still kind of okay with it because I damn sure didn't want to stand in front of people and cry my eyes out. And it wouldn't have changed anything. It wasn't going to bring her back. All I wanted to do was go home and sleep this pain away, but that seemed impossible with my daddy around. My mama's dying was slowly killing him. Well . . . that and the drugs.

He was gone day in and day out. He sold the fridge. Then he sold my mama's couch. And then he hit the lowest of the low—He sold all her old dresses from when she sang in Aces. I kept my disgust out of my eyes and buried it in the back of my throat when he went through all her shit and then left me alone without food. It didn't matter. Didn't nobody give a damn about a project kid. Not Social Services. I was one less person on their caseload. I didn't wanna be there no how. They put you in worse circumstances than where you came from.

At the end of the day, it seemed like all they were chasing was a paycheck, so my little situation wasn't shit to them. I mean, all my daddy was doing was neglecting me. I'd seen parents do worse to their kids and get away with it.

Savior looked out for me though. When my dad went on his drug runs, Savior would bring me food. The last time he brought me a burger, some fries, and a postcard he probably got at a car wash. He told me if I needed anything else to just let him know. Anything.

The card was one of those with a picture of a place, and the place was Rome. Scrawled across the back of the card in sloppy handwriting were the words, *"Keep that head up."* It helped me a little. When it didn't, sleep helped me to forget that my mama, my friend—shit, pretty much all I had—was gone to glory.

My father re-appeared three days later early in the morning. I woke up when I heard the door open. I walked in the living room, scrubbing the sleep out of my eyes, and watched him bring in a plastic sack of food.

He glanced my way. "Hey, baby."

I couldn't name the last time he'd called me that or showed me any type of affection. Half the time he acted like he hated me, and I didn't understand why.

"Hey, daddy," I whispered with a forced smile.

"Look, it's some sandwich meat in here if you hungry."

I nodded and grabbed the bread and bologna out of

the grocery bag. I put a piece of the meat between two slices of bread and sat down to eat. I bit into the sandwich, which really didn't taste like much of nothing to me. Still, I had to put something in my stomach.

My father watched me the whole time I ate, his expression pretty much unreadable. When I was done, I closed the container of meat, knotted the bag with the loaf of bread in it, sat them both on the counter, and headed back to my room.

As I walked past my father, his arm suddenly shot out and secured one of mine gently but snugly, making my heart beat faster. I narrowed my eyes in confusion.

He released me, and I continued walking to my room, feeling uneasy. He followed after me.

I stumbled over my own feet. He was standing behind me. I regained my composure and continued walking, and so did he. My lips trembled as I felt his breath on the back of my neck.

I took another step, trying to increase the small distance between us, but then I turned around slowly to face him. To my surprise, he was crying.

"Now, baby, I don't wanna do this."

Whatever it was, I wasn't waiting to see. I slipped past him and ran for the door. I hoped Savior was outside. I was gonna tell him to fuck my father up, but I didn't get the chance. Before I could take another step or scream, my daddy was on me, and he gave my head a major blow that put my ass out.

Chapter 6

The blow didn't put me out for too long. When I opened my eyes I wished to God that it had. There I was, with my daddy on top of me. When I opened my mouth to scream, he pressed a hand down on it. With his other hand, he tore my only bra. Then my underwear went next.

My words were in my eyes as I pleaded with him not to do this shit. My voice was muffled on his hand. "Daddy, don't do this. Don't rape me."

His eyes avoided mine.

My whole body cringed when he fingered my pussy in a rough manner. The first hand to ever touch me there.

"Please don't do this."

When he shed himself of his pants, I used the opportunity to try and run, rolling off the bed, jumping to my feet, and pumping my legs as hard and as fast as I could. But I wasn't moving 'cause Daddy had a fistful of my hair. He dragged me back to the bed by my hair and flung me down on it. Then he forced my legs apart, pressed his weight down on me, and stabbed my virgin pussy with his dirty-ass dick. All I could do was cry before blacking out again.

When I finally came to, I heard a voice I didn't know say, "How much, man?"

Then I heard my daddy's voice. "Muthafucka, I already told you—Hand me twenty or get the fuck out!"

"All right, damn. She betta be worth the shit."

Courage made me open my eyes. I was naked on the bed, and my legs felt sticky. There was a dirty rag in my mouth, and my arms and legs were tied. I scanned the room. *Two men! Two men!* I blinked rapidly. My daddy and a stranger were standing over me.

I started shaking and shook my head when the man started unbuckling his pants. I struggled on the bed as he put his full weight on my body. I could barely breathe as his dick penetrated me clumsily, and he slobbered all over my titties. All of what he was doing was hurting me.

I closed my eyes and sobbed as he panted in my ear how good my pussy was. And my daddy, he just watched. I didn't want my first experience to ever be this way. *Daddy, please make him stop. Please get 'em off of me.*

"Hurry up, man."

The man kept jabbing me harder every time.

"What, man? I just got started. I didn't even come yet."

"Bust your shit!"

"Is she a virgin, man . . . 'cause she got a tight-ass pussy?"

"Naw, I broke her in myself. Hurry the fuck up!"

"All right, man."

He started pumping harder into me, making my insides sting. My head was hitting the headboard, and his body slamming against mine made slapping sounds. It felt like somebody was taking a stick and ramming it all the way in me. Nothing 'bout it felt good.

I felt a sticky substance enter me and slowly drip out.

He stood and adjusted his clothes. "Man, that definitely was worth the money. I'ma tell every nigga I know!"

I squeezed my eyes shut and moaned.

My daddy got smart after the first trick. After him, he made every guy wear a condom. I had never seen so many men and dicks. Black ones, white ones, Mexican, Cuban, even an Asian. I stopped counting after the seventh man, and I blacked out so many times, it was like I was taking naps instead of passing out. But my daddy didn't care. He was making that dough.

By this time my arms and legs were chafing from the rope and tearing my skin, and my breasts were raw and covered with purple marks from men sucking and biting them. Not to mention, my vagina wouldn't stop bleeding. I got to the point where I stopped pleading with my eyes.

The trade was always sex for money. And my daddy's little operation lasted a good three days. Three days of different men sticking their dicks in my pussy, or their dick and balls in my face, coming all over my breasts, chest, pussy, ass, even my face. Or they'd just spray they shit all over me like they were holding a water hose. Thank God, Daddy kept a rag in my mouth, or else they'd stick they shit there too.

The only time Daddy untied me was to use the bathroom, and he stood in there like a guard dog and forced me back to the bed when I was done. I didn't have the strength to fight him. Most of the time I was so weak, all I could do was look blankly back at the men—young, old, and married—grinding on top of me. Hell, even the mailman wanted a piece of me.

How long was this shit gonna go down? Was it ever going to stop? I figured nobody would come looking for

me 'cause we were still on Christmas break. I had to hope
that it would end soon. My daddy had to have some type
of love for me, but maybe he loved his dope more. Falling
asleep from time to time was the only way for me to forget
what my body was going through.

Suddenly, a commotion woke me up. Somebody kicked
in the door, and there was a lot of yelling. Five men were
on my daddy, whipping his ass.

Fuck him up, please, but don't touch me.

Two of the men held him up while he got punched and
kicked. He howled in pain, but they wouldn't stop fucking
him up.

Then a cloud of darkness seemed to overtake the room,
as a man filled the doorway. He just stood and quietly
watched. With his presence came the scent of some
expensive-ass cologne, offsetting the smell of dirty dicks
and my pussy. He had to be six-four and looked to be in
his forties. He was a buff motherfucker, whose shoulders
filled the door frame. He wore a fresh-ass suit and a trench
coat, and two long braids hung down his shoulders. He
looked straight up Indian with his bronze complexion,
hawk-like nose, slim lips, round face, and long, neat beard.

"Fuck that nigga up!" he yelled.

The men continued to whip my daddy's ass.

The man stepped into the room. "Bring his ass over here."

When they dragged my daddy up to him, the dude
grabbed him by his neck. Damn, my daddy looked so
small compared to him.

"Muthafucka, you get this shit straight right now—You
don't open up a ho shack in these muthafuckin' projects
without my permission. I run this shit. I don't give a fuck if
it's a lemonade stand. Nigga, you ask me! Got it?"

My father nodded his head and hollered out in pain,
blood oozing from his nose and his right ear.

The man dropped my dad on the ground and kicked the shit out of his face. "Dirty junkie ass."

The other men went back to fucking my daddy up.

The man's eyes darted to me. Hell, I couldn't be embarrassed any more. A dozen men had seen me naked and stuck my pussy. Still, I hid my head underneath both my forearms, peeping at him as he zoomed in on me. My whole body started shaking.

"Now, let me have a look at this chick causing so much commotion in the projects."

My heart started pumping faster as he stepped toward the bed. Toward me.

"Word around town is, she got some magnetic pussy. I'm gonna make a lot of niggas mad tonight, shutting this shit down." He bent over and peered down at me, his eyes widening when he saw my face.

He made me just as nervous as my daddy, since I had no idea who he was nor what he was going to do to me. My bottom lip trembled. What if he continued where my daddy had left off?

"Boss?"

He continued to stare at me. "What?"

"Can we kill this sick muthafucka?"

Between hits to my daddy's back, another one of the dudes I recognized off the block said, "Muthafucka's prostituting his own damn daughter. That's Harlem."

He crouched down on his knees and used his silk handkerchief to wipe the combination of dried tears, snot, slobber, and cum off my face. "Let me introduce myself to you, Miss Harlem. My name is Chief."

Chapter 7

I was taken to a hospital and stayed there for a week and a half. They ran all kinds of test on me. The Lord was looking out for me that night because luckily I didn't end up with any major diseases. Nor did I get pregnant. I was almost sure that the grimy nigga who was the first to hit it had AIDS. Hell, maybe even my daddy did. But I was cool, except for the soreness and a yeast infection.

I had a hard time sleeping, with all the nightmares about men touching me, smiling at me, and licking their lips. I had never watched so much television. I looked at soap operas, talk shows, and all the sitcom marathons. And, of course, I watched *I Love Lucy* nonstop.

I hadn't seen my father since the incident and didn't want to. Deep down, I was hoping he'd burn in hell for the shit he did to me.

After two more days passed, the nurse came in the room and told me I was being discharged. She was a sweet lady with a whole lot of sympathy for me. She said she had a daughter around my age and that she couldn't imagine anyone treating someone so precious so badly. She helped me get dressed and told me, "Your brother is outside waiting for you, sweetie. Just sign the release form and you're all done. He came by and paid your bill yesterday." She handed me a clipboard and a pen.

Good, I thought, 'cause I sure as hell didn't have five cents to give her.

My eyes passed over the name, *Keisha Collins*. I signed the form and gave it back to her.

Chief had already prepped me on this part. The day he and the other dudes bust threw my bedroom after they beat my father's ass. He said if I didn't want to be stuck with my dad again I should go along with his plan. So when he passed me to some other dude and disappeared and the other dude carried me to the hospital, gave them a fake name, and told them I was his little sister who was gang raped on her way to a party, I simply nodded and played along.

I didn't know how to react when I saw a Ford Excursion waiting outside for my ass. But there was no Chief in it. The driver, the same guy who had dropped me off there, a tall, lanky, black man with some short dreads, hopped out without a word and ushered me into the back seat. He jetted down the street playing T.I. and jumped on the 110 freeway, exiting on Crenshaw Boulevard and driving around a curved road that went round and round till we were in Baldwin Hills.

We drove up Via Leonardo to this phat-ass oakwood two-story house with big-ass picture windows. My eyes widened as he pulled in the driveway next to a candy apple low rider, and another car—I couldn't think of the name of that one—and turned off the engine. What the hell? I knew we were in Baldwin Hills, the black Beverly Hills.

I hopped out behind him, wondering if the guy was ever going to say something to me. Like the other homes on the block, the lawn was manicured. Wasn't no cigarette butts or candy wrappers on the ground. Just grass and flowers perfectly lined up along the edges of the lawn. And it was quiet. No loud-ass cars speeding past, noisy kids, and wasn't no females fighting or any gang bangers causing trouble.

He used a key to unlock the lavish house. There were high vaulted ceilings, and a big-ass flat-screen TV filled up an entire wall. My dirty tennis shoes seemed even dirtier next to the white carpet and snow-white fur couches. The walls had actual artwork that looked expensive as hell, not like the paper stencils and sketches that were stuck on the walls of my home, and all kinds of crystal gleamed on the countertops.

The driver nodded at me and vanished.

A woman came in the room. "Hello, hello." She strode up to me and extended her hand. She was tall and slender, dark-skinned with rosy cheeks, and had a gap between her teeth, and her hair was in skinny braids balled in a knot at the nape.

"I'm Kenita, and whatever it is you need, I'm here for you, girl," she said in a Jamaican accent. "Are you hungry?"

"Yeah. But I'm a little confused. Ma'am, where am I, and where is Chief?"

She looked at me for a long time and laughed. "You don't know? You home, child. You in Chief's home."

It was hard for me to fully understand the purpose of my being there, but I forgot it for the moment as she piled my plate high with jerk chicken and a spicy rice that I couldn't stop eating. It was that good. I washed it down with fresh lemon iced tea.

"Yes, Chief said he went out and got him a dime piece, whateva that means. I'm not too familiar with some of the slang Americans use. I've only been in his country for the seven months. But now I understand. You're a very pretty girl and so very young."

Her eye narrowed as if she was trying to guess my age but not comfortable flat out asking me.

"You look like that singer. What's her name? Ah . . . Phyllis Hyman. She's dead now. Drug overdose."

I didn't know if I liked the comparison.

"You want more food?"

I shook my head. "No thank you."

"You probably want to go to your room?"

I shrugged.

She laughed. "I love it. So very humble." As I followed after her, she turned her head and added, "That will change."

I didn't respond. I didn't know what she meant.

"Anyway, you will be very comfy here. I do all the cooking and the cleaning, so we'll be spending a lot of time together, child."

The bedroom had the same luxuries as the other parts of the house I had just viewed. The huge bed, a California King, was covered by a very pretty pink comforter that looked like it was made out of silk. There was another huge flat-screen TV, and a vanity table and chairs like the kind my mama had always bugged my daddy to get her. I could just picture her sitting there smiling at her image and humming in that beautiful voice of hers while I brushed her silky hair. Tears starting running down my face at the thought.

"The closet is full of clothes and shoes—" She looked at me. "You okay, my dear?" She came toward me and lifted my face in her hands.

"Yeah, ma'am." I took a step back, causing her hand to drop from my face, and stared down at the carpet.

"Okay. Well, I'll let you get comfortable. You need anything, leave a list for me. I'll get it when I come next time," she said, and in a flash she was gone.

I immediately went to the closet. It was filled with clothes—dresses, blouses, jeans, skirts, velour sweat suits—in all the name brands I had seen other girls wear at school, and some I didn't know. There were also dozens of shoes, from sneakers to dressy heels. I think I tried on every outfit in the closet. Some fit me, and some were a bit too big. Then I slipped my feet in all the nice shoes. A couple were too small, but most of the heels fit me perfectly.

As nice as the items were, I wasn't enjoying any of it. And I knew why. I was alone now more than ever. I didn't care about all that shit in the closet or much of anything else. My mama was gone, and just as I was grieving, trying to make some sense of the shit, my daddy raped me. I really didn't have anyone, and the shit scared the hell out of me. I was a seventeen-year-old orphan who missed the hell out of her mama and couldn't do anything about it. Couldn't nothing I say bring her back.

I prayed to God over and over again that day she died to make her heart pump, but it seemed God just didn't hear my prayers or he just ignored them. Now it was probably only a matter of time before Chief came home and threw my ass out. All this shit was scaring me. I curled up in the bed and cried softly.

For the first time in my life I was able to eat as much food as I wanted, and I'm not talking about that shit my mama bought, like bologna. My mama would get tons of food stamps, but she spent twenty of it on food and always sold the rest. So we either had a sack of potatoes, beans, or bologna. Chief had so much damn food, every time I opened a fridge or looked on a shelf I felt I was in a grocery store. He had all kinds of meats, steaks, shrimp, crab, chicken, ham, and bacon, all kinds of bread and rolls, and fresh fruits every day, like pineapples, oranges, apples, cantaloupes, and strawberries, my favorite.

For the first couple of days I was in and out the fridge every ten minutes. Kenita was fattening me up on Jamaican dishes like curry chicken, beef patties, fried plantains, oxtails and beans, cabbage, rice and peas, and coconut shrimp. I knew in the first two weeks I was there I had easily gained ten pounds, but I didn't care.

Kenita said, "Child, I wish I had your body. I would drive men wild. Just wild."

Day to day was pretty much the same. It was a while before I caught sight of Chief. The only person I ever saw was Kenita. It was hard for me to make phone calls because there was no phone in my room. And it was always tied up by Kenita anyway. But the weird thing was, the phone never rang.

I asked her, "Could I use the phone in your room to make a call?"

She gave me a stern look. "I am not ta let ya use the phone, Harlem, so keep this among only us."

"I will."

I truly had no one to call, except for Savior, and I didn't know his number. But I was hoping to get in contact with Roslyn and then she could contact him for me to tell him where I was. I tried a couple times to get in contact with her, but she was never home. When I was finally able to speak to her, she told me she hadn't seen Savior in a minute. Damn. I wondered where he'd disappeared to. I thought if I could just get to the PJ's I could sure as hell find him. I just had to figure out a way.

When I was of tired of eating I would dip my feet in the pool since I couldn't swim. Or if I was sick of watching television, I would sit and chat it up with Kenita because she never ran out of things to say.

She would go on and on about her boyfriend Simon who was in the Navy. She showed me pictures of him and let me read all the letters he'd sent her. "Oh, I love this man!" she exclaimed one day, hugging one of his pictures to her chest then kissing it. The man, for some reason, reminded me of Savior, and it wasn't because he was dark as hell like Savior. It was something about his eyes. They had the same kindness that Savior's eyes had. It made me sad because I missed him so much and wanted to know so bad where he disappeared to.

And when she wasn't talking about her boyfriend, she was telling me about school. Kenita was a psychology major at California State University. Once I found that out I had a dozen questions for her—What's college life like? What are the professors like? What's there to do on campus?—because I wanted to go so damn bad.

One day when we were sitting in the kitchen, Kenita was doing her homework, and I was eating an apple. She said to me, "Tell me someting, Harlem—Why do you always look so sad? You're such a pretty girl, and you seem so smart."

I shrugged. I guess her being a psychology major, she wanted to test out some of her skills on my ass. "I don't know, Miss Kenita."

"Did someting traumatic happen to ya, someting you don't want to say?"

I took a deep breath. "Well, my mom died not too long ago."

"Oh." She placed a hand over her chest. Then she touched me on my arm. "I'm so sorry to hear that."

I offered a smile and dumped the apple core in the trash.

"That is someting very hard to deal with, especially with you being so young. But it's God's will, and don't ever doubt that, Harlem."

I frowned. That didn't take the pain from my heart away, it being "God's will," or the crying at night, or in the morning when I woke up to the same fucked-up fate, my mama not being there. Was it God's will for me to live the way I did? Was it God's will that I be raped by my daddy and all of them triflin'-ass men? God's will . . . okay.

"Do you know the best way to deal with a loss?"

I shook my head. "No, not really."

"What I have learned about loss is that you shouldn't look at it as a loss. Maybe your mother is now in a betta place. Also think about it like this—You had seventeen beautiful years with your mother while some children don't get to spend any with theirs. They are snatched away with the blink of an eye."

I nodded. She did have a point, but when was she gonna get it that none of this shit made me feel any better?

"What made your mother so special to you? What are some of the tings she did for you?"

I thought about it. I really didn't know how to answer. For as long as I could remember, I took care of myself.

She looked confused by my silence, like she just knew I'd have a reply. "Okay, let's try this. Think of some of the positive qualities your mother had that affected you as a child in a good way."

I guess my mama was funny. And fearless. I knew she was crazy as hell too, and that was whether she was high or not. I also didn't know if that was a good thing. I guess it was good because some of the things she did cracked me up. But she also did some crazy-ass shit.

One day she took me to a parade when I was about eight years old. While we sat in the crowd, my mom was really enjoying the show, but my ass was bored. I started throwing rocks out into the crowd. My mama's eyes flashed toward me and pierced me with a look. I ignored her and kept on throwing rocks.

"Harlem, stop!"

I nodded, and as soon as she turned away I went back to throwing them. She snatched me up and slapped me on my ass.

Suddenly, out of nowhere, a cop rushed toward us yelling, "Don't you touch her!"

I tensed up and prepared for the worst, because Mama hated cops, I didn't know why.

My mom released me and got all up in that cop's face. "Listen, *Officer,* I shitted her out, and I'll do what the fuck I want to her. You ain't gonna get the chance to bust her in the head with a billy club or rape her in a dark alley at night when she sixteen."

His eyes widened. "I'll take you to jail."

"You ain't taking me to jail, muthafucka. The only way you gonna take me out of here is in a body bag, and before you can do that I'll shoot you with your own damn gun!"

There was silence for a moment.

"Yeah, what you got to say now? 'Cause I'll be damned if you get the chance to fuck with my child, get her used to jail and shit."

He looked at my mother angrily, but she just smirked as if the uniform badge billy club, and gun were a joke.

I bit my lip nervously, knowing he was going to haul her ass right off to jail. Instead, he said, "Ma'am, have a nice day."

And we did. We kept watching the parade. I didn't throw any more rocks, and my mama kept on laughing. Every now and then I would catch the policeman casting looks our way, but my mom wasn't bothered a bit.

Just thinking about the way she talked to that cop had me cracking up in the kitchen. Kenita joined me in my laughter, even though she didn't know what the hell I was laughing about. And I wasn't going to tell her either. I didn't need nobody judging or thinking badly of my mama.

Kenita smiled and nodded as if pleased she got me to open up. "Good, Harlem. It's always good to think of your happiest moments with your mom. You have any of those memories?"

"Those were when she would dress up and sing to me."

"Oh. Was your mother a performer?"

"Something like that. A long time ago she sang in a club. She could sing her ass off."

"What was your favorite song your mom would sing for ya? Do you remember the name of it?"

"Yeah. 'Angel of the Morning' by Nina Simone."

She smiled. "Can ya sing a little for me?"

I closed my eyes and attempted to sing the lyrics: "*There will be no strings to bind your hands . . . Not if my love can't bind your heart . . .*"

Singing the song made me think of my mother. And damn! How much I missed her. Soon my lips started trembling, and my words were smashing together because of the sob I was suppressing in the back of my throat. Finally I gave up and stopped singing. I rushed out of the room before Kenita could see the tears fall from my eyes.

I was now seventeen and living in a drug dealer's home. My mama was dead, and I had no idea where my father was. I didn't know if he was dead or alive—and I didn't care. I also knew I needed to go back to school and was wondering if Chief would grant me that wish.

"Where's Chief?" I asked Kenita one day.

"Out of town. He should be coming back real soon."

"Well, I was wondering if I would be able to go back to school."

"Hmmm, I was wondering the same thing, Harlem. That I do not know. I have been instructed to not let you leave, you know, but you can check with Chief when he comes back."

I nodded.

"But until he does, maybe I can work someting out for ya."

"Thanks."

Her solution was to get me the GED study guide. It wasn't what I had in mind, but oh well, what could I do?

I studied day by day. I did the sections one by one. I worked on the math first 'cause math was always easy for me. Then I tackled the reading, writing, then the social studies. The last section I worked on was the science portion. I even took the practice exams in the book.

One day we were in the kitchen, and I asked Kenita for tidbits about Chief.

"Harlem, you very curious. Is there someting you want to know?"

"What do you know about Chief? He seems like a nice man, letting me stay here and all."

"That, he is." She gave me a long look. "He is also very private too."

"Well, what type of man is he?"

"A very secretive one, miss nosy." Kenita giggled.

"I was just wondering—"

"I really don't know too much about him, Harlem."

Another month passed, and it was pretty much the same as the last. I was allowed to leave the house again, but it was just to go back to the doctor and take another AIDS test. Just taking that damn thang and knowing how many men had been inside me gave me apprehension, even though I knew the last test I took was negative and that I had been with no one else. Still, shit, I was scared.

I crossed and uncrossed my legs as the doctor flipped open the manila folder and read the results. And all that nervousness was washed away with two words: "You're fine."

Since Kenita was the one who took me, I begged her afterwards to take me to the projects so I could find Savior. Even though I was terrified as hell to go back to the projects and see my daddy, I was willing to take a chance and go, if it meant being able to catch sight of Savior. I wanted to say sorry for hitting him the day my mother died when he was trying to comfort me. Then I was going to tell him that if the offer he gave that day at the Swap Meet still stood then I would leave with him that very damn moment.

Kenita pierced me with a look. "Harlem, this will indeed be a one time ting," she said sternly, her hands gripping the steering wheel.

I nodded eagerly.

Once there I pulled a cap over my head, hoping that would disguise me a little. First, I went to my old apartment and walked next door to see if Bo Bo was there. Just seeing my apartment made me sick. I started shaking, and my stomach knotted up. Bo Bo was nowhere to be found.

"Shit."

I just drove around with Kenita, asking dudes I knew if they knew where Savior was or even Bo Bo. None knew. And I knew it was stupid, but I went back to Keefee's spot to figure out if they knew. That's where I spotted Bo Bo. He was sitting on their porch and smoking a blunt.

"Stop here please," I told Kenita.

Once she did, I hopped out the car and approached him.

"Harlem, where you been, girl?"

"Bo Bo, where is Savior?"

"You don't know?"

"No, nigga. Know what?"

"Savior packed his shit and hightailed it out of town, boo."

My heart damn near dropped on that stoop. Instantly Savior's words flashed in my head. *"I'm getting out of here real soon. Maybe somewhere quiet, like Colorado. Build a life out there. How about it, Harlem? Would you leave with me?"*

Damn! The nigga had left without me. That shit hurt.

I walked away, ignoring his last words about how he heard about what happened to me and that he was sorry to hear it. I didn't respond. I just slipped back into Kenita's car. I didn't even bother to ask her to take me to the projects again after that. I knew he wouldn't be there. And he sure as hell wouldn't be looking, and obviously wasn't worried about me, so I had to stop thinking about him and focus on me. And that started with me accepting my fate—I was down with Chief for the time being.

Chapter 8

Then Chief came back.

Don't get me wrong, I was living it up in his house. I had a gang of nice stylish clothes and shoes, and I was eating my ass off and hanging out by his pool. Notice I said hanging, because I still didn't know how to swim. Otherwise, I watched TV and even continued studying for the GED. I guess I was getting a little too comfortable and thought he was probably going to tell me to get the fuck out. But I soon learned he had other plans for me.

He came at an unexpected time. I had been eating chips and a seven-layer dip Kenita had taught me to make with ground beef, beans, cheese, sour cream, and jalapeños that was tearing up my asshole as I sat on the toilet when he burst through the bathroom door.

I was so embarrassed, I didn't know whether to stay seated or stand up. But there was no way I was going to stand. I was too busy dropping turds in the toilet, so I did nothing. I just sat there frozen with my eyes wide.

He poked his head in the door and zeroed in on me.

"Baby girl, hurry up with that sit-down and get on out here."

I didn't know what the hell "sit-down" meant, but I hurried as fast as I could, squeezing the digested food out before wiping my ass, washing my hands, and heading nervously out to the living room, where he was waiting. I stood in the doorway wringing my fingers.

He was sitting on the couch reading a letter, one leg crossed over the other. When he felt my presence, he sat it down and beckoned me closer. "Come on in here."

He had his long silky black hair pulled back in a ponytail. His shit was damn near as long as mine. I had to admit, Chief was a very handsome man. He was dressed in some brown slacks that looked like they cost a grip, and a black silk shirt, and black shoes. On his right wrist he wore a Rolex covered with diamonds, and he had two rings on that were blinging. Just looking at them made my eyes hurt. Yeah, Chief was a balla.

With a nervous smile, I took baby steps toward Chief and sat across from him.

He smiled, licked his lips, and scanned my face. As well as my neck, shoulders, breast, waist, pussy, hips, thighs, calves, and feet. He chuckled. "You ain't gotta sit that far away, baby. I ain't gonna hurt you."

I shook my head at myself and went over to sit right next to him.

"How you doin'?"

"Good." I licked my dry lips.

He gestured toward the paper he was reading. "So you okay. Ain't got nothing, I see."

"Yeah." I clasped my hands in my lap.

"Good. Chief had to make sure . . . 'cause if you wasn't, I couldn't do nothing for ya, baby."

"Uh-huh."

"So by now, I know you know what the program is, right?"

I nodded, even though I didn't really.

"How old are you?"

"Seventeen."

"When you gonna be eighteen?"

"Next year."

"Cool. Well, you know Mr. Chief been looking out for you these past six months, right?"

I nodded. "And I really appreciate it too." I knew he was going to tell me to leave, but where was I going to go? I didn't even want to think about it.

He didn't respond. Just kept staring at me, his eyes roaming my face then my body.

"Well, can I get a ride?"

He looked at me funny. "Ride?"

"I thought my time was up here."

He laughed. "Time up? Girl, you not going nowhere. You don't get it, do you? You my woman now."

Chief clearly laid out the rules for me. I was his kept woman. Even though I wasn't a woman yet. I wasn't even eighteen yet. But I guess he didn't give a damn. His rules were simple—no drugs, no crazy-ass parties, no other niggas but him, no job. My only job, according to him, was to sit and look pretty. And I had to be accounted for at all times.

"It's hard to find a pure chick nowadays," he told me. "Most bitches in Cali fucked in, out, and over. Them niggas in the PJ's pulled some shit over on you, but you still right. And you cleaner than any ho I've met elsewhere. Shit, at least you had an excuse. You were tied to a bed and raped by them fools! Would you believe there are some women who would have done that shit voluntarily?"

I shook my head.

Chief also wasn't playing when it came to where I had to be and whatnot. "I'm a powerful man. You deal with me, you gotta work with me. No sneaking or creepin'. And the one thing I will not tolerate is a distrustful, disloyal woman." His eyes narrowed when he said that, and his mouth was frowned up like he was eating something sour.

When I asked him if I could go back to school, he told me it was out of the question.

"You want Social Services all in your business? Girl, please. Your ass will end up in some home where niggas going to be doing worse shit than what your pops did to ya. Believe that."

That scared the shit out of me. *Fuck Social Services!*

"Study that GED. You seem like a smart girl. Pass it, and in a year or maybe even less, when shit is not so hot, I'll send you on to college."

That got me extra excited. "Thanks for everything, Chief." I leaned over and embraced him. He smelled so damn good.

"No problem. Now go on and put on something nice. I'm taking you somewhere special."

Clad in a slinky black dress that stopped at the bottom of my thighs and which had an open back that went all the way to my rump, and some heels, I stepped out with Chief in a silver Benz. The car drove so smooth, I felt like I was floating as he cruised on the highway.

He took me to a fancy restaurant called Crustacean. I had never been to a restaurant that fancy. There was even someone playing the piano. It was crazy. We were served lobster and some prawns that looked like huge shrimp. I couldn't get enough, and he ordered lobster tail after lobster tail. I was sopping the meat in so much butter, my fingers were greasy.

Chief just laughed and told me to eat as much as I wanted. He didn't have to tell me twice. He poured some wine for me. I had never drank the stuff before. He said I needed it to unwind, so I allowed myself two glasses of the stuff before pushing the pretty glass away. I didn't want to make a habit of having any addictions or weaknesses. I had seen firsthand how they can ruin a person's life.

When I was too stuffed to eat anymore he took me "home." That sounded so weird to me then, but that's what it was to me now.

Once we arrived, Chief wrapped his arm around my waist and guided me into the master bedroom, his room I guessed. It was in a part of the house that I hadn't been invited to see.

It was larger than mine and had a masculine touch in the way it was decorated. Everything from the carpet to the bed and decorations were coal gray and black, from the big-ass rug that looked and felt like real fur when I rubbed my feet against it to the blankets on his bed. There was a wide-ass fish tank in the room with all types of weird-looking fish swimming around, and a fireplace. Chief must have been obsessed with those flat-screen TV's because there was another one in his room.

I smiled when I saw rose petals on the floor leading a trail to the bed.

Chief stood behind me and slipped my dress off my shoulders so I was in only my underwear and heels. I shivered slightly, a little nervous about what was about to happen.

He slipped down on both his knees, pulled off my shoes, and slipped my panties off so I was totally nude. Then he pulled me into the bathroom, where there was a huge Jacuzzi-like tub filled to the top with water and suds.

"Go ahead and get in," he told me.

I did and shyly watched him undress until he was nude like me. He was a big husky nigga, powerfully built with a muscular chest, arms bigger than my thighs, and muscular legs, tattoos on his chest and arms. One had the abbreviation for Los Angeles in big letters across his back. He had a hairy body with a trail of silky hair that started at his pecs and led a trail down his stomach to his, Lord, big-ass dick that looked like it belonged on a horse and not on a man.

Chief joined me in the tub. Like a baby, he bathed me gently, starting from my feet and going up my legs. His hands were having an effect on my body. The shit felt good too. I didn't know if it was okay for it to feel that good. He then took a shampoo that smelled like coconut and washed every inch of my hair. His hands rubbed all over my body, and where his hands stopped his kisses began. "Damn, baby, you fine as hell." He gave me gentle pecks all over my skin. Then he used his tongue. He pulled me into his lap and began kissing me slowly, first a peck, then my bottom lip was in his mouth, and he taught me how to use my tongue to play with his.

Soon, it became second nature to me. My hands curled around his neck, and I was returning his kiss with passion.

He lifted me to my feet, water splashing as he lifted me out of the tub, carried me into his room, and placed me on his bed. As I lay on my back totally nude, he stared down at me like I was a feast.

His mouth began working from my neck to my collar bone to the mounds of my breasts. He went lower and kissed my stomach and my hips. Then he raised my thighs and placed kisses on the inside of each. He placed more on my ankles. When he got to my feet he took each one and nibbled on my toes, making me squeal. Then he spread my legs apart and put his head between them. I felt his tongue enter me, setting my insides on fire. I cringed and twisted my body every which way from the pleasure.

As he licked me like I was an ice cream cone, he used his fingers in pleasurable spots then followed with his tongue. His hand kept flickering on my clit, while his tongue eased in and out of me. My legs started shaking, and I felt a weird sensation take over my body.

As cum oozed out, he lapped it up with his tongue. "Your pussy taste good, baby," he said in a husky voice.

Then he settled between my legs and entered me.

There was no pain, just an intense pleasure as my walls stretched to accommodate his dick. His eyes bore down on mine. "You like what daddy doing to you, Harlem?"

I moaned, losing control.

He kept the tempo extra slow. He started playing with my breasts, licking them and squeezing my nipples, as he guided himself in and out of my pussy smoothly. With my legs gripped tightly around him, he thrust himself a couple more times inside of me.

I moaned loudly and clutched his back as another weird sensation came over me. I never in my wildest dreams thought that having sex could feel that good.

Chapter 9

Chief snored loudly in bed. His arm was wrapped so tightly around my waist, I had to wake him up so I could go to the bathroom.

He got up early the next morning to shower and get dressed. When he saw me watching him he winked.

When I buried my face further in the covers, he laughed, strolled over to the bed, and straddled my naked body. He kissed my lips. "Ain't no need to be shy now, baby. I done seen and felt all you got going on." He reached down and patted my rump.

"I know." I couldn't think of anything else to say.

He used the side of his hand to stroke my right cheek. "Damn, girl, you fine as hell. I can't keep my head straight. Let me get up out of here."

"Wait, Chief." I sat up in the bed and pulled the covers more firmly to my chest. "Would it be all right if I went to the mall or something?"

He stared at me a minute. "Naw. You wanna get out the

house, you wait for me to come back." And with that he left.

I didn't see him again until about four days later.

Kenita became my best friend in the house. We cooked together, I helped her clean up, and she quizzed me for the GED. But shit, there were times where I was tired of being cooped up in the house. Chief noticed.

When he came back to see me, he took one look at my moping face and told me to get dressed. He took me to the skating rink off Crenshaw and 48th Street. On Fridays it was hip-hop night, so mostly young people my age and in their early twenties came on this night. Then afterwards they went to In-N-Out to eat.

I was having a ball, but the only thing was, he wouldn't skate with me. He sat at a table on the phone but watched me as I spun around the rink dancing to the music and laughing. I wondered if Savior had ever brought girls there? Each time I stepped off the rink to sip my soda or get a bite of the food he ordered for me I begged him to join me. He waved me away and continued his phone conversation. I felt like he was babysitting me instead of being my man.

"Come on, Chief," I pleaded as I backed toward the rink.

He waved me away again. "Go on, Harlem."

I pouted and turned around and clumsily bumped into a young man, causing both of us to fall, him on his back and me on top of him. His Lakers hat flew from his head and landed near my leg. I picked it up for him. We both laughed, and he helped me to my feet. He was a tall boy about my age with braids and braces on his teeth. As I read it I noticed him cheesing.

"Hey, you wanna skate one with me?" he asked, lingering.

I glanced back at Chief. He was back on the phone paying me no mind, so I figured it was okay. "Yeah. That's cool."

It was the new song by Snoop Dogg. I allowed him to hold my hands, and we danced to the song like we were on a regular dance floor. I had my hands in the air yelling, "Hey," and he kept up with me, bopping his upper body to the beat.

I laughed when he attempted to do the "Crip walk" in his skates. I did the "lean back" dance and then took my body all the way down to the ground, and the guy pulled me back up.

When the song ended, he continued following me. "Aye, you got a number?"

I shook my head. "I got a boyfriend."

"Aww, come on, man."

Just then Chief's head shot up and he was looking our way.

I backed away from the guy as quickly as I could because Chief didn't look too pleased. I shook my head. "No. I'm cool."

The guy kept on yapping. "Come on, baby, baby. Let me do you after school like some homework, girl!"

I laughed and kept skating away, but I noticed that Chief's expression got meaner with each step I took toward him. He had the phone to his ear, but his face told me he didn't miss a beat of what just went down.

I sat down next to him and started unlacing my skates and bopping my head to E40. Chief's eyes weren't on me, though. He was mean-mugging the dude.

I slipped away to return the skates and get my shoes. When I came back and sat down I put my shoes on and stood. "You ready to go?" I asked.

He ignored me and placed one hand in the small of my back and pushed me forward. I started walking briskly to stay ahead of him.

When we got to the exit, I paused, and he slapped my ass to propel me forward. I didn't hesitate. I jogged a couple steps to walk at his requested pace.

He handed me the car keys. "Go get in the car," he ordered.

I did as I was told, and once I was settled in the car, I watched in the rearview mirror as he strolled back inside the rink.

Five minutes later a car pulled in, and I craned my neck to follow it as it shot past me. Five guys hopped out and ran into the rink.

Chief came out at that same moment, stopped and took three drags of a blunt, ground it out with his boot, and headed to the car. He hopped in without a single word to me.

A few seconds later the five guys emerged dragging a young guy out. I heard him shout, "What's the problem, fellas?"

A fist was the only reply he got. That and a foot in his ass as they whipped on him. I looked on horrified as his hat flew off and his braids were flying every which a way. It was the guy I had danced with.

"Chief!" I shook his arm. "Make them stop hitting him!"

Chief tapped his fingers against the steering wheel while the guy got his ass tapped.

Fists and feet were flying and connecting with him, and he was screaming in horror.

I tried to reach for the door handle but felt a steely arm on my hand. I tried to pull away, but the grip was way too strong.

"He disrespected me," was all he said.

"He's just a fucking kid like me!" I yelled, tears rushing from my eyes at the pain I knew he was experiencing because of me. "Why are they doing him like that? Because he danced with me?"

He ignored me.

"Chief, it was only a dance. It didn't mean nothing. You know I'm down with you."

He turned his eyes to me. "Are you?"

"You gotta ask me?"

Chief pressed down on the middle of the steering wheel. When the horn sounded the beating stopped.

I breathed a sigh of relief and hoped he wasn't hurt too bad.

As Chief loosened his grip on my arm, I snatched it away and scooted as far from his ass as possible.

During the drive, he tried to brush his hand across my face, but I knocked it away and gave him the meanest expression I could. When he put his free hand on my knee I slapped it away, hating him in that moment.

I refused to look his way or utter a word to him the whole ride home. I wasn't so sure if this little arrangement was going to work. I didn't know if I could voluntarily be with someone with such a bad temper. Yeah, my daddy had a bad one, but I had no choice in that matter. He was my daddy.

When we got home, I snatched my body from the car with much attitude and marched toward the house. Chief tried to wrap an arm around my waist, but I moved away to prevent it.

"You still not talking to me?" He held his hands out like he didn't do anything wrong.

"You didn't have to beat him up."

Once inside I went straight into my room and closed the door, and he didn't bother me.

Chapter 10

The next morning, I almost freaked out when I felt something licking one of my feet. Then I felt teeth sink into my skin. I shrieked and fell out of the bed.

Expecting to find a rat, I yanked the covers off the bed to find something furry crawling toward me.

I laughed and scooped up the most adorable puppy I had ever seen. It had the cutest face with long floppy ears, and the little thing was covered with golden brown hair. I think it was a cocker spaniel.

"Still mad at me?" Chief asked, leaning against the door frame and puffing on a cigar.

I swallowed the reminder of my anger from last night and smiled. "No, I'm not."

"You like her, baby?"

The puppy kept licking me in my face.

"Yeah, I do."

"Good." He turned to go but stopped and said, "Oh yeah, if you don't want what went down last night to happen again you betta keep unnecessary niggas out of your face." Then he was gone.

I blocked his words out of my head and decided on what to name the little puppy. "I'ma call you *Lady*," I told her and nuzzled her face with mine.

I couldn't wait for Kenita to come back and see Lady. And since she wasn't here, I used her excursion to my advantage.

I took a dash outside to give the puppy some air. We walked down the driveway and a little further down the street. No one was home, so I figured Chief wouldn't find out. And if he did, so what? I was only taking the puppy for a walk. What harm was it doing?

The puppy was cute but bad as hell. She kept trying to bite her collar. When I tried to gently pull her by the leash she would yank her body back. At one point she even got tangled in it. But she was so cute I couldn't get mad. I leaned over to unhook the metal leash from her neck before she strangled herself, and untangled the other end that was around one of her legs and preventing her from walking.

"You are a silly little doggy."

Once I had her free, I attached it to my belt buckle and leaned over to tickle her tummy. I laughed when she angled her body so she could try to lick my fingers.

A kick in my ass sent me flying. Before I could even get up or see my attacker I was socked in the back of my damn head. Pain clouded my vision for a minute.

"You think you can move in on my muthafuckin' nigga? I'm with Chief, bitch. You just a fuckin' fill-in, off-brand bitch!"

As I rose to my knees she kicked me in my side, causing me to fall on my back. "Yeah, look at me, bitch."

A very pretty, angry-looking female stared me down for a moment. Her skin tone was a shade lighter than mine, and she had "doe-brown" eyes and full lips. Her hair was short and layered and piled on top of her head, but some slipped out and hung on the side of her face. She was taller than me and slightly bigger and didn't look much older than me.

As she charged after me again, I lifted my leg and kicked her in her stomach, making her grunt and stagger backwards. I stood and instantly we both started throwing blows.

If it's the one thing my daddy taught me to do, it was to fight. I wasn't a violent person, but I could defend myself if need be. And a couple times in the PJ's I had to get down, but I always did my best to avoid it. The only time I did get down was when a bitch put her hands on me.

My mama always said, "You can call me everything but a child of God, but if you put your hands on me, muthafucka, that's the end of you!"

I swung like Tyson and drilled her right cheekbone, her chest, and upside her head. Her head swung in every direction from the blows.

I knew she had to be from the projects because when she saw I was whipping her ass, she punked out and pulled out a switchblade.

I grabbed the dog chain from my belt clip and wrapped it around my hand so half of it was hanging freely. My heart started to slam in my chest. I squatted and waited for her to make a move.

As she lunged forward and swiped her blade, I backed up and swung, bashing her in the face. The metal split her bottom lip, and blood spilled out.

"Bitch!"

I didn't have time to be calling her names. I waited for her to begin her A-game again.

She lunged forward and swiped her blade again, this time barely missing my neck.

I stepped in and struck her again. It made her weak. I moved in on her again and continued to bop her in her head with my wrapped up fist over and over until the blade fell from her hands and she hit the pavement knocked out. I stopped and took a few deep breaths to slow my heavy breathing down as the adrenaline pumped through me.

I spied Lady not too far from us in a corner chasing her tail, not bothered by what just happened. I shook my hand and scooped her into my arms. I knew one damn thing— No man was gonna get me caught up in some shit like this again. I had to get the fuck away from Chief. Far away.

I walked back to the house and let the puppy down to run around the living room.

I didn't want to steal, but I found a wad of bills in Chief's bedroom, in one of his drawers. My heart started beating when I saw the gun there too. I didn't bother it though. I just grabbed two of his twenties and five one-dollar bills. I just needed enough to catch a bus the fuck out of there. Shit, he had hundreds, fifties, and twenties. I didn't think he'd notice the small amount I had taken. And, besides, I'd be gone by the time he came back.

I didn't know where I could go. I had no family in Cali or anywhere else, but maybe if I could get back to my area I could find my friend Roslyn, who was my only hope at that point.

As bad as it sounded, I was prepared to strip at that after-hours spot for the rest of my life to escape Chief. I patted little Lady one last time. She whined and chased after me, but as much as I wanted to, I couldn't take her little butt with me. I peeked at her through the little crack in the door before I shut it completely. I could still hear her whining and scratching on the door.

I didn't feel like waiting around for a cab to come, so I walked around to find a bus stop. I walked about two blocks before I found a bus stop. I breathed a sigh of relief when I found the seat at the bus stop to be empty. *Perfect.* I didn't feel like sharing it with no wino or some pervert who hung out at bus stops asking for spare change or pussy.

According to the schedule, the next bus was set to come at four forty-five. Since I had no watch I didn't know how much longer I had to wait. I knew it had to be around four though because when I left the gas station it was three-fifty.

Traffic was speeding past me. I almost pissed when I saw Chief's driver fly by in the Excursion.

"Shit!"

I put my head down and covered my face quickly, hoping he didn't see me, but as he followed traffic and got to the end of the curve, he broke and made a U-turn.

I hopped up instantly and ran in the opposite direction, looking over my shoulder. T.I. was blasting, his way of telling me he was close on my heels. I increased my speed and hit another street.

From the corner of my eye I saw him leap from the SUV, and he was on me in a flash the way a fucking chee-tah effortlessly snatches up his prey. The fucking driver, without a single word, plucked me in the air and carried me to the truck.

Hell, I fought, though. "Get the fuck off of me!" I yelled, swinging my fist in the air and kicking. It didn't make much of a difference; it just made me tired.

He dumped me in the back seat and hopped in the

front and drove back to Chief's house. I wasn't going no damn where, and I now had to face Chief.

Once we got back to Chief's house, he yanked me out the car and forced me in the house. I fell in a heap on the floor and lay there for a moment catching my breath.

Then I heard, "You trying to leave me, Harlem?"

Chapter 11

Fear slid into my face after I raised my head and saw Chief standing over me.

"Girl, I'ma ask you again—Are you trying to leave me?"

I tried to rise.

"Stay the fuck down and answer my question."

"Yes!" I rose to my feet and got all in his face, despite his order. "I don't wanna be here. Did you think I would, while you mess around with other females and get me caught up in shit? Please. You don't run me, Chief. I'll go wherever the fuck I wanna go, and I just so happen to not want to be here."

He gave my cheek a blow that sent me flying into the coffee table.

I screamed loudly as a stinging heat rushed to my face.

With a flash he pressed me into the table and grabbed me by my hair. "Listen up, miss bitch, don't ever question what the fuck I do or who I do it with. You are officially my fucking property. You belong in this muthafuckin' house, and that's where you gonna stay. You try this silly shit again and I'll blind your eyes out!"

I covered my face with my hands and cried, not bothering to tell him about the girl who had attacked me.

He was unmoved. I heard him unbuckle his belt and unzip his pants. He sat on the couch and took his dick out. "Come over here so I can show you how to suck a dick."

Being Chief's woman became my nightmare. The kindness he had originally shown was now replaced with brutality, and I dreaded living in his house. Although this was the last place I wanted to be, I knew that I was stuck from the day he'd carried me out my old house. I wasn't dumb enough to test the waters, so I just tried to stay in my place. But, damn, I sure was in a fucked-up place.

The only person in the house I could trust was Kenita, but after the shit went down with me leaving, he fired her ass, even though it wasn't her fault. Her mom was sick so she called off that day. I felt so bad for her, and I knew it was my fault. If I hadn't left, she wouldn't have been fired, but Chief didn't give a damn.

She came back one day while I was taking a shower. A little while before that Chief had made me put on some black lingerie that consisted of a nipple-less bra and some lacy thong underwear and some black boots that went all the way up to my thighs. He fucked me every way imaginable, on my back, sideways, on my knees, standing up, with one leg on the wall, standing up and the top half of my body bent over, me on the bed and hanging halfway off the bed, making my as dizzy ass hell. The last position we tried was fucking in a chair. Then he ate my pussy for what seemed like an hour and had the nerve to want me to suck his dick just as long. He had every ounce of my body sore.

As I was showering I could hear shouts coming from the living room. I threw on a towel and rushed out of the bathroom. I saw Kenita with tears in the corner of her eyes, and it seemed like she was struggling to not let them fall.

"Kenita, you heard what the hell I just said—Your lousy services are no longer needed in my crib."

"Chief, ya joking, right? I'm not going anywhere."

"Who jokin', you fuckin' foreigner bitch? I'll show you how much I'm jokin'." He snatched her purse off her arm and tossed it outside.

Kenita went off. "You should be ashamed of yourself keeping that young girl locked in here like a prisona, *bumbaclat!*"

I turned away so Chief wouldn't see me snickering silently, but turned back around quickly when I heard him raise his voice.

"Bitch, you betta get on before I have your ass deported. I know somebody who works for Immigration. One call, bitch, and your ass will be running naked through a fucking jungle with your titties bouncing and zebras chasing your ass."

Her eyes widened. She looked defeated, like she knew that waging war with Chief would be useless. "All right, Chief." Then she finally noticed me in the room. "Goodbye, Harlem."

I smiled sadly. "Bye, Kenita. Take care."

"Good luck to ya!"

She gave Chief one last glare—"Bumbaclat"—and walked out the door.

Once the door was closed Chief turned to me. He

chuckled, picked me up, and carried me back to his room, where the fucking continued.

It was the last time I saw Kenita, and as time went by, I really missed her.

Chief replaced her with a sixty-year-old black lady named Gladys, who was five feet, if that. She walked around the house in her black wig with bangs from one ear to the other and hummed like she was on a damn plantation. She rarely uttered a word to me and watched me like a damn hawk.

My only friend in the house was Lady, and I treated that puppy like I gave birth to her. She ate with me, hung out with me all day, and even slept in the same bed as me. But when Chief came home, he always gave her a kick in the ass that sent her flying from the room.

Then I became his fuck slave. He used my body day in and out, taught me the way he liked it, how he wanted to be touched and fucked. I got it right because I didn't want to make him angry and have him fuck me up. And, yes, Chief was a very skillful lover. In all honesty I loved and craved his touch. I asked myself time and time again how someone I feared could make me melt the way he did when we were in bed. He took me to heights I had never been before, so I had no problem sharing my body with him. I began to wonder how many other young girls he had shacked up in beautiful houses.

When it was time for me to take my GED Exam, I was escorted there by Chief himself. He even went as far as to sit in one of the little desks next to me. Then he damn near wanted to strangle the little white lady who told him he couldn't be in the testing room and that he had to leave.

"Young lady, your father needs to wait outside while you take the exam," she said in a choppy voice.

I hid my smile.

"Let me go before I pop this bitch," he said loudly. "I'll be outside. Hurry up."

Shit, this was one request I wasn't going to grant. I took my time, like the book suggested, dividing my time evenly for each section so that I had more time for the part I struggled the most with. I read each question twice and underlined important context clues. I even did the process-of-elimination thing. The book suggested that I put a check mark by a question and come back to it later if I wasn't too sure of the answer.

Once I was done with the test, I went over each and every answer again to make sure I was okay with it and that the circles were filled in completely.

"Thank you for taking me," I told him as we were going home.

He rolled the steering in his hands as he made a right turn. "Now you know daddy been doing a lot for you, Harlem. I got you out those grimy-ass projects away from your sick-ass daddy. Keep you laced, your belly full. You live under a nice little roof, and you get this good dick too. Now I need you to do a little something for me."

I nodded, wondering if I really had a choice in the matter, and what the "little something" was.

Chapter 12

I had to make sure I didn't look nervous the next day. I thought the dress was way too short. My ass was damn near hanging out, and my nipples were poking through the top. My hair was flat-ironed and hung around my shoulders and back. And my face was packed with makeup so I looked not only sexy, but older than seventeen. Today I was Tupac, and all eyes were definitely on me. Many a man were looking my way and offered to let me cut in front of them in the long-ass line at the county jail. And, of course, the females, unless they were gay, were rolling their eyes at me and mumbling under their breath, but that's 'cause their dudes were checking me out.

The security guard with the handheld metal detector kept licking his lips at me. He looked like he wanted to scoop my titties in his hands as he swiped the wand over them. When the detector made a beeping sound, he asked, "It that your bra?" He licked his lips at me again.

It always made me cringe inside. I hated when men

licked their lips at me. It made me feel dirty, fucking impure.

"Yeah, it has a wire in it. Ain't nothing down there, see." I stepped closer to him, careful not to lift my arms, and pressed my breasts against his chest so he got a feel of my nipples. That put his mind right where it needed to be.

The fuck-off was doing a job observing all the curves and crevices of my body, and I let him, so he wouldn't suspect shit.

"Damn, baby," he whispered in my ear, "let me take you out."

"Naw." I shook my head. "I got a man in here."

"So? I don't give a fuck. These niggas in here can't do shit for you, but cause you grief, run up your phone bill, and have the damn post office out of stamps. And then when they ass get out, they gonna bring you AIDS they got from taking it up the ass."

I smiled and shook my head again.

"Girl, I'm serious. Why don't you let me save you some grief, and at the same time"—He paused and pressed his hard dick up against me—"introduce you to my johnson?"

I gave a flirtatious laugh. "Who said he was a detainee?"

"Then who is he?"

"Baby!"

The guard's head shot up toward the warden as he signaled for me at the entrance.

"Hey, boo," I said and slipped past the guard.

I really put on a show, giving him a long tongue kiss, which he returned with far too much tongue and slobber. Shit, he was old enough to be my daddy's daddy. Short, black, and fat as fuck. With dentures.

But I told myself it could be worse. I could be kissing Mr. Berry right about now. Or pushing up on the man-looking lesbian at the front gate who I couldn't get past unless I took the paper from her that had her phone number on it.

She muttered, "Damn! That muthafucka be pullin' all the fine bitches, with his ugly ass. He must be 'kickin' them down with ends.' "

I walked in behind the warden to his office, feeling like this shit was déjà vu. And though I was playing this role very well, I couldn't wait to get the shit over with.

Chief wasn't playing when he taped me up. There were places on my body I almost forgot about. One baggie of the shit was taped on the back of my neck behind my hair. One was in the valley between my breasts. One in the small of my back above where my ass dipped out. Two underneath both my arms, in my armpits. One was taped to my pussy, and one between the crack of my ass. And I had two more taped under the arch of each of my feet.

"Is it okay if I go in the bathroom and do this?" I asked him.

He sat on his desk and shook his head. "Not a chance. How I know you gonna give me all of it and not try to keep some of the stash?"

I rolled my eyes at the fat fuck. He was full of shit. He just wanted to see my bare ass. I stripped out of my clothes under his eyes, shook them one by one so he saw they were empty. I laid them flat on the floor and did the same thing to my heels. I slowly peeled each taped bag of cocaine from my body.

I was bent over, my ass all up in the air, trying to get the tape off my pussy hairs.

"Do you need any assistance?" he asked me in a husky voice.

I flicked him off. Then I shrieked as some of my hair came with the tape. I dropped the bags on his desk one by one then posed nude in front of him, so he could make sure there was no more shit on me I was trying to cop. Inside I felt like a slave at an auction.

Of course he had to be an even bigger ass and examine me "more closely," making me stand there while he lifted each of my breasts and inspected, stuck a finger in my pussy, then split apart my butt cheeks. Yet, his hands lingered a little longer than they needed to on my ass as he rolled my cheeks in his hands. The fucking pervert was making my skin crawl.

"Okay," he finally said, "you can get dressed now."

Once I was fully dressed and on my way out the door, I yelled, "You fat, black bastard. You wish you could hit this pussy!"

I cried on the way back to the house. I caught the driver looking at me, but he said nothing, just had a blank expression on his face.

Once home, I went straight to Chief's room. I would have preferred my own, but he told me when he was home that that's where he wanted me to be. I stripped out of my clothes and hopped in the shower. I scrubbed my body raw and wiped all the silly makeup off my face, as if that would rid me of my latest humiliation. Nothing could make it right. I grabbed a towel and wrapped it around me.

When I walked into the bedroom, Chief was sitting on the bed.

He nodded at me. "How it go?"

I forced a smile. "Good."

"Come here, Harlem."

I went over, and he pulled me on his lap, even though I was still wet and water was dripping on him.

"You got out without any problems or suspicion?"

I nodded, pulling my bottom lip in.

"That ain't bad for your first time in the game, baby." He patted my rump. "You know what you are now, don't you?"

I shook my head. "What?"

"A cold piece of work—a hustlin' bitch." He threw the towel to the floor, pushed me flat on the bed, and started caressing my breasts.

Chief had me, his "hustling bitch," hit up several other jails. He took me all over the state. Only, one time I had to do the shit I almost didn't get out that muthafucka. I had to make it seem like I was seeing an inmate and when I got to the visiting unit I would pass the shit off to one of the corrections officers.

The fucking jail was no joke. I waited in line as usual in my little get-up. I had on some short shorts, which made my ass look three times bigger than it already was, and a halter-top. Chief had me put my hair up in a bun at the crown of my head, which didn't look suspicious because it was hot as hell that day. When I got inside, the security guard with the metal detector was already eyeing me in the line before I even got up to him. I had five people ahead of me, but he was already salivating.

Finally he got through the four people in front of me with the quickness. An older black woman was up next, but she turned to me and said, "Go ahead, dear. I need to find my son's booking number."

"Thank you, ma'am."

Silently I recited in my head the booking number of the dude I was supposed to be visiting. His name was Pierre, and he was supposed to be my baby's father. I stepped to the guard, my sexy smile already planted on my face.

The security officer was looking impatiently out the

window. He shook his head and muttered, "Fucking pigs and department of justice always trying to step in, like we don't do our fucking job right."

I turned my head slightly and almost shitted on myself when a police truck slowly pulled up in the parking structure. But that wasn't what alarmed me. It was the type of police vehicle. The one that carried drug-sniffing K9's.

I continued to watch them as the officer jumped out and went to let the damn dog out the back. I thought quickly.

"Oh shit!" I clutched my stomach desperately. "I gotta use the bathroom."

He looked at me funny and pointed across from him. "The ladies restroom is that way."

"Thank you." I rushed past him, pretending I had the shits.

Once there, tears shot out of my eyes as I locked the door, and hoped no one would come knocking and catch me before I got rid of the shit I had on me. I went into the vacant stall, pulled off my clothes, and yanked the taped baggies off my body, ignoring the pain. Once I had all eight of them, I ripped each bag open, careful not to spill any of it, and dumped the contents in the toilet. I flushed it quickly, and then again, to make sure all the coke went down the drain. I stood at the sink naked and rinsed the baggies out. When all the white powder residue was washed off each bag, I wrapped the bags in about ten paper towels before dropping them in the trash.

But I wasn't done yet. I turned off the cold water and turned the hot water on full blast, took more paper towels and some soap from the dispenser, and scrubbed my body. I scrubbed so hard I wanted to cry. I scrubbed until my skin was damn near bruised and the paper towels were shredding on my skin. I ignored how painful the hot water was on my body, and slapped more water all over until I was convinced there was no cocaine residue anywhere on my person. Then I lightly scrubbed my clothes. Thank God, I'd learned at school from the D.A.R.E. officer that a dope dog can pick up even the smallest amount of the drug.

When I walked back out, the security guard offered to let me get back in my spot in line. I looked around for the police and K9 and saw them walking through the jail entrance about ten feet away from me.

I glanced at the prisoner's name on the sign-in sheet. When I saw another woman's name scribbled across the first line and the time 12PM, I thought of something slick. "Oh hell, no, this muthafucka did not have this bitch for a visitor! And he knew I was coming. Fuck that nigga. Let that bitch put some money on his books." In a huff, I turned and walked past the guard, and the crowd, which was staring at me like I was crazy. I walked out the lobby and continued walking until I was at the pick-up spot.

A few minutes later the driver pulled up. It seemed I had stopped breathing from the moment I had entered that bathroom. I climbed in and leaned back in the seat so relieved that I was sucking in air, almost hyperventilating. Now the only problem was explaining to Chief what happened to his shit.

My legs were shaking as I stood in the doorway and bit my lip, not knowing what kind of a reaction I was going to get from him once I told him I flushed his dope down a toilet. I doubted that if I explained the situation to him he would give a damn about my fear. All he wanted to hear was that I got the job done right.

I stepped into the house and slowly walked up the stairs to Chief's room. He was on his chirp phone and sitting on his bed. I guess he used that chirp all the time because it was a prepaid phone and couldn't be traced back to him. I never saw him use the phone we had in the house, and I never heard that muthafucka ring either. The only person who ever used it was Kenita.

He studied me for a moment, an amused look on his face. I knew that look would vanish the moment he found out what went down.

"What's up, Harlem?" he said as he sat the phone down, not hanging up.

"I have to tell you something."

He patted the bed next to him. "Sit down."

I obeyed.

"Aye, dawg, let me hit you back." He sat the phone down and looked back at me. "How did the run go?"

I took a deep breath and scratched at my scalp nervously. "Well, that's what I want to talk to you about. See . . . umm—"

"Spit the shit out! What happened? I got shit to do." He knocked a fist into his open palm, making a loud sound and making me jump.

"I couldn't bring the drugs in. I got to the door and a police officer with a K9 dog was coming in, so I had to dump them down a toilet. I'm so sorry, Chief." I closed my eyes, waiting for my body to be filled with pain—either a smack across my face or a punch in my stomach.

Chief busted up laughing. "That was only a test, Harlem. That's a hard jail to bring drugs into. Ever since an inmate went AWOL, security been tight like a muthafucka. I just wanted to see if you could do it. Don't trip. It wasn't real shit. That was just flour. I figured if you could get that in, you can get the real thing in. I guess you can't. You not as slick as I thought you were. Don't worry, I got somebody else for the job."

He dismissed me and went back to his phone conversation.

Although he never made me go back to any jails, I damn sure was put in another risky situation.

The next time he had me dress up, the driver dropped me off at a fancy-ass hotel to meet some nigga named Rico.

I walked inside carrying a big-ass Dooney & Bourke bag filled with cash. This time I was getting the pick-up. I met the dude downstairs at the small café. The deal was he was under tough-ass surveillance from the cops, so I had to make it look like he was my man, who I was meeting for a light dinner then a little romp in one of the rooms upstairs. I was dressed conservative that time in a white blouse, a pearl necklace, and a pair of black slacks, and my hair was brushed back in a neat ponytail that was braided. I strolled into the hotel and went straight into the little restaurant inside. The only thing was, Chief didn't tell me what the nigga looked like, but he would know what I would be wearing.

I almost went to the wrong dude, a guy who was seated and eating dinner alone. When I heard, "Lola," the code name, I immediately turned on my heels and walked over to a man who looked like he was Costa Rican.

Rico was a handsome man, tall, with a muscular body. He had curly hair and a neatly groomed goatee. He wore a suit and wasn't the type of dude I expected to be involved in this line of work. But underneath that suit he was no better than Chief. He was a fucking criminal too. He grabbed me, and I was forced to give him a long kiss. Only, I didn't mind so much because he wasn't bad to look at. Not at all.

He pulled out the chair for me. Since we didn't know where the narcs could be, we played lovey-dovey and continued to kiss and hold hands during the whole meal. We ordered pasta, which we shared from one plate, for effect.

For dessert, I fed a slice of raspberry cheesecake to him before leaning over and kissing him again. It seemed by the glazed look in his eyes and the way he was eyeing my titties that he didn't mind too much about making out with me either.

After he paid the check he got up and pulled back my chair. I stood up, and he wrapped his arm around my waist. We smiled at each other and walked up the stairs to our room.

Once we made it to the second floor, anxiety hit me. Yeah, he was playing a role in the restaurant during dinner, but what if he was thinking about flipping the script and maybe trying to do something crazy to me. Like try to get the dough in the bag without giving up the dope, and killing me if need be. I had no way of protecting myself. No gun, no knife, nothing.

He opened the door, and my smile faded when I saw the dark room.

"Hit the fucking light switch," I ordered, like I was somebody.

He chuckled. "Anything for you, *chica.*" He walked a few feet away from me and flipped them on.

I nearly jumped out of my skin when I saw another man lounging in a chair in the room facing the door. But that's not what scared me the most. It was the big-ass bazooka he had pointed at me.

I placed my hand over my chest and demanded in the most confident and pissed-off voice I could find, "What the fuck is going on, Rico? Do Chief know about this?"

Rico laughed again, as did his heavily-armed friend.

"We're not afraid of Chief."

Well, that was a first. I almost wanted to shake their hands.

"Now, lessee what you got in the bag."

As he took a couple steps toward me, I took a couple back. "You ain't seeing shit until he stops pointing that goddamn gun at me." I didn't have much to lose. If they were gonna kill me they would have done it already.

They both stared me down with menacing looks.

I glared up at Rico. "I'm not playing."

After a pregnant pause, they both turned to each other and burst out laughing again.

"You know what," Rico said, "I like you, *chica.*"

You ain't gotta like me. Just have your boy put that fucking gun down.

Even though Rico's man laid the gun on the bed behind him, I wasn't gonna relax until I was the fuck up and out of there.

I handed them the bag and leaned against the wall while they went to work. Within five minutes they had counted the twenty G's in there and re-stuffed the bag with their shit for me to take back to Chief. At a glance I could see it was some type of weird-looking pills.

When he tossed the bag back, I casually pushed myself off the wall and followed Rico out the door. Behind us the other dude yelled something in Spanish.

My head shot around, but before I could say something smart, Rico said, "Don't worry. He said he likes you, and that maybe, just maybe, a beautiful *chica* like you would consider coming and working for us."

Chapter 13

I had been counting down the days until my GED test score would come. Maybe finishing school didn't make a difference to some, but shit, getting my diploma and going to college meant something to me. Just because I was from the hood didn't mean I didn't see the importance of getting an education and knowing how much having a college degree would help me.

When I saw the white envelope with my name on it, I squealed and ripped it open. My eyes flew over my scores. Not only did I pass the shit, but my scores were higher than the damn passing scores!

I wished my mom was alive so I could show her. I was anxious to share my news with someone, so I ran into the entertainment room where Chief was. He'd been entertaining guests the night before. I didn't know they were still there though.

"Chief! Chief!"

Seven sets of eyes swung to me, making me feel self-conscious in my little shorts that read on the booty,

"CUTE," and I had on my hot pink tank top with no bra underneath and no shoes on my feet.

This was the place Chief came to unwind, and my ass was rarely invited in there. Chief's entertainment room was the biggest room in the whole house. There was a pool table in there, a big-ass stereo system so loud that when he played music you could feel the vibrations from the bass all over the damn house. Must have shaken the block too, 'cause once a neighbor came banging on our door, telling us to turn the music down.

Chief went to answer the door with his gun. He yanked it open and pointed the gun directly at the neighbor and said coldly, "Muthafucka, you trespassing. I could blow your ass away and get away with it."

The neighbor never came to our door again. But, I guess, to avoid any other neighbor from getting the balls to come to his door, he had some soundproof walls installed. The entertainment room had not one, but three flat-screen TV's, and it was stocked with a DVD player, an Xbox, and PlayStation. Across from the biggest TV were two red suede couches, the other two TV's were on the walls. There was also a stocked bar and bar stools in the back, and chains divided the bar from the small dance floor, where there was a DJ stand. Chief also had a portable stripper pole set up in the room, which I didn't remember seeing in there before. It was like a mini-club. Whenever I went in the room when Chief was there, it always smelled like weed, and today was no exception.

My eyes flew around the room. There was cups of drink all around, and niggas was smoking blunts. There were even lines of coke laid out on the glass coffee table, along with some of those weird-looking pills.

Chief, Solomon, and a dude named Nicky were seated

at the table. Two dudes were shooting pool, and two others were seated at the bar.

Chief stared at me through glazed eyes. He was high as fuck. He sat down his dominoes. "Harlem, you know what I always wanted to ask you?"

"What?"

He grinned. "Can you play dominoes, baby?"

I shrugged. "Yeah, I guess, but no better than anybody else."

"Girl, as smart as you are you mean to tell me you not good at slapping bones?"

"No, not really."

"Well, let us be the judge of that. Sit down over there."

I sat at the round table at the empty chair.

Chief chuckled. "Now this is the catch to the game, Harlem, 'cause we bored as fuck with the usual game and we wanna spice it up, and just when we was thinking of a way to liven up thangs, here you come along."

I bit my bottom lip, wondering if it was such a good move to barge in on them.

"Now here's the catch—For every game you lose, you have to take off something. Cool?"

I narrowed my eyes at him, as I took in what he was asking me to do.

All the niggas at the table were frozen, waiting for my next move. Ugly-ass Solomon was smirking 'cause it was just up his alley to see me naked so he could lush on me.

I could not stand Solomon. Whenever Chief wasn't looking, he was winking at me and eyeing me in a sexual manner. The look I always gave him told him I wouldn't spit on his cross-eyed ass. Hell, when he was staring at my titties he was probably seeing four of them. And he was real sneaky about it. He made sure he never did it when Chief was looking. Once, he even went as far as to rub up against me and then pretended like he bumped into me by accident.

I scooted away from him and muttered, "I'll tell you about a cross-eyed muthafucka—Half the time they can't see where the fuck they goin'."

His reply back was, "I'll tell you about a ho—Half the time they can't keep their mouth shut."

But he was Chief's boy, and they were close. So I doubt Chief would've believed me if I told him he made passes at me.

"Chief—"

"You ain't gotta do nothing that's a big deal. Hell, we all high, so you probably win any damn way."

I tilted my head to the side and tried to keep the annoyance off my face. After a moment of silence I said, "Just one game, you promise, Chief?"

"One game."

I closed my eyes and pretended I was at home with my mother, when we used to play together. I watched him throw a couple pills in his mouth that he washed down with a small bottle of Hennessy, while Solomon put the dominoes on the table face down. My heart sped up as he shuffled them.

Solomon shoved seven dominoes to everybody at the table to start the game. Nicky's whole face lit up, and I knew why. He probably got the big six.

I bit my bottom lip as he put it in the middle of the table.

I looked down at my dominoes. I didn't have a six or anything to make six. Solomon had one, and Chief had one, so I tried to pass.

"It ain't fair for you to get away with passing, Harlem," Chief told me.

"What?"

"I consider passing losing, so every time you pass, you need to take off something. Nicky, since you picked the lucky six, pick what she takes off."

My eyes burned into Chief's. Then they shot to Nicky's. I prayed he'd refuse to go along with this shit.

He licked his lips at me. "Take off your blouse."

"Chief—"

"A game's a game, Harlem. You agreed, so take that shit off." His eyes bore into mine, making me drop the dominoes out of my hands and lift my tank top over my head.

If I had to pass again or if I lose, I'd be assed out, because all I had left on was my underwear and shorts.

Chief started laughing and saying, "Tickled bitties!" Nicky whistled.

Embarrassed, I kept my head down. I wanted to cross my arms over my chest.

"Pick up your bones, Harlem, and let's finish the game."

I did as he told me.

The next person to go was Solomon. He made six again with two dominoes. Chief followed. Then Nicky. This time I was cool. I put it down a match to what Solomon put down, like the rest of them did.

Now Chief put down two more dominoes, one with a six, another with a three.

I took a deep breath as Nicky was able to put something down to match it and Solomon, but I didn't.

"Go on, Harlem. Let's keep this game going."

I put down two dominoes, hoping Chief would be too drunk to know that they didn't match.

Chief took one look at the two I put down and shoved

them away. "Get that bullshit off the table, Harlem, and take them ass shorts off."

The two dominoes fell to the floor.

I pleaded with his eyes. But he was too busy looking at his remaining dominoes.

At this point a few of the other men in the room were crowding around us, and all their eyes were on my titties. Now they were watching as I stripped out of my shorts.

Chief just looked at me and chuckled. "Now play your hand right, Harlem."

I tried to bend over to retrieve the other two dominoes.

Chief barked, "Naw, your cheating ass lost them. Use what the fuck is on the table."

That meant I only had one domino left to play. I looked down at my hands to avoid all the eyes lushing on me.

"Play your shit, Harlem!" Chief slapped the table, making the dominoes rattle.

I looked down at the only domino in my hand. My hand started shaking. The board had sixes and threes, and I had a five. I had to pass again. I paused nervously, hoping Chief would let me go. "I pass, Chief," I said quietly.

"What?"

"I got a five."

"You know what that means."

"No, Chief."

"Take your shit off!"

Now all the men were crowded around the table, and I had no choice but to stand up to my feet and take off my underwear. Then I stood naked in front of all of his friends. All side conversations had stopped.

Chief stared me down. "Sit over there where everybody can see you."

I walked slowly to the small couch across from the table,

wishing I could sink into the cushions. I'd never felt so uncomfortable and embarrassed as I sat there waiting for him to tell me I could leave.

He didn't. Instead he forced me to remain seated on the couch, ass buck-naked, until the game was over.

Nicky won.

I kept my eyes on the floor, not wanting to meet anybody's gaze.

Then I heard Chief say, "A deal's a deal, man. Fuck it."

He looked even higher than he was when I first walked in the room.

I heard him ask Nicky, "What you want her to do, dawg?"

Nicky whispered something.

The next thing I knew, Chief pointed a finger at me. "Play with yourself, Harlem."

I looked at his friend, who was taking a long drag from a blunt. "Huh?"

"Nicky won. He get to pick what you do."

My eyes widened. "No, Chief, I don't wanna do that. You said play a game of dominoes. You are really tripping." *To hell with my clothes.* I stood, turned my back on him, and rushed to the door. Then I heard a click that made me stop in my tracks.

"Don't do that, Harlem. Don't fuck up my high. Do what the fuck I tell you to do." The muthafucka had a gun pointed directly at me. "Give my nigga a show. You act like I'm asking you to give him your damn liver."

Them fucking tears came pouring down again. I hesitated as I begged Chief with my eyes not to make me do something like this. So degrading, so embarrassing. So nasty! But he never dropped the gun. Just raised it to my head and repeated his order.

I walked back over to the couch and sat down facing them. Shame filled me.

"Cock open them legs," Chief said.

His friends stood still as statues as I revealed my pussy.

"Do it right for Daddy, and do it slow," Chief urged.

I closed my eyes and placed my shaking hand over my pussy. Then I stuck my finger in myself and pulled it out. It was making the men yell and laugh like I was really entertaining them.

"Look how tight her pussy is," Nicky said.

"Slide in some more fingers," Chief ordered.

I obeyed by plunging two fingers into myself.

"Now lick them."

Dudes in the room grunted, moaned, and whistled as I slipped my finger in my mouth and tasted myself. I wanted to throw the fuck up.

"Tell her what to do, Nicky," Chief yelled. "Damn! It's your fantasy, ugly muthafucka."

"Play with your clit," Nicky said in a nervous voice.

I tried to keep my tears in the corner of my eyes, as I rubbed my hands over my clit.

Then Chief told me to use my other hand to fondle my titties, and the grunting continued.

I was feeling sick at all the men I knew were leering at me. My hands were making my own skin crawl.

Then I was told to open my pussy lips wide, so they could see the inside.

They went crazy.

"Stroke it until it get wet," Chief said to me.

I stroked myself for a little longer.

"Okay, Harlem," Chief said, "that's enough. Get the fuck out!"

I hopped up off the couch silently and, in a quick pace,

left the entertainment room. I went into the bathroom to rinse my mouth off and wash myself off of my hands. Then I tossed on a nightgown, and lay in the bed and cried until I dozed off.

A few hours later Chief's loud voice woke me up. "Bitch, what the fuck is wrong with you, getting naked and acting like a freak in front of my homeboys?" He punched me in my stomach, knocking the breath out of me.

I had my mouth wide open, but no sound came out. Tears ran down my cheeks at the pain.

Without another word he walked out of the room.

Okay, it was official. I hated Chief. Everything about him. The way he walked, the way he talked. How he used his height and power to make me do the most humiliating and fucked-up shit. He told me constantly how he thought I was so precious, fine. Beautiful even. Smart. But yet he treated me like I was some ho out in the street, pretty much making me his drug mule, then making me blow his punk-ass friend. That shit was not love. No nigga ever showed me love, except for Savior. But the feeling that he was gonna some day rescue me like he did before were long-gone thoughts. No matter how much I thought about him, I came to the conclusion that he didn't give a fuck about me either. That's how I felt. Or more so, I forced myself to feel that way.

From where I was looking I may have been young, but I'd lived a fucked-up life and was on my way to a fucked-up future. I truly didn't know how to get myself out of that mess.

After a three-day hiatus, Chief popped up. I sighed inside because I wished the big bastard had stayed where the fuck he was.

I was sitting on my bed brushing Lady's hair. When she saw Chief, she snarled at him, making her cute little face look so vicious and ugly. I held my lips in to hide my laugh. When he tried to pet her, she snapped her head back and nicked one of his fingers.

He leaned over and smacked her so hard, she fell from the bed. "You little bitch!"

As she whimpered and ran out the room, I cut my eyes at him.

"Okay, I'm sorry. Damn! You act like you love that dog more than you love me? Why is that, Harlem? Huh?"

"She never hurt me, Chief, and lately it seems like that's all you do."

"Is that how you feel? I hurt you?"

My look said it all.

"Look, the other night I was fucked up off that X, out of it, baby, else that shit would have never went down. Them niggas knew I was out of it, and they let it go down anyway."

"Yeah, whatever." *Because you popped ecstasy that makes it okay? Shiiit.*

He chuckled. "You ain't letting that shit go, are you?"

I ignored him and pulled strands of Lady's hair out of the brush.

He stroked his beard and studied me carefully. "Here then, baby girl. Damn!" He sat two velvet boxes in my lap. "Look at them."

I huffed out a deep breath and opened both the boxes. One had a beautiful tennis bracelet. The other was a matching necklace, and they were blinging! Despite their beauty, I handed them back to him. "I don't want them."

Now he took a deep breath. "You know it's a lot I can deal with, but not with you being mad at me, or that silent treatment shit y'all silly women like to do."

Get the fuck over it! I wanted to yell. *I don't like having to perform like a porno star!*

"Well, get dressed. Something real pretty. I'm taking you to a party."

Chapter 14

Stepping out with Chief to the Century Club, I was dressed in a cream-colored dress that slinked over my curves and had a slit that went all the way up my thigh, and some flashy-ass heels by Jimmy Choo—whoever that was. I styled my hair in a side ponytail that hung over one shoulder. Chief had on a fly, cream-colored suit with matching hat, his hair hanging down underneath. And, yeah, he looked handsome. All the females were checking him out, and the males were checking me out. But what those females didn't know was that he was no knight in shining armor. And, as for me, hey, I was pretty, but I was damaged goods.

We went right in the club. No line for us. As we walked around, I noticed a lot of people from the projects in there. Girls I knew were pulling me each and every way, asking if I was okay after what went down, and if my daddy was locked up, and did I still miss my mom.

Chief shoved them out of my way. "She don't wanna hear that shit. Bitches, move!"

Chief led me right to the VIP section, which was filled
with his friends and their lady friends, some of whom were
their hoes. In all, there were about twenty different guys
and their dates. This twenty included all those who were at
his house the day I had to play with myself, including
Solomon. I wondered how his date could look at him in
his fucked-up eyes without cracking up. Did she wonder if
he was looking at her or someone else? I always did. And
when he was having sex with her and on the verge of coming, did his one eye cross more, roll up in the back of his
head, or straighten out? The guy who won the domino
game, Nicky, was there too, and the dude was fucked up.
One of his eyes was closed shut and damn near purple, his
bottom lip was huge, and one of his arms was in a sling.
Every time I looked his way, he avoided my gaze, but every
now and then I caught him mean-mugging me. I simply
smirked and looked the other way.

They sipped Moet, Hennessy, and Hpnotiq and chalked
it up.

Chief said, "Fuck Cristal," and kept downing glasses of
all kinds of shit, but when he offered me some, I declined.
I sipped on a soda instead.

I was bored. I wanted to get up and dance to get rid of
this pressure in my chest. I was dressed to kill and I knew I
looked nice, and being Chief's lady, I had more clothes
than I could've ever imagined having when I lived in the
projects. And I knew all the other women in there wanted
this spot. But I didn't.

Project life, the violence, not knowing if when you
walked out your front door you'd ever come back, or the
chance of getting your head blown off, just sitting on your
stoop, I'd take that back any day. Still, you took a chance
and you sat out there anyway. All of it—I'd take it all back
in a minute if I could escape the life I lived now, never

mind the roaches, rodents, the cold-ass house in the winter, barely having food, and not having clothes while all my friends were decked out. Only thing was, I just didn't know how to get away.

I was so absorbed in my own thoughts I didn't know what the sudden chatter was all about. Voices grew louder, and I heard a lot of laughter.

Chief jumped up and yelled, "My nigga! About fucking time." He embraced a tall guy.

Chief's shoulders were so broad, I couldn't see past them to see who the guy was, but when Chief pulled away my heart skipped a beat. It was Savior! All the other dudes followed suit, giving him hugs.

I simply sat and stared at him, but I made sure my face didn't show what I was really feeling.

When he turned his head, his eyes connected with mine. He lost his composure for a moment, but his smile came back instantly when another dude gave him a bear hug. But his eyes were still on me. He was bigger than the last time I saw him, his shoulders broader, his chest wider. Shit, he was almost as big as Chief. And now his braids were replaced with a bald head.

I put my head down for a moment and nervously pulled my bottom lip in.

"Here, muthafucka. Come and get a drink, man. Where the fuck is that waitress?" Chief shoved him down next to me and pushed a drink in his hand.

When his thigh came into contact with mine, I jumped up from my seat. "I'm going to the bathroom, Chief," I said, and slid past them both.

"Harlem, tell that sorry-ass waitress to bring up some more bottles of Moet. It's a celebration, bitches!"

Everyone laughed, except for Savior, who continued to watch me.

I stumbled out of the room and down the stairs to the restroom, which was packed with females, touching up their makeup and messing in their hair. I assumed they were hoping to score a man or a damn sugar daddy. I didn't really need to use the bathroom, so I stood and watched them for a moment, waiting for a stall to be empty. When one was available, I stepped in and sat on the toilet seat, trying to catch my breath.

Savior was here. *After a year he fucking reappears. Did he get another job, go back home to see his mom, get another woman? Maybe he got married. And what is he doing back here? And more importantly, why did he leave without me?* A dozen more questions filled my head, and I had no answer to any of them bitches. One thing was for sure; he never came to see me again after my mom passed, so maybe that was the confirmation I needed that he really didn't care what I was doing. I mean, I wanted him to punch out Chief and say he was taking me away from there. Even shoot his ass if he had too. I wouldn't be hurt. No, sir. I know the shit sounds corny, but I was hoping he would pick me up in his arms and carry me out of that club and into a new life, no worries about the future. We'd go somewhere like Paris, or where I would love to go—Rome.

Harlem, kill those thoughts. It's good to dream, but it's just not going down.

I left the restroom and went to the bar to get the waitress' attention. She was serving someone at the other end, so I drummed my fingers on a bar counter that held an abandoned drink. I was in no hurry. Any time wasted at the bar kept me out of the fucking VIP section and away from Chief and Savior.

I felt someone was standing behind me. I turned my head, and my heart started beating again. I acted indifferently, like I didn't care if Savior was in the room when, deep

down, shit, I did. I wanted to leap into his arms and hug
him and cry my eyes out about what I'd been through.
About what I was still going through. And here it was again,
I was thinking that maybe, just maybe, he could get me
out of it. But my voice of reason came back in my head.
Harlem, Savior ain't thinking 'bout you. I glanced at him.

He just stared at me with a blank, unreadable expression. He twisted his lips twisted to one side then to the
other side of his face.

"What the fuck you looking at?" I yelled.

He just laughed, making me madder. It wasn't one of
them laughs when someone is laughing with you, 'cause I
wasn't laughing. It was one of those laughs when you knew
they were laughing *at* you.

"Well?" I snapped my head to the side then rolled it
around in a circle. "What do you want?"

"Chief told me to check on you to make sure you was
okay down here and to make sure no dude was all over
you."

"Gee, what a nice little puppy dog you are, Savior."

He aimed a finger at me. "Bitch, I know you not talking."

That got me for a minute. The color drained from my
face. Still, I pretended I didn't care. I made barking sounds
at him and rolled my eyes to the ceiling.

He took my right arm and pulled me closer to him,
causing me to wince a little at the pain of his grip. He
whispered furiously, "I ain't nobody's fucking flunkie! You
the one who shacking up with the nigga, giving him pussy
at his beck and call. For what? So you can lay up on your
ass and wear this kinda shit, like some gold-digging tramp?
Harlem, that's exactly what the fuck you are. I been watching you for the past ten minutes. You just like the rest of
these bitches in here. You enjoying this shit"—He yanked

at my dress—"not me, so let's get that shit straight right fucking now." He shoved me away so hard, I almost fell off the bar stool.

"And what the fuck you know about what I do and what I want, Savior?"

"I know enough. I used to think you were different than those project chickens. I thought you had some substance to you. I was wrong. You ain't got no integrity in you. Hell, you don't even have self-respect. And it seems to me you right where you wanna be—somebody's kept ho." He pulled me by the collar of my shirt.

"Fuck you, nigga. You ain't shit no way." I picked up the glass of half-filled drink and flung it directly in his face.

Savior scowled when the brown liquid hit him. He stood up to me like he wanted to slap the shit out of me, but he simply grabbed a napkin, wiped his face, and backed away from me.

I slid off the bar stool and sauntered off in the opposite direction, although we were heading back to the same place. I wanted to stop him, tell him the truth. But would he really give a damn? He did, after all, leave without me, despite his promise, and it wasn't just that my pride got in the way. *Fuck Savior.*

But even as I walked away, my eyes began to water because of what he said. Damn, it hurt. Imagine, the one you loved all that time fucking hated you. And I didn't know why. What I also didn't know was why I didn't hate him, even though I wanted to. Damn, I wanted to.

Chief didn't pay me no mind when I went back to the VIP section and sat down. He continued downing his drink and entertaining his friends. He thought he was a real comedian, and they laughed at him like he was. He acting like he was Nino Brown and shit, with his shirt unbuttoned and a Hennessy bottle in his hand, singing "Super Freak" like he was Rick James.

When Savior came back, he smirked at me then sat across from me, making me shift my body and face the other way to avoid his mocking gaze.

"Sorry it took me so long," he said, his eyes on me. "I had to tell some simple-ass bitch about herself."

I bit the inside of my mouth to fight the urge to go off on him.

"That's right," Chief said. "Tell these bitches!"

Chief bumped into me. He turned around. "I'm sorry, baby." Then he bent over and started kissing me, using extra tongue and slobber, with his drunk ass.

I spied Savor's eyes on us, and his look of disgust. I guess this was my time to smirk, but I didn't.

By two AM my ass was ready to go, but people were still partying. Chief had disappeared with Solomon and three other dudes to smoke some weed. They said they'd be in the parking lot.

I was stuck there, forced to sit under the evil glare of Savior. And when he wasn't mean-mugging me, Nicky was still shooting evil stares my way. I rose and walked past both of them and the other people partying and went out on the balcony to get some air from all the heat in the damn room. I was hoping Chief would hurry the hell up so we could go home. I took a deep breath of the fresh air but exhaled quickly when I suddenly heard what sounded like a woman crying.

I walked over to the opposite edge of the balcony and stared down at Chief and his other four flunkies. There was a girl down there too standing in front of Chief. She looked familiar as hell.

"Chief," she whined.

Solomon snuck up behind her and kicked her in her ass, making her fall forward.

She stood up quickly and got all in his face. "Don't touch me, you cross-eyed fucker!"

One of the other dudes raised up her skirt, revealing her thong.

"Stop!" She turned and slapped his hand.

Chief leaned against one of the cars and laughed louder.

"Chief, why you doing me like this?" She rushed toward him again. "You know how I feel."

"How you feel, girl?"

"I love you."

I heard the heels of his shoes slid against the gravel on the concrete as he got in her face. "What? Love? Y'all hear this ho?"

"I do," she said in a shaky voice.

"Shit, you was a jump-off ho. You got the game twisted."

"What about all the shit I did for you—bringing dope up in the county jail for you, the fucking transports I did, and entertaining your punk-ass friends?" She was flinging her arms as she spoke.

Chief stepped to her and gripped his hands around her throat. "Look, bitch, you was the one who wanted to get crazy and pop up where I rest my head, getting in my damn business."

"But I was just jealous," she said in a high-pitched voice. "Bitches in the projects was saying a new girl had stepped to my man and was laying up with him. I was just going after what was mine."

He shoved her away. "What was yours? Bitch, you think you runnin' me? You crazy."

She came running right back up to him. "No, Chief, I

thought I was your chick. I been down with you for over a year."

"Yeah? Well now your pussy is tired to me. It lacks 'lasticity."

She was now crying hysterically at his cold-ass words, but his buddies were busting up laughing at his comments.

"But me and my family ain't got nowhere else to go now. You know they threw all our shit in the street."

Chief studied the girl and stroked his beard. "Let me ask you a question, Tina—Are you loyal?"

"You know I am, Chief. Whatever you want, you know I'm down."

In that next moment I watched horrified as she bent over against Savior's car and Solomon and the other three dudes ran a train on her, fucking her one by one.

Chief just laughed and watched, singing between each chuckle, "It ain't no fun if the homies can't have none."

She looked like she was being tortured. Solomon was the roughest with her, yanking on her hair and smacking her on the ass as he rode her.

I felt a chill run down my back as one dude after the other jammed their dick into her and she let out moans of pain, not pleasure, that I later couldn't get out of my head. I stepped away from the balcony rail and turned away with tears in my eyes for the girl, even though she was the one who had attacked me with a switchblade.

Chapter 15

I sat by the side of the pool in my bikini soaking up all the sun the next day, trying to forget about the night before and how embarrassed I was seeing Savior and him seeing me with Chief. His words had been coming and going through my head all night and day: "... *you right where you wanna be—somebody's kept ho!*"

I shook my head, but the thoughts weren't going anywhere. I felt like shit. And in all honesty, I was a well-kept ho. Didn't want to be, but hell, that was my title. And that wasn't the only thing on my mind. I thought about that girl and the nasty shit she had to do to prove her loyalty to Chief. I wondered if I would ever be in her position. It wasn't as if I hadn't degraded myself already.

The evil maid from hell came outside and instructed me that Chief was calling for me.

I wrapped my sarong around my hips and went to his room, where he was lying on his bed, ass buck-naked and stroking his dick. I lowered my gaze, not in the mood for no fucking with his nasty ass.

As much as I enjoyed sex with him before, I hated it two times over with him now. It got to the point that he made my skin crawl. I knew I had no choice though. Before the night was over I'd either be on my knees or on my back, but never on top though. It seemed to me that Chief had some serious power issues. Once I tried to get on top of him while we were having sex, and he body slammed me so hard on the bed, he knocked the breath out of me. Crazy ass.

"Come in, baby. I got a surprise for you."

I stepped in the room.

"Come on and give Chief a kiss."

I slipped on the bed, crawled to him on my knees, and did as he requested.

His hands gripped my ass and massaged my butt cheeks as he slipped his tongue in my mouth.

I closed my eyes and continued to kiss him the way I knew he liked to be kissed.

He pulled off my sarong, slid my bikini bottom off, and began slipping a finger in my pussy. His kissing became rougher, and I know, when I felt someone slip their tongue in the crack of my ass, that I wasn't imagining things.

I pulled away from Chief and turned on my back to find a young girl about my age crouched on her knees less than a foot away from me. "Chief, what the f—"

"Relax, baby." He pulled me back on top of him. "Remember I said I had a surprise for you?"

I twisted my head and mad "dogged" the girl. She was black with beautiful mahogany-colored skin and a short haircut that framed her pretty face. She was real skinny too. She had a tongue piercing and was ass buck-naked, with a facial expression that said, "Down for anything."

Well, I wasn't! When she tried to touch me again, I backed away to the edge of the bed.

Chief laughed. "Relax, baby. Let's have a good day."

I shook my head. "I can't do that!"

"You really ain't got no choice in the matter, so lay the fuck back," he growled, gripping the back of my ponytail.

As I lay back on the bed, my heart was in my throat as she slowly approached me like a cat. Chief sat up and watched, fascinated, as she crouched between my legs. First, she started rubbing all over me, cupping my buttocks in her hands and kissing me all over my neck. Then her hands snaked up to my titties. Then more kisses to my stomach. She scooted her body up, and her tongue flickered over my nipples, while her dark eyes held me, wide-set, penetrating. Then her hands started stroking my face.

I resisted the urge to knock them away.

Chief grunted, and I looked his way. He was sitting there stroking his dick so hard, I thought the outer skin was going to slide right off. When Chief felt the girl (who I wouldn't dare touch voluntarily) was giving me too much attention, he started tripping and wanted us all over him.

I had the top of his body, and she the bottom. I kissed him, while she sucked his dick. As I was bent over, one of her hands slinked over my ass, and she slid a finger in my pussy and started to stroke it rapidly. While Chief wasn't looking, I pushed the bitch's hands away from me. I was disgusted as fuck, but I had no choice. Never fucking did. Either it was perform a threesome or probably get fucked up.

He wanted her to stroke his back as he fucked me. Then, between fucking me, he wanted her to suck his dick again, which she did with a whole lot of enjoyment. Then he wanted me to sit on his face so he could eat my pussy in front of her.

She lay back on the bed, watching and finger-fucking the hell out of her pussy, as Chief's tongue slid into me.

Nasty bitch!

She then crawled over to Chief and pulled one of his hands to her so he could penetrate her with his finger. As he did it, she started screaming and grabbing her titties.

Chief slapped me on my ass. "Get on your knees, Harlem." He followed behind me on his knees and slid his dick in my pussy.

She positioned herself underneath me and started raising her head and licking on my titties and squeezing my clit between her fingers. Chief pumped into me hard and came like I never felt him come before.

But we weren't done. With him you're never done till he said so. Next, he made the girl dry-hump me while he watched and continued to rub his dick up and down, until cum shot from his dick to the damn wall.

Still, we weren't done.

In the bathroom, he sat on the toilet and watched while me and the girl took a shower together. Then he hopped in too and had me hold on to the shower head while he fucked me. Meanwhile, she crawled out of the tub, lay on the floor, and once again finger-fucked herself.

Chapter 16

I woke up the next day to find Chief watching a tape of the three-way. That made me wonder what else his sneaky ass filmed. But I doubted he would voluntarily tell me. He was sitting there relaxing and smoking a cigar, while my pussy and the girl's head were on the widescreen in the entertainment room. I hid in the corner as he watched.

His cell phone rang. He used the remote to turn the TV off. "This Chief, man. What's up, Savior? Oh that's going down in a few days, man. Yeah."

I snuck back into his room, but I could still hear the conversation.

"What house got stuck up? Awww, shit! Man, I'm on my way."

I jumped back into his bed, my mind made up.

Once I saw his Benz speed out the driveway, I snuck back into the entertainment room and pulled the tape out the VCR. Then I struggled to find a spot to put it in my room. I was so busy doing it, I didn't notice that the housekeeper watching me. I made a face at her, and she smacked her teeth and walked away. *Hopefully Chief won't notice it missing.*

Later that night as I was in bed dozing off, I felt a sharp pain in my neck. I opened my sleepy eyes to find Chief's angry face hovering over me.

"I'm going to ask you one time and one time only— Where the fuck is my tape?"

"Chief—"

Bam! He threw me from the bed into a wall.

As I fell to the floor, pain shot threw my right shoulder.

Chief came behind me, grabbed me by my hair, and bashed my forehead into the carpeted floor.

I screamed again and pointed underneath the bed, hoping that would stop his assault on me.

"Get the muthafucka."

I crawled on the floor in such a hurry to grab it, I banged my own head into my bed. I shook it and reached under the bed for the tape.

"Hurry the fuck up!"

I stretched my fingers until I felt the edge of the tape. I curved my fingers around its edge and pulled it toward me. I stood back on my feet and handed it to him.

He wouldn't take it though. Instead he pulled off his belt, held me by one of my arms, and started swatting my ass with it. I kept screaming over and over again, telling him that I was sorry, but he kept whipping my ass until there were welts crisscrossed all over my behind.

When he got tired he shoved me on the bed. "Don't ever touch shit that belongs to me!" He scooped up the tape.

For the next ten minutes I had to lie in bed on my side because my ass was on fire. Meanwhile, Chief went back into the entertainment room. The door was closed, and I didn't dare enter it. I did, however, sneak over and put my ear to the door. I couldn't hear much, but one thing was for sure—Chief wasn't gonna let go of that tape.

I was soaking my sore ass in a tub filled with warm water and Epsom salts when Chief barged in the bathroom, no smile or apology for what went down the night before, just a cold-ass nod.

I nodded back.

"Aye, when you get out of that tub, I got something for you to try on in the room." With that, he shut the door behind him.

I got out of the tub quickly, grabbed a towel, and dried my body off. I was extra careful and gentle when it came to my behind because it was still sore from that ass-beating he gave me the night before.

When I walked into the bedroom, I was expecting to find some hoochie mama dress or a sexy outfit he wanted me to wear. Instead I noticed there was a big sweatshirt on the bed and a pair of jeans in my size. I read the lettering on the shirt and smiled—*California State University Dominguez Hills.*

My heart started to pound and I was hit with a rush of excitement. Did this mean Chief was going to let me start college? It had been some time since I had passed the GED. I smiled and hugged the sweatshirt to my chest. I wanted to study social work. I was going to join all the clubs they had on campus: drama, art, dance, an Afro-centric club, a club for helping the environment, and a club for big sisters (if there was one). Count my black ass in. I was going to do sports. Hell, maybe I'd even join a sorority.

With Chief doing this shit for me, maybe he wasn't so damn bad after all. He just needed to work on his temper.

He walked into the room. "Try the shit on, Harlem."

I dropped the towel, put on a bra and panties, and slipped into the sweatshirt and jeans. I knew there was excitement in my eyes. Once I was done, I stood in front of him silently.

He examined me for a long time, twisting one of the rings on his finger. Then he nodded to himself and said, "Yeah."

"Thank you, Chief. When do I start?" I asked breathlessly.

His eyes narrowed. "Start what?"

I gestured toward the shirt. "The college."

"What the fuck you talkin' 'bout, Harlem? You ain't startin' no college. You goin' to Vegas to do a drug run with Savior. The sweater is just a decoy to make y'all look like some college students hanging out there for spring break. Now throw some shoes on, pack you some shit, and march your ass downstairs. And you betta hurry."

Chapter 17

I sighed when I found Savior sitting in the living room sipping a soda. He had a mocking kind of look on his face when I stood in front of them.

Chief smiled. "Aye, dawg, don't she look like one of them *edjamacated* bitches that go to that school?"

Savior shrugged. "Yeah, she'll do, I guess." He was dressed like a college student too in a plaid Ecko shirt, a pair of dark blue jeans, and Timberland boots. He even wore a pair of glasses, which took the edge off his normal thuggish look.

"Y'all make sure you don't just drop the shit off and jet. Y'all need to lay low when y'all get out there and shit."

Great, *I had to be with this bastard, who for some reason hated me.* And at the moment, I hated him just as much as I hated Chief.

Chief watched us pull out of his driveway like he was some proud, doting father, when he really gave a fuck only about himself and was sending us like lambs to the slaughter. What if we got caught and never came back? Did he think about that or even care?

The truck was filled with silence, and I kept shifting my weight from my sore bottom to my thighs, to ease some of the pressure.

Savior ignored me, and just blasted the stereo. He was playing Anita Baker. *Weird.* I expected him to be blasting some gangsta rap, but that's what he chose, and I had no problem with it.

After an hour had passed I asked him, "How long is it going to take to get there?"

"Look, don't start asking me twenty-one questions. We get there when we get there, so sit tight and shut the fuck up."

I sucked my teeth and turned my body in the opposite direction. "Why do you have to be so fucking mean to me, Savior?"

"How do you expect me to be?"

"Shit! Nice."

"To you? Hell no. I can barely stand you. You lucky I even agreed to be bothered with your triflin' ass—"

"Fuck you! Fuck you! Fuck you!"

"You know what, let's fix this now—Don't say nothing else to me!" He turned the radio up as far as it would go and put his concentration back on the road.

I looked out the window and wiped the tears that started running down my cheeks. I caught Savior looking at me too. He looked a little sad even, but he didn't respond.

Moments later, I attempted to go to sleep, but I couldn't.

When his cell phone rang, he turned down his radio and answered the call. "Hello?"

I knew it was a female on the other end because his

whole demeanor changed. He smiled instantly, and his voice turned from being harsh to husky and sexy, hurting my feelings even more. Why couldn't he be nice to me? Why couldn't he talk to me in a husky, sexy voice?

"What's up, mama?" He paused for her to respond then said, "I'm cool, just working." He paused again and gave me that evil-ass look again. He turned back to the road, and the look faded. "Yeah, I can talk. So what are you doing?" Pause. "Oh, you in bed? What are you wearing?" He chuckled. "The pink? That's the one I bought for you."

I gritted my teeth and rolled my eyes.

"You better behave yourself and wait for daddy to get back. Yeah. Make sure you have that shit on when I come home too. Yeah, baby. You know I like to see you in that. It's my favorite on you." He paused again.

Whatever the bitch said made him chuckle, a sexy chuckle that rolled off the back of his throat.

"I miss you too. All right, baby. I'll be home soon. Be good. I don't want to have to spank you. Bye."

I was tempted to snatch his phone and call Chief just to show him how the shit felt, but I figured Chief would say something like, "Harlem, what the fuck you callin' me for?" and hang up. And, plus, there was a fucking lump the size of a mango in my throat, preventing me from saying anything. Not to mention, I couldn't stop myself from crying again.

After another hour had passed, my back was hurting from the position I was in, and my ass was aching from the welts.

Savior noticed my pain. "You wanna stop and eat somewhere?"

"No, I'll be okay." I knew we needed to dump that shit as soon as possible.

Once we drove through Vegas, we passed all the nice

hotels. I saw the MGM, Stratosphere, Caesar's, and whatnot, but we wasn't going to any of those. He drove past it
all into a seedy part of Vegas that looked ran down as fuck
to a raggedy-ass hotel, our drop-off spot. And it wasn't like
you saw in the movies where you go into a warehouse and
dudes come out with guns, holding briefcases and shit,
testing the product to see if it is legit and exchanging the
product for the money. It was more cool, more sophisti-
cated. Hell, we simply left the truck outside with the keys
in it in the parking lot, took our shit out like we were traveling, and got a hotel room. The guy working there didn't
have to utter a word. He just made a quick phone call and
got us a room. There was nothing else to do after that,
other than wait till they brought the car back.

The only thing I didn't like was being in the same room
as Savior. But it had double beds, so we were cool.

Once we went to the room, Savior went into the bathroom. I used the time to slip off the sweatshirt, pull off my
jeans, and slip under the covers in my bra and underwear.
I got as comfortable as I could on my stomach and wished
I had bought some painkillers, but my pride prevented
me from asking Savior to get me some. Hell no.

Later that night, I woke up to see the room light on and
Savior pacing back and forth across the room. I put my
hand over my eyes to shield the bright light.

When he saw I was awake, he marched in front of me
and yelled out, "What the fuck you doin' with my boss?"

I sucked my teeth and gave him an ugly look, rolling my
eyes, and twisting my lips to one side, not knowing where
a comment like that came from. Without answering him, I
lay back down on the bed and presented him with my
back.

"No, you gonna answer my question, Harlem." He
reached over and grabbed me by one of my shoulders.

"Get your ass off of me, Savior."

"Answer my question!"

I was sick of muthafuckas demanding shit from me, putting their fucking hands on me without my permission too. "Here's an answer, muthafucka—'Cause I don't owe you shit." I balled up my fist and knocked the fuck out of him.

He fell back and almost hit the floor. His eyes widened, and he came after me again.

I slapped him right across his face this time. Then I pounced on him and tossed more blows until he was covering his face and telling me to calm down. But I wouldn't. I just kept on hitting him as hard as I could until he grabbed both of my hands in his. But he couldn't control my mouth.

"Savior, do you have any idea what I been through? After I lost my mother, huh? You wanna know what happened to me? My daddy knocked the shit out of me, ripped my fucking clothes off of me, and raped me. And it didn't stop there, he tied me to my bed, ass buck-naked and let fucking men rape me for twenty dollars a pop. Not once, not twice, but over and over again, until my pussy started bleeding. Until it wouldn't stop. Let me give you a damn visual—I had men on top of me, sticking their nasty, dirty, grimy-ass dicks inside of my pussy and busting nuts all over me while my daddy watched. Was you there? Did you come save me? Hell no. You boned the fuck out without me! I didn't have nobody. And every day I prayed you would come back and get me out of that fucked-up house. I kept that stupid-ass postcard you gave me. And all that time when you didn't come, guess who did? Chief. He came and got me, he whipped my daddy's ass, he cleaned me up and gave me a place to stay, food, and clothes. And for that I am very fucking grateful. So before you start running your fucking mouth about me and calling me hoes and bitches, think on that shit. 'Cause when the shit went down with my father, you were nowhere to be found. And for the record, I'm not with Chief for money. I'm with Chief because I have nowhere else to go. And since you got all the fucking questions for me answer this— Where were you, huh, Savior? Where the fuck was you?"

Then as I started crying, I mean, really bawling like I was a baby, his hold loosened a little more with each sob, until he was holding me and stroking my hair like I was a little girl.

In my ear he was telling me, "Shush. I'm home now. Everything's gonna be okay."

Savior held me for a long time. We didn't talk or nothing. He just gave me the hug I had been needing for the past year.

"Go ahead and go back to sleep. We'll figure this out in the morning," he told me.

I nodded, sniffed a couple times, and lay on my stomach. The movement caused my underwear to ride up in my butt, giving me a Murphy.

"What's this all over your ass?" he asked me.

I didn't answer. If I told him Chief had spanked me like I was a child, he would have asked why he spanked me. And I'd have to tell him I hid Chief's tape. And then he'd want to know why I hid the tape and then I'd have to tell him the tape was me with Chief and another girl fucking. I would be too embarrassed. And Savior would probably bounce on me then, let alone the other shit I had done.

"Don't tell me—naw, tell me. Did Chief do this to you, Harlem?"

I looked away and wouldn't answer him.

"Harlem!"

I thought of a quick lie. "It got pretty wild one night when Chief and me were havin—"

"You know what"—He rose to his feet and raised a hand, halting the last bit of my sentence—"don't bother telling me about you and Chief's sex life. I got something for that swelling though."

He left and came back about ten minutes later.

I felt fingertips on my bottom. I turned my head and saw Savior rubbing something on it. "What are you doing?" I demanded, trying to get up.

"Relax, baby."

I was marveling at the fact that he called me *baby*.

"Are you sure 'Mama' is okay with you rubbing on another girl's ass?"

He chuckled and continued massaging the cream into my butt cheeks. "I didn't know if you were going to fall for that or not. That wasn't no girl, Harlem, it was somebody that had the wrong number. I just said all that shit to piss you off." He laughed again. "I see it worked."

I tried to pull away, but he placed a hand down on my waist, gently pressing me into the bed so I couldn't get away.

The laughter was still in his voice. "Girl, stop tripping. I said I was just playing with your ass. Ever since I saw *her*, the only woman I've had on my mind is *Harlem*. Ain't nothing changed that."

"Whatever," I said, but I wasn't really mad. In fact his words had me cheesing from ear to ear. I buried my face in the pillow so he wouldn't see that.

"Anyhow," he continued, "they say this stuff is supposed to work quick. Does it feel a little better now?"

I nodded, busy thinking about how his hands had my coochie tingling.

Chapter 18

Savior took a deep breath. "Look, Harlem, we are going to have to talk about a lot of shit."

I sighed. "Like?"

"Like where I been all this time. You know it hurts me to know that you think I would just up and leave you like that."

"You did," I shot back.

"I didn't. I was locked up. So whoever told you I went out of town is a damn lie."

"Bo Bo told me and that's your boy, so why would he lie?"

"Because Bo Bo liked you too and shit. Obviously Bo Bo is a hater. Look, a couple days after your mom died, I tried to come and see you, despite your daddy's warning for me to stay the fuck away. I wanted to see how you were and I knew your daddy wasn't doing much of nothing for you. So I offered to kick him down with some bills to at least get you some food and shit."

"Did he take it?"

"You know he did. But he also warned me to still stay the fuck away, or I would fucking regret it. And I did. I think it was your pops that dropped a dime on me. Cops got me. I did this big-ass transport—a transport that sets niggas up for life. That's what I was doing for Chief."

I was confused. "Then why are you still doing transports, Savior?"

"Chief never said it, but me getting arrested for a little baggie and shit, the decoy? Harlem, you don't know how a hustler's mind works. Chief thinks I'm soft right about now, that my mind wasn't completely on the job at hand. And it wasn't. So I have to prove myself to him again. That's why we here."

"I don't get it. What was the decoy?"

He calmly explained it, which made me love him more for his patience with me. It made me think of all the times Chief prepped me for the drug runs about the way each institution operated, and if I didn't understand right away, he would yell at me so loud, I would jump.

"I got arrested because the cops found a baggie in the front seat. That was the decoy. We always do have a decoy if we got some heavier shit. Then once you dump the heavier shit, you get rid of the decoy and you smooth sailing. Only thing was, after I dropped off the big shit, my mind was so on getting back to you, I forgot to get rid of the decoy. I ended up getting pulled over, and cops found it in the front seat. But one thing I swear to you is that I wrote you letters and shit. I sent you cards. What you don't understand is that you were the only thing I looked forward to while I was in that fucking box. Getting out and seeing you. And not just seeing you, being with you." He paused before adding, "There's something about *Harlem* that makes me want to be an honest man. Something about you that makes me want to give you the world, or as close as I can to it and hope that it's enough."

I closed my eyes briefly before opening them and looking at him.

"So after I did that year, the first thing I did before I changed clothes—anything—was to come and see you. I told myself, if your pops got in my way, I was gonna knock him the fuck out, get you out of there. I didn't care about nothing else but that. I risked everything when I did the transport. Had I not been able to deliver that shit and the cops got to me sooner, I would be buried underneath the jail. But, hell, I did the shit for you. I got sick of seeing you there, seeing people fester off your hope and give you despair in return. That shit you was dealing with, you didn't deserve it. Shit, and I knew we were both young. Hell, we're still young. But I just wanted to get you out of there, out of that project life before you made yourself at home. I was hoping we could get away. Maybe get a place far out, and you could go to school or some shit. Maybe we could have opened up a business. Now, I'm not very book-smart, but I could have put the money up. Plus, I'm good with my hands."

He was reminiscing like he thought this shit was still possible, even with Chief and the way things were now. And I didn't have the heart to tell him it wasn't, not without a time machine.

He leaned forward and rested his hands between his legs. "I'm telling you, I had my speech all planned on what I was going to tell you and I had fifty *G*'s waiting for me. The only other missing piece was you. So when I came back to the projects to find out you was gone and down with Chief I was"—He shook his head, reliving the moment—"Man, I can't even describe how I felt."

"I'm sorry it had to be like that, Savior."

"I was too. And I've been angry with you for a long time. But, baby, to know what they did to you, Harlem, it kills me." He started crying.

I reached over and wiped the tears off of his face. "I don't want you to hate me no more, Savior."

He grabbed my hands in his and kissed my fingers. "Baby, I don't hate you. I never hated you. I was just covering up because I loved you and it was killing me to know you were with Chief. I never stopped loving you, Harlem."

Damn. Never stopped loving me? Who would have thought anyone was capable of loving me after everything I had done? But then again Savior didn't know about all the stuff that I had done.

So he didn't ask for nothing from me. There was no pressure for me to do anything that night with Savior. We just talked. I told him about that night, how I met Chief to all the men who hurt me that day. It made him so mad. It was the first time I had talked about the incident since it happened. And Savior hung on to every word and as I cried, he cried right along with me. Then he held me until I drifted off into the calmest sleep I had in a long time.

Chapter 19

"**W**ake up, baby."

I felt lips on my eyelids, and I opened them slowly to find Savior staring down on me, a smile on his face.

"The shit is done! Come on and get up. It's your day. Whatever you wanna do, we'll do it here."

I yawned, rubbed the sleep out of my eyes, and thought about it. What did I know about Vegas? "What is there to do out here?"

He traced my bottom lip with his finger. "A lot of stuff. Let's see, we can go to brunch, then gamble. There are places for you to go horseback riding while I'll chill—I ain't getting on no damn horse."

I laughed and snuggled under the covers.

"Or we can go to the arcade at Circus Circus, go ride an ATV, go on a helicopter ride. What? Whatever you wanna do, Harlem, this is your day."

"Wherever. Just out of this ugly-ass hotel."

"Girl, I just got my tour guide on and that's all you got to say?"

I laughed again. "Boy, you crazy."

He joined in on it. "Okay. Go get dressed."

I rose to go jump in the shower. Whatever medication Savior had given me worked. The welts were slowly fading from my bottom.

I had just washed my hair when I noticed Savior knocking on the sliding shower door. "What's wrong?" I asked him, opening the shower door slightly and slipping my head out.

He had a weird look on his face, like he was fighting himself. He had a small container in his hand. "I wanted to know if you still had welts."

For some reason I wasn't shy about my nudity in front of him. I turned the water off, slid open the shower door completely, and showed him the marks on my behind. He stepped in the shower in his boxers in an attempt to put some medication on me, but I pulled it out of his hands, set it aside, and started kissing him. I rubbed his head and slipped my tongue deep into his mouth, tasting every crevice.

His hands gripped my hips, and he was returning the kiss fiercely. He leaned my head back and started kissing on my neck. Wet, hot kisses that trailed down to my breasts. He rubbed them in his hands first, allowing his fingers to rub over my nipples, making me whimper in pleasure. Then he tasted them with his mouth, kissing them with the same intensity as he did my mouth. His hands rubbed and gently stroked every inch of my body. Then he made me hold on to the shower head while he crouched down on his knees and tasted my pussy, while rubbing a finger over my clit repeatedly.

I moaned out load and gripped the shower head as tight as I could because I felt my knees growing weak and I started shivering. My juices flowed out of me and into Savior's mouth.

"Come here, baby." He sat on the edge of the tub and pulled me into his lap.

I was confused at first, but he showed me how to ride him slowly and how to take him all the way inside of me.

He kissed me and moaned against my mouth, "I love you."

And I was getting turned on all the more. I started moving faster on top of him as he guided me, stroke after stroke, until both our bodies grew weak and we came together.

I held onto to Savior's hand like he was my man, as we strolled down the Strip and took in all that Vegas had to offer. We went into shop after shop, but I wasn't interested. I just enjoyed walking with him. He made me feel so damn safe.

We gambled for a bit. I only played the quarter and nickel machines, even though Savior was feeding my hands with dollars after dollars. Shit, I wasn't crazy. I wasn't giving the machines money like that.

"Go ahead, baby," he told me, "try your luck."

As we stood near the craps table, Savior pressed behind me, his arm around my waist. He kissed my neck and placed the dice in my hands.

"Savior, how much you gambling?"

He chuckled. "A *G*."

My eyes widened. "You trust me with gambling that much money?"

"I trust you. Wherever you wanna throw it to, you do it."

I placed the dice to his lips to let him kiss them. Then, with my eyes closed, I threw them. I kept my eyes closed tight.

Savior screamed, "You won it, baby!" He kissed me on my neck.

I squealed in delight at the sight of all the chips the dealer was pushing my way.

Then we went to Circus Circus, where Savior and I got on all the crazy rides. Then we went to the arcade and played games for a couple of hours. I had to drag Savior to the Dance Dance Revolution game. They had it at arcades in Cali, and the line to play it was always long. It was a dancing game that had a screen full of different-colored arrows, and whatever arrow came on the screen, your feet had to step on it. And it played music that kind of sounded techno.

"Come on, Savior," I pleaded, trying to pull him by his arm.

"Naw, Harlem, I said I'm cool."

I laughed. "What? You too hard to dance?"

"Gangstas don't dance."

"You know damn well you ain't no gangsta, your heart too good. So come your ass on."

He huffed out an impatient breath and stepped on the machine. To him it was a very "unthug" like thing to do, but I was starting to see he had a hard time saying no to me.

The music came on, and the lights flashed, telling us where to put our feet. Although I caught on quick, Savior didn't. I cracked up at his stumbling over the pedals on the machine.

Then we went to another casino, where they had lions chilling.

The last stop was the MGM. As we walked through it, I asked Savior, "Ain't this the one where Tupac was killed?"

He smirked. "Yeah. But that nigga ain't dead."

We dined at Morton's Steakhouse, where I had one of the best steaks I ever tasted.

On the way back to our room, Savior asked me, "You still on that Rome kick?"

I laughed. "Always."

"Well, I was thinking, why not somewhere more local? Like maybe here."

I stopped walking. "Savior, stop playing."

"I ain't playing, baby. We don't have to go back to Cali."

I cut him off, waving my free hand.

"What? You wanna go back to Chief?"

"Believe me, Savior, I don't. But we can't just settle somewhere. I'm thinking about you."

"Don't think about me, think about what you want. You love me, don't you? Or do you love Chief? Seems like he wants to be your daddy, as opposed to your man."

"You should know what I want, and who I want to be with. And the only person that has ever been is you. That ain't changed, so don't even think like that."

Savior was jealous, but believe me, he didn't have to be.

"Anyway, baby, if you say you care about me and you want to be with me, shit, I'm offering you that now. I know it's not a lot, but that offer I had way back when, hell, Harlem, it still stands."

I smiled and brushed my knuckled across his face. "Savior, we need to think this through, and now ain't the time to make no big moves either. He'll come looking for us. And you know he don't play when it comes to his money."

His lips were poking out as he looked at me. He was mad I wasn't saying yes. He kissed my fingers.

We continued to walk back to the room. "Remember this. I got a crib in Chino that Chief don't know nothing about. It's on Adams. The only gray house on the block."

"Okay." I hoped I could remember the street name, just in case.

Chapter 20

He got a phone call. It was three in the morning, and I had a pretty good idea who it was. I remember, right before me and Savior left Cali, Chief told us to lay low out in Vegas until he called for us to come back. So that was probably him telling us to hightail it home, but damn, I didn't want to do that shit.

Savior flicked on the light, confirming my fears and my dread. In a husky voice he said, "I got the call. You know what that means. We gotta leave today."

Without much talking, I got up and pulled on some clothes.

Savior watched me with a defeated look on his face. He was sitting on the bed and watched me slip on some pants. He pulled me by my waist and buried his face in my stomach. "Don't make me send you back to him."

"Just until we figure something out, Savior, only until then." But deep down I knew I should have stayed with him. I was going back into a war zone with Chief.

Before we left, I made love to Savior one last time.

I knew it was a stupid thing to do because Chief could find out about it, but we both couldn't resist. It was bad enough that when he came home, before he did anything else, he would come straight to my pussy, sniff it, then stick a cold-ass finger in it. He said it was to make sure I wasn't fucking around.

So I douched afterwards and made sure Savior's smell wasn't on me before we set out for the long ride home.

Savior held on to my hand as we pulled into the driveway.

I stared at him a long time, wanting to kiss him, hold him, and have him make love to me again, because when we made love, not only did it feel good, it felt right. Like that's where I was always supposed to be. With him. But he let my hand slip from his, and we both went into the house to meet up with Chief.

Chief grabbed me and placed a long, wet kiss on my lips while he rubbed on my ass. I felt embarrassed and bad for Savior. His jaw was poking out, and there was an evil look in his eyes, like he wanted to rush Chief.

"Damn, man, let the girl get in the house halfway before you attack her."

Chief chuckled and let me slip past. "Shit, man, if you had a woman that fine, you'd be all over her ass too."

Little did he know.

I found out a little secret about our maid. Ms. Gladys liked to steal from Chief. All that money he left around his room seemed to be too much of a temptation for her. The first time I caught her, she was packing a twenty in her bra as she vacuumed his room. I said nothing though.

The next time he went away and I saw her slipping dollars in her clothes, I was ready. While she was in Chief's room, I yelled out, "Gladys!"

She sucked in a breath, and her eyes shot up to the ceiling. They were buck as hell. All I could see was white.

"You fast-ass girl, why you sneaking up on me?"

With both my hands on my hips, I said, "I'm telling Chief."

"Why, Harlem?" She adjusted her wig, but her eyes were still wide.

"Because I want Chief to see what kind of staff he got working for him."

She squinted her nose up and snarled, "I knew your ass was a troublemaker."

I laughed. "You the troublemaker, old woman." I clutched my chin in my hand, like I was in serious thought. "Hmmm . . . and I wonder if we take this to Chief who he would think is the real troublemaker?"

Her evil look was replaced with fear. "No, please don't tell him."

"Oh, now you begging, huh? You wasn't begging or being nice to me when you were spying and trying to get me in trouble. Now I'ma tell you what—You betta lay off of me. No more spying on me, stay out my room, and most important, stop running back and telling Chief my every move. You got that? Or I'm snitching on you."

"Yes, yes." She started wringing her fingers and smiling at me.

That was a first for that shit. I shook my head at her.

"You hungry?"

"No. But do you have a phone in your room? 'Cause I need to use it. In fact, I'm gonna need to use it often. Is that okay with you?"

She nodded and rushed out of the room, without putting the money back.

I ignored her and went into the room to call Savior.

Chapter 21

I wasn't too stupid though. I stayed extra slick with mine. Chief was slowly loosening his tight hold on me. But only a bit. While he was home he let me take Lady for a walk, but only to the corner. And I was able to go to the grocery store with Gladys and his driver. He even gave me some spending money to buy some of the goodies that I liked. I really didn't want to go, but it was a chance for me to get out the house. I kept most of the fifty he gave me and bought Chief a jar of macadamia nuts. I knew he liked them. And I was hoping if I was nice to him, he'd be nice to me.

All it did was get me a fuck from him I could have done without.

The next weekend he surprised me by calling me into the kitchen, where he was sitting down at the table and Gladys had something cooking on the stove.

He studied me for a moment.

I stared down at my feet. I didn't want to give anything away about my relationship that was forming with Gladys.

"How you been feeling about your situation, Harlem?"

"Good, Chief." *I fucking hate you and everything else about this life.*

He licked his lips slowly, curving the tip of his tongue around his edge of his mouth. "Gladys got some shit going on in her family this weekend. And I ain't gave her no time-off since she been here. So you gonna be here for the weekend alone 'cause I got some shit to do that can't wait." He locked eyes with mine. "Your punk ass is not to leave this house."

I nodded.

He aimed a finger at me. "Don't take the kindness I been showing you as a weakness 'cause Chief ain't hardly a weak nigga."

I nodded again.

"Be a good girl, Harlem."

"Okay, Chief."

I know I promised Chief I'd be a good girl, but hell, I lied. I wasn't perfect. Gladys had already warned me that he would be back in a week. He must have really trusted her, 'cause he never told me when he was coming back. But I knew she would be back that Monday.

Savior pulled up at a nearby restaurant where I was waiting and greeted me with a warm hug before escorting me to his truck.

"Where are you taking me?"

"It's a surprise."

I sat back excited.

He took the freeway, and we went to a city called Buena Park, to a place called Medieval Times. I remembered it was a place my school went on a field trip, but I couldn't get the money up and had to stay home that day.

I clapped my hands together. "Savior!" I squealed as he

pulled into the parking lot. "How did you know? I always wanted to come here!" I leaned over and kissed him.

He chuckled, parked the car, turned off the ignition and said, "Come on."

I was so excited throughout the whole show. While we were entertained, we dined on chicken, corn on the cob, thick, buttery bread, and apple pie *a la mode*. I ate two slices. The combination of hot pie with rich crust, "ooeey-gooey" sugary apples and sweet, creamy ice cream was too good to eat only one.

Everything was eaten without utensils. When I was done with my second piece of apple pie *a la mode*, Savior licked the sugary sweetness off of my fingers. He just chuckled like I was the cutest thing on the earth. The way proud parents look down on their baby, that's how he was looking at me. And he was making me blush and cool down.

"No. Don't do that. Do what you were doing. Enjoy yourself, Harlem."

I smiled and went back to nearly jumping out of my seat, I was so into the show.

When the show was over, the fun wasn't. Savior guided me to a hotel. With his arm curled around my waist, we slipped inside the fancy suite.

I squealed as I looked around the room. "Savior, what is all this?" I walked around and found rose petals on the bed. There was a bottle of apple cider and two wine glasses on the table, and a huge crystal bowl on the floor filled with bubbles, and scented oils lay next to it.

"It's a knock-off spa. For you. Now come on."

I hid my smile as Savior sat me down on the bed, kneeled in front of me, slipped off my shoes, and dipped my feet in the warm, scented water. His hands caressed the bottom of my feet to the tips of my toes, making me tingle inside. Once he washed them with a soft sponge, dried them off and added lotion to them, he pulled out nail polish and polished each of my toes in a deep red color.

I giggled at the level of concentration on his face.

"Don't move."

"Okay."

After he polished my last pinky toe, he paused for a moment and asked, "Are they dry?"

I laughed. "No, Savior."

He lifted my feet to his face and started blowing on them one by one. When he was convinced they were dry (they weren't), he told me, "Take off your clothes and lie flat on your stomach, Harlem."

I obeyed.

He slipped a towel on my lower body, and within seconds I felt something drip down on my back. It was joined by Savior's hands as he kneaded my flesh between his fingers, making me purr. He rubbed up and down my back, my shoulders, my neck, and my sides.

"That feel so good, Savior," I whispered.

When his hands accidentally brushed against my right nipple, I moaned and turned my body over slightly so he could touch it again. He did. And then my front was covered with the oil that was on my back.

I opened my legs, and he slipped between them. His lips found mine, and we wrestled tongues until we were both moaning. His hands roamed my body, and I rubbed my hands up and down his back.

I rolled over so I was on top of him. I kneeled between his legs, tore off his belt, and unbuttoned his pants. I pulled down his boxers, grabbed his dick, and put it in my mouth, making him close his eyes and throw back his head.

I bobbed up and down on it, wanting to give him as

much pleasure as my mouth could offer him. I pulled it out and licked around his shaft, tracing its long length with my tongue then encircling the tip.

Savior's fingers were playing in my hair, his voice hoarse as he moaned.

I slipped it back into my mouth and sucked so hard, my cheeks popped in and out.

He took a finger and slipped it in my pussy and stroked me as I deep throated him, and used his other hand to play with my nipples.

"Ahhhhh," I moaned loudly at the pleasure and started sucking his dick at a harder and a faster rate. My titties were jiggling in his hand, and I licked around his balls and stroked his dick again. When his warm substance, which tasted sweet, filled my mouth, I swallowed it.

He lifted me straight in the air and right down on his dick. I moaned as I felt my pussy stretch and pulse each time it came into contact with his dick. He pumped into me fast and to the hilt, and all I could do was yell. He grabbed both my breasts in his hands and massaged them.

I jerked on top of him, until I felt us both tense up. Too tired to even move, I collapsed on his chest, and he continued to rub my back.

Chapter 22

As I expected, Chief wasn't home when I came back to the house. I went up the stairs to his room in hopes I could slip into bed and be asleep, just in case he came home early, which wasn't likely. I remembered Gladys had said he told her he'd be gone for a week, but still I didn't want to take any more chances. I pulled off my clothes, dumped them in the dirty clothes, and pulled back the covers, about to slip a leg in.

"Where the fuck you been?"

I froze. I didn't even bother to look at Chief, who I knew was standing in the doorway.

The muthafucka was big as hell, but moved like a mouse. Within seconds, he was towering over me.

"I ahh—"

Wham! He punched me right in my face.

I fell back on the bed, and my legs and hands shot up to ward him off. This didn't help though.

He slapped me hard across one cheek and then the other.

I started crying and begging him to stop.

He grabbed my ponytail and dragged my ass from the bed.

"The mall!" I lied. "Chief, I went to the mall to spend the rest of the fifty you gave me, that's it!"

My lie was so wack. And I had no stuff to support it. And even if I did, he'd told me not to leave.

My head was throbbing, but he wouldn't let up as my head thumped on each stair, and my body was going every which way as he continued to drag me. I landed in a loud thump on the bottom stair.

"You wanna be out in the street? Bitch, you can go out and make me some money."

"No, Chief. I'm sorry."

He pulled me to the door then marched me outside to his car. "Get your ass in the car."

"Please," I sobbed, not knowing what he was going to do, and also because I only had on my panties and bra.

He held me in one arm, opened the passenger door with his other, and shoved me inside.

I cried and sunk as low in the seat as I could while he got in the car and sped out the driveway and down the highway. As he drove, I noticed the big, beautiful houses disappear. He drove down Crenshaw, past Slauson, and made a left on Manchester. He drove down a little ways, and I had never seen so many liquor stores, motels, and churches. The farther he drove, the uglier the neighborhood got.

Soon we were on the dirty-ass block of Figueroa, where a cluckhead was walking back and forth and prostitutes were hanging out. And this is exactly where the car slowed down, on the ho stroll. This spot was fucking famous for hoes. Young hoes. And this is where we stopped. I curled into a ball and kept my eyes closed.

The next thing I knew Chief was getting out the car and yanking me from it. "Get out!"

I fell on the curb beside the car and shot to my feet quickly. Despite my pleading and crying, he drove the fuck away, leaving me there. I shivered and wrapped my arms around myself to ward off the cold, goose bumps suddenly surging and forming on my skin.

I backed up into a corner in front of a liquor store that was closed. I really didn't know what to do. I didn't want to walk because that would have drawn attention to myself, and I didn't want to wait there because it would seem that I was a ho like the rest of the girls on the street. The prostitutes were on the other end on the street, and one of them saw me and started pointing at me.

Soon one of them came flying over to me, titties bouncing in the air and yelling, "Bitch, back the fuck off our block! Yeah, bitch, I'm coming and I'm talking to you!" She got all up in my face.

I could see she was tore the fuck up. One of her two front teeth was missing, her cheeks were sunken, and her lips were purple. But, even still, through all of that, I recognized her, and she recognized me.

When our faces were inches from each other, she froze for a moment, and the anger in her face left and was replaced with fear. She backed away from me and ran back to her group. It was the girl who had attacked me that day. The one who was also at the Century club that night. And now she was a ho? Tricking for money? And, man, she looked bad. Nothing like when I first saw her. Damn! I wanted to ask her, "What happened to you? Was it Chief?"

I started crying even more at that point and praying God would get me out of this mess. All I could do was wish this was a pure nightmare and that Chief would have some type of decency and come back to get me.

A car pulled up nice and slow. The passenger next to the driver poked his head out the window and asked, "You trying to get fucked, baby?"

I shook my head.

"Come on, man, 'cause them bitches down there are tired."

I waved them away.

"Damn, you fine. And I like that outfit. Step closer to the car, baby."

"Naw."

"Awww, come on, cutie."

The driver leaned over the passenger and winked at me.

I ignored them both. I stared down at the dirty-ass ground that had new spit, dried-up spit, old black gum, trash, and shit. I was out there barefoot.

In a flash, before I could even blink, one of the dudes from the car ambushed me and tried to drag me to the car like Chief did earlier.

I started kicking and screaming at the top of my lungs, fighting for my life that didn't mean much of shit, but I didn't wanna go out like this. As I struggled, my hair in my face blinding me, I fought him as best I could, but he held on tight like I was a rag doll.

I had flashbacks of my daddy forcing himself on me, and all those other men too, and it made me fight all the harder. I yelled Chief's name over and over again until my throat ached.

The man had me in front of him and an arm hooked around my neck, so I couldn't get away. "Damn she got ass."

One of his hands reached down to touch my butt. That move caused his grip to loosen on me a little. That's when I snapped my head back and butted him in his mouth.

He dropped me to the ground. "Trampy-ass bitch!"

I crawled to my feet and took off running, leaving him to nurse his mouth. I ran down the block and turned the corner, my heart pumping wildly in my chest. I quickly looked behind me to see if he was anywhere near me and suddenly collided with a large frame. I screamed again when an arm shot out and grabbed me.

"Relax, Harlem."

It was Chief.

Behind me, the dude had just hit the corner and was coming toward us. "Muthafucka, I seen her ass first!"

Chief secured me to his body, with one arm, then aimed his gun at the guy with the other.

"Aww, shit, man." He stood as still as a statue. "My bad, dawg."

Calmly, Chief said, "Get on, nigga, before you get wet."

Terrified out of my mind, I squeezed my eyes shut and buried my face into Chief's wide chest. When I opened them, I saw the guy pivot on his heel and run away like he was in a marathon. I cried and clung to Chief, my whole body shaking. My tears and snot smeared his shirt.

"See what happens when you disobey me?"

I nodded.

"You lucky I got a little love for you, else I'd let them niggas run a train on you just on strength."

"Yes, Chief."

"Shut up! You need to appreciate what the fuck you got and just how good your little ass got it."

I nodded over and over again.

"Now come on."

I followed him back to the car.

Chapter 23

When we got home he ordered, "Go get in the shower."
I slipped past Lady, who was scratching at my feet. I
hopped in naked and let the water cascade down on me. I
couldn't stop the tears from falling and mingling with the
drops of water. I crouched down low in the tub and wished
the water would just swallow me up. I would have stayed
that way, if it wasn't for Chief banging on the door and
telling me to get my ass out before my pussy shriveled up.
I turned the water off and wrapped my body in a towel.

At the mirror, I stared at my face for a moment. Both of
my cheeks had red marks of them, and my ears were still
ringing. A patch of my hair was ripped out, and a couple
of strands in that patch were still hanging on for dear life
to my bleeding scalp. I went ahead and tore it from my
head and dumped it in the trash.

In my mind I tried to think of a way to get the hell out,
but every time the thought came, the repercussions of
leaving had me too fucking scared.

I dried off quickly, put on a robe, and stepped into Chief's room.

I had never seen a man more obsessed with his dick. He would sit in the bed and stare and stroke it like you'd pet a dog or a child. And that's exactly what he was doing.

Without taking his eyes off of it, he asked, "What are you going to do for daddy?"

I dropped my robe and crawled into the bed fully naked. I slipped between his knees and proceeded to suck his dick. I wanted to bite his shit or bend it backwards until it popped off.

He moved his hand through my hair and forced me to take him fully in my mouth. I felt him on the back of my throat. He got impatient and flipped me on my back and started playing with my breasts.

I was dying inside. I didn't want any man, except for Savior, to touch me like this.

He tongued my nipples, and I was getting really sick. But I moaned like it was the best feeling in the world. He went down to my pussy and tongued it, and I felt nothing at all.

"Why you not wet?"

"I am, daddy," I lied.

When he started licking my clit, I started screaming and thrashing my body from side to side so he'd think I was getting off. But my love for Savior and hate for Chief wouldn't let me.

He climbed astride me, pushed his dick in me, and started pumping. Only, I was so dry, my pussy started making farting sounds.

I tightened my legs around him, dug my fingers in his back, and yelled, "Fuck me harder, daddy!"

And he did. So hard, in fact, my head was hitting the headboard, and yet, I still wasn't wet.

The more he pumped, the more he noticed. "Why the fuck you not comin'?"

"I am, baby."

"Why you lyin', bitch? Daddy's dick ain't good enough for ya any more, ho?"

"It is, it is!" I was trying to come, but I couldn't.

My eyes bucked to the ceiling when he reached for my neck and started choking me. "Harlem, you tryin' to mess with my manhood?"

I couldn't get any air in my mouth. It felt like my lungs were sewn together and I was going to throw up, as I struggled with Chief. I gripped his hands with mine, but he was way stronger, and on a mission. He pumped and choked. Each time he entered me, his hands got tighter on my neck.

I felt weak, and my hands dropped. I was damn near passing out when he bust a fat nut into me and shoved me away and left me struggling for breath. I couldn't stop my hands from shaking as I rubbed my sore neck. I couldn't stop coughing, and my eyes were leaking a fluid. My nose was also running.

He went into the bathroom, expressionless, and came back wiping his dick with a towel, which he dropped on the floor, and got back in bed. "Sleep your ass on the floor with the dog."

I curled up next to my puppy and did exactly as I was told. And as humiliating as it was, I would have slept on the floor with Lady every day to avoid sleeping with that evil, dirty muthafucka.

Chapter 24

There were times where I wondered why Chief was as cold as he was. What made him that way? It seemed like he took pleasure in hurting me and controlling my every move. The little outings he used to take me on didn't happen anymore, and now he was gone again. He called to check on me to see if I was there. And when it was Gladys' day off, you'd better believe he wanted to know I was there, so he'd call periodically throughout the day. The threats he gave me were out of the ordinary. Nothing like "Bitch, I'll kill you." No, no, no. He was more creative with his punishments if I stepped out on him. He'd say, "Harlem, if you step foot out the house I'll blind your eyes out," or "I'll cut you till the white meat shows." Or then there was the expression, "Stuff my fist up your asshole."

But my personal favorite was: "I'll cut your pussy in half."

After the last beating he put on me, every time I saw Gladys she gave me a look of pity. Hell, I even saw sympathy in her eyes. And since I was so down, I didn't feel like giving her attitude anymore. Nor did I need to; she was off my back.

I thought a lot about what my options were at that point. My birthday was approaching and maybe Chief would let me leave. Right. That wouldn't happen. Chief felt like he owned me. Shit, I'd just have to be brave enough, have good planning, and think of some type of escape. Maybe start snatching money from him so I could buy a ticket to somewhere. I didn't care where. I could get a job and maybe even change my appearance so I didn't have to constantly look over my shoulder. But I'd probably do that, regardless.

All in all, I didn't care what I had to do. More and more, I doubted my decision to turn down Savior on the offer he'd made to me when we were in Vegas, to stay there and not go back to Chief. It was so stupid of me to come back to California. Who knows how happy we could have been? Maybe it wasn't the best choice to make, but it made no sense to jeopardize both our lives at this point. But then again maybe Savior's life and my life were already in jeopardy. Maybe anyone who had any type of dealings with Chief would live to regret it. He was fucking ruthless. He had no sensitivity to anything.

Lady was still limping after he threw her against a wall for pissing on the carpet. He called Gladys all kinds of names when she burnt a hole in one of his tee-shirts, or if dinner wasn't to his satisfaction, which was crazy because Gladys could cook. But it was the same way with Kenita. He would say, "That African bitch think she betta than me 'cause she was born in the Motherland."

I started to tell him she was Jamaican, but didn't bother. Let him live in his ignorance. He lived in it this long.

He smacked me upside my head so often, I became used to it. It was almost on a schedule. Because no matter how fine Chief was, and how much money or nice things he had, he was still an evil-spirited person, plain and simple.

The crazy part about Chief was that as much as he degraded me, he had the nerve to have a jealous streak. One day his friends, along with Savior, and the cross-eyed bastard, Solomon, were over, and they were watching a boxing match. Gladys and I were cooking together, while Lady was sprawled out on the floor near our feet.

We made Buffalo wings, French fries with cheese and bacon, and I showed her how to make the seven-layer dip Kenita had taught me to make. When I took some of the food in the entertainment room, I felt Savior's eyes on me, but I wouldn't look his way.

One of Chief's friends made a grunting sound as I leaned over to put one of the platters on the table. I ignored it, but Chief didn't.

He said slowly, "Muthafucka, you disrespectin' me, dawg?"

The dude put his hands in the air as if surrendering. "Chief, I'm just having some fun. Relax."

"What?" He pulled out his nine and aimed it at old boy's head. He was quick to pull out that gun!

No one in the room moved.

"Chill," the guy said.

Wrong word. In that moment, any word was the wrong word. He should have just shut his ass up.

Chief slapped the dude so hard with the back of the gun, he passed out on the floor. "Wake up, muthafucka." Chief crouched down at the man's head and slapped him over and over till he woke up.

This was all interesting to me because I recalled not too long ago I masturbated in front of him and his homies. But since he was high, he felt that excused it. But I think it was about control. If he didn't authorize shit, he wasn't down with it. And he damn sure didn't like people making a fool out of him. And that's what ol' boy was doing.

"And all y'all, y'all see her?" He gestured toward me. "Get a good look, niggas. I'm giving y'all permission. Y'all see her face, her skin, them pretty-ass lips? See them titties, her small-ass waist, them hips and—turn around, baby—that ass? Yeah, she fine, muthafuckas, and she mine. Y'all hear that shit? She belongs to me. And I'll kill a muthafucka execution-style for stepping to her, friends and family included."

I was looking in another direction, and I was hoping Savior was too. The last thing we needed was for Chief to find out about us. All hell would break loose.

The more time went by, the worse he got. He was almost like a bitch, so damn needy. Every time I saw Savior the strain to leave was there, but I wanted to leave on my own terms. I wanted to be an adult so that there was no way anyone, law and all, could have control over me.

Whenever Savior came over to handle business he would plead with his eyes. And I noticed his attitude toward Chief changed—his dislike for him was noted. Sometimes he barely looked at him, and he rarely laughed at his jokes like he used to do. And it made me real, real nervous. Because what if he exploded one day and Chief and him went at it? Nobody could win a war with Chief. He was too fucking powerful. Savior didn't have the army Chief had. I doubt anybody did.

Chapter 25

The next month, Chief was in one hell of a good mood. He got a new operation going. I heard him telling someone on the phone. He was branching out of the projects and over to another side of town.

"Yeah, man, this shit sounds very lucrative ta me," he said into the phone.

Ghetto fabulous ass. And a friend of his was fresh out and coming through soon.

One afternoon we got a knock at the door, which didn't happen often. Since Gladys was in the kitchen cooking dinner and Chief was in the bathroom taking a shit, I went to answer it. The man standing on the porch was as tall as Chief and buffer. He was dark-skinned with brown eyes, very handsome, except for the long scar across his right cheek. He wore his hair like Chief did, long, pressed, and hanging down his back. He also dressed the same way. He wore a black shirt with some brown slacks, and his shoes looked expensive as hell. Looked like they were made out of alligator. And there was something about his eyes that looked familiar, but I didn't really give it any thought. I figured it was just the fact that his style reminded me so much of Chief's style that maybe that was why he seemed so familiar.

When he lowered his head to look at my face it was like he was seeing a ghost. "What the fuck?"

My head snapped back confused as he continued to stare at me. When he wouldn't respond I asked, "Can I help you?"

"Man . . . ahhh . . . you—?"

I cleared my throat. "Huh?"

"I'm sorry but you look like someone I used to know."

I narrowed my eyes at him. "Who?" I knew I should have asked him what his name was, or allowed him to come in, but curiosity got the better of me.

Just then, an arm curved around my waist and jerked me out of the way.

"What's up, nigga?" Chief exclaimed.

Chief and the man hugged. When they released each other, both men turned to me, noticing I was still standing there being nosy.

"Go somewhere, Harlem," Chief ordered.

I hesitated. I was still observing the guy, and silently my eyes were asking him to answer the question I had asked previously. I rushed away when Chief swatted my butt.

I heard the man say, "She looks familiar."

Chief said, "She just another pretty bitch."

They stayed in Chief's office for a long time. First, I heard laughter. Then I heard shouting and cursing. Next thing I and Gladys knew, things were being slammed into the wall, and we heard the sounds of glass shattering. Although we couldn't hear exactly what they were saying over shit being thrown, the one word we did hear used over and over by both men was "spot."

Finally they left the office, and the guy had an angry scowl on his face as he walked to the door. Once there, he passed one final look my way. Chief came out the office next with a cigar in his mouth, obviously unfazed by whatever just transpired. His face nowhere as heated as the guy at the door.

The anger then faded, and the man looked at me with a kind look on his face, like he was looking at his own daughter. "Goodbye, young lady."

It seemed like he wanted to say more, like he was struggling to get something out. I gave him a little time before I smiled and said, "Bye."

He turned back to Chief, changing his expression to a more evil one. "Seems to me you can't follow the codes. I'm home, and these streets are mine, Chief, and you know it. I was kind enough to give you the projects, but now you getting too greedy. You know damn well Rickerson Village is mine. Give that idea up or lose both. This is my last warning. You swoop in on my shit, and I'm tearing your shit down. The smartest thing you can do is be content with what you got, 'cause no matter how hard you think your operation is, I don't think you that. But the choice is yours."

Chief calmly puffed on his cigar. He blew out a cloud of smoke before saying in a quiet hiss, "Get the fuck out my house, Stuckey."

And I knew for sure I knew that name from somewhere. I just couldn't remember where.

The next day I couldn't resist calling Savior from Gladys' room and telling everything that went down. I told him what the guy looked like, how he was dressed, and the exact conversation he had with Chief. I even told him what the man said to me.

"Why do you think he stared at me like he did, Savior?"

He chuckled into the phone. "You don't know by now? All men stare at you like that because you're a gorgeous woman, Harlem."

The compliment had me blushing. "That's not what I mean. He looked at me like he knew me."

"It's probably because you heard about him from around the projects. Long before Chief had the PJ's on lock, he did. He was running things. But he went in for ten years. During that time, Chief came into power and took over where Stuckey left off. Now that Stuckey is home he wants his spot back. Only, Chief ain't being so accommodating to him. Chief's trying to take over territory Stuckey claimed, instead of allowing him to set up shop there."

I wasn't listening. *The name Stuckey . . . where the fuck have I heard that name?* I thought back to the look on his face when he saw me and what he said. *"I know someone who looks just like you. Looks just like . . ."* Then I thought about his name again. *Stuckey. Who had mentioned that name before?* I gasped. Mama did!

"Savior, I think my mom knew Stuckey."

"It's possible. You don't hear the name *Stuckey* too often.

"Wow! What a small world." I then digested Savior's words about Chief and Stuckey feuding over Rickerson Village. "So what does this all mean?"

"It means that Chief and Stuckey are about to go to war and a lot of niggas are about to get wet."

Chapter 26

I didn't have the time to figure out the relationship my mother had with Stuckey. I was hit with a whammy of shock. I was late. Try almost two months late. At Gladys' urging I took a pregnancy test she had smuggled in the house.

"How do you do this?" I asked her.

"Let me see."

We both read over the directions and pulled out the plastic applicator that looked like a thermometer and sat it on the sink. I peed in a small plastic container, used the little plastic squeeze to get some of my piss, and squeezed it into the little applicator. It said in five minutes I would know if I was pregnant or not. If I was, it would be two pink stripes across the small applicator. If I wasn't, it would be only one pink strip.

I leaned against the sink and bit my nails down to nubs and waited for five minutes to pass. The shit was taking forever. Meantime, I wondered whose baby it could be, Chief's or Savior's?

I counted down the date. Judging from how late my period was, it would seem that the baby was conceived when I went on the trip with Savior because when I came back home Chief had disappeared again and I didn't see him for another two weeks. So, if it was Chief's, I wouldn't have been so late. Deep down, I hoped the baby was Savior's. Having a baby with Chief would trap me forever. But then again, if it was Savior's baby and Chief found out about it, he would kill us both. Despite this, I still hoped the baby was Savior's.

Maybe this was a sign from God and my opportunity for me to leave Chief for good. Or maybe I was just a damn fool to be happy about having a baby. And regardless of whose baby it was, I was going to keep it. Hell, this baby was now my inspiration to really leave Chief like I had been planning to. It wasn't just about me any more. I had a baby growing in my womb that needed to be as far away as possible from Chief.

I smiled thinking about holding a baby in my arms. I would be the best mother that I could possibly be. I would never mess with drugs, I would eat healthy, walk, play music for my baby, even while he or she was in my belly. I would read to them when they were small and take them to the park. Yep, I was convinced I would be a good mother. I was prepared to give that child everything they needed to be happy.

"Harlem. It's time!"

I grabbed the applicator and read the results. My eyes widened at the two bright-ass pink stripes across the screen. I was pregnant. I smiled and felt a tear slide down my cheek. "It's positive, Gladys!"

Gladys snatched the tube out of my hand, scooped up the other stuff that came with the kit, and wagged a finger at me. "No good for Mr. Chief to see this. I'll go put it in my car." She stuffed everything in a bag and rushed to the living room.

I took a quick look in the mirror and just like I saw in those movies where women would look in the mirror at themselves and imagine how they would look once their bellies poked out, I did the same. I imagined eating all that crazy shit women ate and wondered if I'd have those same crazy cravings for things like pickles and ice cream like I saw on *I Love Lucy*. Or would I be throwing up and unable to keep any food down? Maybe I'd blow up like a pig, eating everything in sight.

Baby names tumbled over in my head. If it was a girl, I would probably name her something like Naya, Adara, Mikayla, or Kenya. But then I thought of an even better name. I could name the baby after my mama. Aja. And if it was a boy, something powerful like King or even Malcolm. I liked the name Ashanti too. I learned in school in my history class that it was the name of an African tribe in Ghana.

Then I thought about Savior. In that moment I knew for sure I was leaving Chief. I was going to tell Savior I would leave Chief, had to get out now. I had too much to lose, and I wanted this baby more than I ever wanted anything.

I rushed into Gladys' room and grabbed the phone and sat on her bed. I punched his number and put the phone to my ear.

"Who you callin', Harlem?"

Shit. My voice was caught in my throat as I hung up the phone. Chief was standing in the doorway of her bedroom.

"Gladys told me to order a pizza."

"When it's comin'?" he demanded.

"I—I—in twen—"

"Why you stutterin'?"

The phone rang in my hand. I closed my eyes and couldn't stop shaking.

Chief sat down next to me on the bed and snatched up the phone. "Who in the fuck is this?"

No one said anything, so I knew it was Savior calling me back.

Chief slammed the phone down. He started rubbing his beard, studying me slowly. "What I'm trying to figure out is who the fuck is calling my damn phone. 'Cause don't nobody got the number to that muthafucka, not even Gladys. So it's gotta be somebody you talking to. But the question is, Who the fuck you talking to? You don't go out unless it's with me, so you don't have nobody to call. Unless you calling party lines. Is that what you doing, Harlem, when you get bored? You know I'm a jealous man, baby, so tell me the truth so I can go on about my business."

He asked me in such a calm way I thought, if I agreed, he would lay off me and I would get away with a simple chastisement.

After a pregnant pause, I nodded my head at him, beads of sweat on my forehead.

He nodded back at me. "I figured that's what it was."

I sighed in relief when he rose from the bed. But he rose only halfway and took his elbow and slammed it directly into my stomach. I fell back on the bed as the sharpest pain I ever felt spread into my abdomen and back. I opened my mouth to scream, but no sound came out.

Chief leaned over and whispered in my ear. "Bitch, what I tell you about lying to me?" He slammed his elbow into me again.

I couldn't breathe for a moment. Paralyzed with pain, I was choking and gasping. I prayed he didn't kill my baby.

Chief rose from the bed and walked out of the room.

By the next morning, I wasn't pregnant any more. I woke up with severe cramps in my stomach, a pain in my lower back, and a warm liquid in my crotch. Matter of fact, the sheets were soaked with blood.

I knew without a doubt Chief had killed my baby. My heart beat loudly in my chest. I examined the substance between my legs and saw a thick glob of blood, and after an even closer inspection, I saw little clot-like particles in it. I clutched my stomach. When I stood up, more blood shot out of me.

I went into the bathroom to run some bath water and sat in the tub, hoping the warm water would stop me from bleeding, but it didn't. It snaked out of me and reddened the water in the tub.

I bled the whole day. That baby was long gone. At that point there really was nothing left for me to live for. I couldn't deal with this, all this shit. Some way, it had to end. I slid my fingers over the razor blade, wishing I wasn't so scared and could slice through my flesh. It seemed like that would be the easiest thing to do. Just fill a tub with water. Yeah, it would be the punk's way out. But try as I might, I couldn't use that shit, so I did the next best thing.

I found pills in Chief's medicine cabinet. It was the Vicodin he had left over when he had one of his teeth pulled. I remembered he cried like a baby, the hardest nigga in LA crying because his tooth was pulled. I shoved them one by one down my throat. I lost count after the ninth pill.

Once the bottle was empty, I cupped water from the

faucet in the palm of my hands and washed the pills down. I thought about my mama and how long it had been since I saw her. How much I missed her. How much I needed her.

The telephone rang.

I walked into the bedroom and picked it up. I put it to my ear without bothering to say hello.

"Baby . . ."

I recognized Savior's voice instantly. I wouldn't answer, so he continued to talk.

"Miss you. Listen, I got a plan. Remember what we was talking about the other day?"

I gave a long sigh into the phone.

"I just have to find a way to get to you."

My heart started giving my body long, slow pumps, like a flower budding suddenly, or a cake puffing up in an oven over and over. I'm sure that's how my heart looked inside my body. I hung up the phone and ignored it when it rang again.

My head was spinning, and my body felt like it was floating. My legs felt like jelly. I walked out of the room and attempted to go down the staircase. I struggled at first and felt so weak, I had to grip the railing with both my hands.

As I made it to the bottom steps, my legs gave out, and I collapsed. And my body rolled down the remaining steps before I felt the hardness of the floor.

I felt hands on me. Gladys was shaking me and yelling my name. I couldn't respond. My body felt so weak. I couldn't move my arms, and my head felt heavy. My body was like dead weight. All I wanted to do was sleep.

Gladys was crying. That's all I heard before I drifted into blackness.

Chapter 27

I was dreaming. I had to be.

"Come on, baby, I have a surprise for you."

I smiled as Chief took my hand and guided me through a door. I stepped inside and saw my old apartment, the one I had lived in with both my parents, and everything looked the same. I tried to pull away from Chief, but he held me in a tight grip and pushed me into my old bedroom, where my father was standing. I looked at him like he was shit, and my eyes widened when I saw a needle hanging from his arm. When he stepped aside, I saw ten more men behind him, and they were licking their lips at me till they were all moist and shiny with saliva.

Someone shoved me onto the bed, and instantly my daddy climbed on top of me. I struggled under his weight and screamed. He started ripping my clothes off. I was yelling like crazy and swinging my fists at him wildly, pulling his hair, trying to scratch his face.

Suddenly, the door burst open, and Savior came running toward me and my father. He lunged after my father, but Chief pulled out his gun and fired it into Savior's chest. Blood leaked from his body, and he collapsed on the floor.

"Savior! Savior! Don't die! Please don't die!"

"Harlem? Harlem? You having a dream. Wake up." Someone was shaking my body gently.

My eyelids fluttered open, and once they came into focus, I stared into Savior's face.

He leaned over, looked behind him, hugged me, and whispered, "Baby, I have been losing my mind over you. What were you thinking?"

I looked away.

"You gotta answer me, Harlem. What made you do that?"

I cleared my dry-ass throat and rubbed the sleep out of my eyes. "Don't hate me," I pleaded in a hoarse whisper.

"Aye, what I tell you about that?"

I touched his bottom lip with one of my fingers, happy he still loved me.

"Chief sent me over here. He said Gladys called him after she called 9-1-1 and said you were taken to the emergency. I'm glad you okay."

I looked down embarrassed. But I guess I wasn't thinking straight after I lost the baby and realized I would never get the chance to feel it grow inside of me and truly love him or her. I felt like shit. I felt hopeless, like there was nothing for me to look forward to. I wanted to live a regular life, go to school, be able to be with who I wanted be with. And without a doubt I knew that person was Savior. And most of all I wanted to feel safe, not feel like every other day I would have to do all kinds of nasty shit to satisfy my so-called man, or do illegal stuff, or feel like at any given moment I would get my head bashed in. I didn't like the life I was living at all, despite the luxuries.

And most of all, I didn't feel like I had anything to offer anyone, including Savior. Yeah, I was cute, but shit, that's all I truly was, a cute face with good pussy for men to fuck. How far can you get on that? And what the hell can you accomplish with it? Shit, I was a ho, trash, a damaged package. I done shit I still have trouble looking in the mirror about. I knew Savior cared about me, but would he after he knew all the shit I had done for Chief?

And I couldn't really get free of Chief to be with Savior the way I wanted to be. Truth be told, I didn't think I'd ever truly be free from Chief.

I stretched my body and moaned. My stomach was sore as hell.

"You can't look at me, Harlem?"

"I'm ashamed." I couldn't tell him about the miscarriage. He would probably kill Chief.

"You ain't ever got to feel like that. You just made a mistake."

There was a tap on the door. A doctor, a white man who looked like he was in his late twenties, slipped in the room. He had to be twenty-eight, I thought.

"Hello. Harlem, right?"

I nodded.

"I'll give you some privacy, Harlem." Savior walked out the door and quietly closed it.

The doctor flipped through my chart and pulled a pen out of his jacket pocket. "You took a large amount of pills, young lady. You want to tell me why?"

"I wasn't feeling good."

He bit on the tip of his pen. "We had to perform a D and C on you, not to mention we had to pump your stomach. Well, were you aware that you had a miscarriage the day before?"

I nodded.

"I see."

Duh. "What's your point, doctor? You got one?"

"Well, young lady, if you took these pills because you miscarried—"

"I didn't."

"I was going to say, you're a very young girl, you'll have plenty of chances to have—"

"No disrespect, doc, but I don't want to hear this shit. You and me come from totally different worlds. While your mother and father were teaching you how to ride a bike, mine were both shooting up. Now, all I want to know is if my information is confidential, and if you can burn my file?"

He stuttered over his words. "Yes, yes, it's all confidential."

"Good. When my boyfriend comes, don't bother telling him I lost a baby . . . unless you wanna see me carried out of here in a body bag."

After all, I wasn't one hundred percent sure who the baby's father was.

He reddened in the face, but he looked like he felt sorry for me. "I won't. Who is your boyfriend?"

There was loud yelling outside. "What fuckin' room she in? 'Cause the bitch up front said room ten. Y'all need to get your shit straight. Y'all stupid muthafuckas getting all this money in vain." Chief swept through the room like a hurricane.

"That's my boyfriend."

"Go on an' leave us for a few, *doctor*." Chief looked at the young dude like he was covered in shit.

"Certainly." He took one look at Chief's tall, buff, thugged-out ass and nearly ran out the room.

Chief approached me slowly. His eyes scanned my face as he leaned down and stroked my hair, something he never did even when we were fucking. "Baby, was it that bad? I'm sorry you felt like you had to do this to yourself."

Chief saying sorry? What the fuck is this?

"I know what the problem is. I have been neglecting you. Ain't been home giving you the time and affection you need." He nodded to himself. "You wanna go out and shit, be around people your age you can have fun with. You're like a caged bird right now. You couldn't take the loneliness any longer, huh? Between you and me, if I had to stay up in that house day in and day out with Gladys' crazy, old ass, I would have taken them pills a whole lot sooner than you did."

I laughed softly.

"That's why you went on the party line, right?"

I nodded, lying for the second time about that damn party line.

"Well, it's over now. I'm not gonna make you feel like shit. Let's just put this behind us."

Dear God, now I know I'm not the most spiritual, but please let this man have a little decency. Enough decency to free me and send me on my merry way so I can have a chance of a halfway normal fucking life. Sorry for cursing, God, I prayed silently.

Chief pierced me with an evil look. "Harlem, are you listening to me?"

I nodded.

"I know just what you need. You want a little freedom, right? Well, we gonna have a little fun this weekend to take your mind off of all this shit. I'm throwing you a pool party for your eighteenth birthday, and, baby, it's gonna be off the chain!"

Chief spared no expense for my party. He hired a DJ, had a full bar for the guests, had the shit catered. The menu was lobster, shrimp scampi, crab legs, shrimp cock-

tail and salads, potatoes, and various fruits dipped in alcohol. There were all kinds of drinks for the guests to get
fucked up on, and they were served in huge, carved-out
pineapples and coconuts. He made the theme a luau, a
Hawaiian feast. He even had a hair stylist come in and do
my hair. She flat-ironed it so it was silky and hung down
my back.

When my makeup was done, I was given a Hawaiian
skirt that wrapped around me and tied in the corner of
my waist in a knot. My bikini top was made out of two coconuts that hid my titties and were attached to strings that
crisscrossed on my back. The rest of the women were
dressed in the same way I was, and the guys wore Hawaiian
shirts, pants or shorts, and sandals.

The party was nice, and under different circumstances,
I would have enjoyed it, but because of my fucked-up situation, I just couldn't. I sat on a lounge chair by myself
watching people have a good time.

Chief was getting his drink on too. In fact, the nigga was
fucked up. Twice I saw him pop pills in his mouth. It was
that ecstasy he had used the night he made me suck his
friend's dick. I saw him take them before he disappeared
inside the house with a dude who had been over a couple
a times, and his girl. She was very pretty, I noted, with a
very curvy frame, and her hair was bleached blonde and
looked nice on her. She wore a throng bathing suit, with
no skirt, cover top, or sarong covering up her ass.

I hoped they stayed in there. Chief was very unpredictable when he popped that shit. Sometimes when he
took it, he would leap on me and fuck me roughly and for
hours. Afterwards I couldn't walk straight, and my coochie
would be sore as hell. Usually, I'd end up soaking in the
tub.

I watched the partygoers dancing. I imagined it was me

freaking the hell out of Savior, like one girl was doing to this guy. I had seen Savior earlier playing cards inside with Chief and some other dudes, looking like this was the last place he wanted to be. He even brought me a gift, but he kept his distance.

I rose to go to the buffet table and drown my sorrows in some lobster and butter. I hadn't been eating well since the day I tried to kill myself. I put a couple of tails on a plate and grabbed a small container of butter and some salad. I tasted the food standing up. The lobster didn't taste as good as it did that day Chief took me out, but that's because I wasn't as excited as before about eating lobster. Back then my nose was wide open. Now there was nothing to be wide open about. I had seen too fucking much to be considered young, even though I had just turned eighteen. I was an old soul. I may not have been aging on the outside, but I had aged on the inside for sure.

I stabbed some salad with my fork and dipped it into my mouth. All the vegetables in the salad were fresh, as well as the salad dressing, but I wasn't tasting a damn thing. I threw the plate in the trash.

Gladys was drying her hands on a towel and making her way over to me. "Harlem, Chief want you."

My stomach started knotting up. I nodded, scratched my head, and went into the house. The door to his bedroom was closed. I opened the door blindly. When I saw what he was doing, I gasped and took a step back.

The lady who earlier had walked in with Chief and the other dude was on the floor, ass buck-naked on her back, and Chief was crouched over her, sniffing white powder laid out in skinny lines off of her stomach.

She giggled and tilted her head back so she could see me. "We switching today, Harlem. You got my man, and I got yours. He's in your room waiting for you." Then she added, "Go easy on him, girl."

I narrowed my eyes at her as she threw her head back and sighed, like she was anticipating something. Then I looked at Chief. He wasn't even looking my way. He was too busy using his nose like a vacuum and sniffing the white powder off her abdomen.

Sure enough, her man was in my room. The door was slightly open. From the small crack I could see his nasty ass sprawled across my bed, ass buck-naked, touching his dick, and obviously waiting for me.

Well, I hate to burst your bubble, buddy, but you not bursting a damn thing in me. I ran from the house and went back outside to the party. I knew I might be in trouble for not going to his friend, but I was willing to take a chance that day. I couldn't go through with that shit, no fucking way. I would deal with the consequences later.

Chapter 28

Iwas lying on a lounge chair talking to some girl who I'd met at the party. She was telling me that she had just graduated high school and was on her way to college. She was going away to some school in Georgia. I was so envious of her.

"I'm going to take up social work. I want to be a social worker." She stuffed shrimp cocktail in her mouth.

"That's good. There are a lot of kids out there who could use people who care about them." I know I could have. I didn't bother telling her that I shared the same dream to be a social worker.

She nodded her head excitedly. "Yeah, you're right. Aye, this is a bomb-ass party. My friend over there in the pool said your man Chief paid for everything. You are so lucky to have a man like that, girl!"

"Looks can be deceiving," I commented dryly.

"Girl, I can't even get a man to take me out to Denny's."

We both laughed at that comment. I knew, without a

doubt, I'd take her life in a heartbeat. And the sad part was, she would probably take mine too.

I glanced up in time to see Chief making his way over to me. Boy, if looks could kill, I'd be sliced and diced, laying in that salad.

He took one look at the young girl who was staring at him in awe like he was a King Kong or something and said, "Get on, bitch."

Her eyes bucked as she took a sharp intake of breath and scurried away.

Now folks stopped dancing, people stopped eating and talking, and all the attention was on us.

"Go on in there with old boy like I told you. You owe me."

The closer he got to me, the more I smelled the pussy on his breath.

Since there were more people around, I figured he wouldn't try anything stupid. "Why I owe you, Chief?"

"Why? 'Cause nothing in this world is free, Harlem. I spent a grip on this party, and you gonna have to work it off. You should know by now you don't get shit voluntarily from me. And, more importantly, this is your fucking position, my pleasure, whatever it may be, so play it, bitch."

"I ain't going in that room, Chief. That dude looks nasty. And, besides, he has a damn woman. I'm sure one of these other girls will be willing to do it. But I'm cool."

His eyes were shooting fire my way. "You gettin' a real smart-ass mouth. I ain't ask no other ho, I asked you. Get the fuck in the room."

I backed away from him. If I had to fight, if he threw me out, oh fucking well, but I wasn't going to sex his friend. Enough was enough. "I'm not go—"

Chief lifted me up and threw me over his shoulder, my

hair hanging in my eyes and my head banging against his hard shoulder as he carried me.

I pushed the hair out my face and looked in dread as he paused in front of the swimming pool.

"Maybe this will bring you back to the real world. In that world, Harlem, you don't ever say no to me. I'll kill you, and I don't give a fuck who's around."

"Chief, don't drop me! I can't swim!" I clutched his shoulders, then his shirt, to stop him from throwing me in the pool, but this didn't help.

He released me, and I fell straight in. I struggled as soon as my body came into contact with the water. I was kicking my legs and flinging my arms. Water was rising, or I was sinking, because it quickly crept up to my neck. I struggled to float, but couldn't.

"Help me, somebody!" I managed to get out before water seeped into my mouth.

"Naw, bitch, you bad. Swim the fuck out. Aye, mutha-fucka, did I say touch her?"

My head snapped to a girl who had extended a hand to me. At Chief's words, she pulled it back.

I couldn't hold myself up any longer. My eyes were blinded by my tears, and the chlorine in the water was stinging them. I slid my body up, only for it to ease right back down. And nobody would help me.

The music had stopped, and people were leaving. Some crowded around the pool and looked at me like I was the entertainment.

"Help me!" I screamed, struggling to stay afloat.

No one did. Then I was completely under. Water had filled up my nostrils, and it felt like my lungs were closing in. Still, I was fighting, but it felt like my body was sinking rapidly to the bottom.

Somebody dived in. I held my arms out, and they effortlessly swam to me, yanked me, and pulled me up out of the water.

Once I could breathe, I took in a mouthful of air. Then I started coughing and belching and found myself looking into the concerned eyes of Savior.

As I clung to him, Savior held on to one of my arms and leaped out the pool. Then he pulled me out.

Chief laughed. "She ain't talkin' shit now, is she?"

Savior ignored him and continued walking, carrying me in his arms. People were brushing past us and leaving, while others continued to watch. Some looked on with pity, some had blank expressions, some looked anxious to see what was gonna pop off next. And some went right back to partying, like what just went down didn't. Chief didn't follow after us.

Once inside Savior lay me down on the couch.

My breathing was still ragged, my eyes were red, my nose was burning, and snot was running out of it.

"You okay?" Savior asked me.

I nodded, but I really wasn't.

"Good." He rose and stalked angrily to the door.

"Savior!"

He turned around and said, "You need to leave before he kills your ass. Because when he does, I'll be in jail, 'cause I'll kill him." He slammed out the house.

I lay there for a while, not knowing what my next step in the shit was. One thing was clear, I had to get the fuck up out of there. I couldn't stay another day. I just didn't know how to leave. Could I say, "We're just not compatible," or "Chief, we have come as far as we can. Now I think it's time"? Hell no! There was only one way I could do it and that was to escape. I just needed to figure out how.

Someone tapped me on my shoulder. It was Gladys, and in a couple of words she made the decision for me.

"We leavin' tonight," she said firmly. She slipped something in my hand and dashed away on her little legs.

I looked down at a small can of pepper spray.

Chief never came to me and said he was sorry for nearly letting me drown. I was in his room, like usual, when he was home.

He barged in the room with two females. One was looking at me like she wanted to fuck me, and the other was mean-mugging me for real.

"Get the fuck out," Chief ordered.

I did gladly, and with a hidden smile. He just made it easier for me to escape, because I wouldn't have to be under him.

Chapter 29

Gladys had my nerves on edge. Was she really going to help me, or was she setting me up? I couldn't be too sure, and with every passing second I wanted to reconsider my decision and apologize to Chief. Because I knew when his high came down he was going to tear my ass up. Since he had the bitches in the house, we couldn't leave until they left. We wanted to make sure he was asleep before I stepped out of the house.

I peeked out the crack of my door as a naked Chief and the two chicks passed my room and he escorted them down the stairs and to the front door. I heard the creaking of the wood as they walked down the staircase. The females were giggling.

I snuck out of my room and hid in a corner of the small space just above the top step. I could hear a smacking sound. I saw Chief kissing one girl, then the other, and grabbing on their asses, as he did it. I looked away disgusted.

"Bye, Chief," they chorused. Then they slipped out the door.

As soon as I heard it close, I rushed back to my room, jumped in my bed, and partly hid under my covers. But, damn, I forgot to turn off the light.

Chief came back up the stairs, his thundering footsteps pounding every stair on the way up. Then after a few seconds, the sounds of his heavy-ass feet stopped.

I froze, and my heart started pounding. I squinted my right eye to a slit to see him standing in my doorway, his dick hanging limp and cum leaking from it and dripping on the carpet.

He reached down and grabbed it, studied it for a moment, then scratched his balls. His head shot back up to me again.

I shut both my eyes again quickly and pretended I was asleep.

His feet slid across the carpet, and soon I felt myself being pushed into the bed, and the bed being pressed into the floor.

When I opened my eyes, Chief's dick and balls were all up in my face, and I could smell pussy all over them. He was standing up in the bed, straddling me between both his legs. "Suck my dick," he ordered.

The thought of doing that made me want to gag, but when he punched me in my neck, making me unable to breathe for a moment, my mouth shot open.

He jammed in so far into my mouth, I had to breathe out of my nose.

"Suck it right, Harlem, or, bitch, I'm gonna hurt you."

Now I knew what pussy tasted like, although I would have preferred not to, as I deep-throated him and was forced to lick around every crevice of his dick. He pulled his dick in and out of my mouth like he was fucking my pussy. My head hit the back of the headboard, and tears were stinging my eyes as I tried to keep up with him or risk making him angry.

"Lick my balls."

I obeyed, although there was barely any saliva left on my tongue. I had to rub it against the roof of my mouth to moisten it before I swirled it all around them.

Chief had his head tilted back. "Yeah, bitch, you know who the boss is around here. You know who runnin' shit. That pussy, mouth, and ass is mine." He kneeled on the bed, snatched me up by my ponytail, and rammed his dick right back in my mouth. He shoved it in and out in quick inserts, at the same time rubbing his fist against it like he was jacking himself off. And each time he did, it was hitting me in my face. He released it and gripped my breast underneath my shirt and twisted it so painfully, I wanted to scream. But I didn't.

"Now there it go. I'm about to bust, and you betta swallow all of it." His legs started shaking, and he released a nut in my mouth.

I coughed but swallowed it as it eased down my throat.

"Swallow that shit and love it!"

I was swallowing not only his cum, but the dried-up leftover cum from the pussy that was on his dick.

He pulled out of my mouth, pumped his shit some more, and as more oozed out, he let it drip all over my face, neck, and breast. Then he stood and stared down at me like I wasn't shit.

I didn't move an inch until he exited my room.

After I cleaned myself up, I let a little more time pass before I crept up to his bedroom door. I slid closer to it and pressed my ear to it. I could hear him snoring. I relaxed a little and went back into my room.

Pure relief was what I felt when I saw the beams on

Gladys' Volkswagen flash. It was the signal to get my ass out of the house as fast as I could.

I tucked the spray in my pocket and exited my bedroom as quietly as I could. My hands wouldn't stop shaking, and my kneecaps were bumping into each other. I was sure after the fuck-fest Chief had with those tramps he was asleep now. Still, I tiptoed down the stairs. The target, the living room door, was in my sights after I had passed the sixth step. I had about nine more steps to go.

I was glad the stairs were carpeted and didn't make a sound as I descended them. I didn't hold on to the rail because it would have made a sound as I went down. Once I reached the bottom, I made even smaller steps toward the door on my tippy-toes, because there was no carpet there and it was possible to hear my feet hitting the floor. I had half a foot of distance left. I took a deep breath and extended my hand to reach the door handle.

"Harlem!"

I jumped, and my eyes flew to the bottom of the stairs where Chief was standing. I froze up only for a second. Then I turned back around to unlock the door, but my shaking fingers kept slipping off the knob. By the time I managed to get it unlocked, Chief had already closed the distance between us and snatched me up by my ponytail.

"How many fucking times do you think you can pull stupid shit like this?"

I closed my eyes briefly.

"You are giving me a dozen reasons to butcher your ass." He shoved his fist into the side of my face, catching my nose and causing me to fall backwards into the door.

Blood spilled from my nostrils. The pain was intense, but I ignored it. I was watching for his next move. I slid the pepper spray out of my pocket. I felt for the safety catch on the small canister, flipped it off, and hoped the nozzle was fully open.

When he lunged at me again, I held the can up to his face and sprayed it like a wild woman. The first blast hit his forehead before running down into his eyes. I never saw him howl like he did when that combination of peppers clouded his vision.

He started running around the room, like a blind man, bumping into shit, and I took off, out the house, down the porch steps, and into Gladys' car. She put her foot to the gas pedal and got out of there like a bat out of hell.

I let out a moan. I forgot to grab Lady.

Despite Gladys' urging, I refused to stay with her at her cousin's house in Ontario. She didn't need any more drama. I had got her caught up in enough. There was only one place I was going to go, and couldn't nothing change that.

"This is it," I told her as her car pulled up on the street next to a small gray house. I looked at the windows. All the lights were off. But Savior's truck was outside, so I knew he was home.

I turned to her and said, "Thanks, Gladys. You really looked out for me back there."

She leaned over and hugged me, and I hugged her right back. And I didn't let her go. I started to cry. Then the crying turned to sobbing on her shoulder. I clung to her tightly. When I finally pulled away, I saw tears running down her face.

"Call me, Harlem." She handed me a paper with her address and a phone number.

I waved at her one last time before I stepped out the car. Then I walked up the steps to the door and knocked.

Savior opened the door and looked half-'sleep. He just stood there staring down at me looking surprised as hell to see me on his doorstep. He was a shirtless with a pair of sweats on.

I heard Gladys start her car and drive away.

I bit my lip, knowing I looked a mess. My nose was swollen, and there was dried-up blood on my face. I smelled like pepper spray. "Ahh, Savior, you said—"

He stepped over his threshold, grabbed my hands in his, and hugged me deep and long. Then he pulled away to get a closer look at the bruises on my face. His eyes teared up. "Baby, what happened to you? Tell me."

That was when I lost it. I broke down and mumbled through the crying, "I'm sorry I didn't try to get out sooner."

He carried me inside to his bedroom, where he lay me on his bed and stripped me out of my clothes. He came back with a warm face towel and washed my face.

"Savior, I gotta tell you something."

"Sssh. Come on and let me put this shirt on you."

I held my arms up, while he slipped a long white tee-shirt over my head.

"Get some sleep, and we'll talk in the morning."

I nodded and relaxed on his bed. I had never felt safer.

When I woke up in the morning, Savior was wide-awake on the couch, with gun in hand.

I approached him slowly. "Hi."

He smiled and tucked the gun underneath a pillow, but I had already seen it. "Hey."

I sat down next to him. "Did you get any sleep last night?"

"Yeah."

"Don't lie, Savior."

He chuckled. "It don't matter. What matters is that *you* got some sleep. What matters even more is that you finally left Chief."

"Yeah, I finally did." I folded my legs underneath me and looked around his apartment. It didn't have all that fancy shit Chief had, just a comfortable long brown couch with a lot of pillows, a TV, DVD player, a coffee table, stereo system, and Xbox. That was it.

He rubbed my right thigh. "Whatchu thinking about?"

I looked down. "That I got you in some deep-ass shit, Savior. Chief might try to kill you."

"He don't know I got this place, for starters, and by the time he does realize you here, we'll be long gone."

I raised my head back up. "What do you mean?"

"It don't take a fool to know that Chief did that shit to you. Or to know that once he figures out you left him and that you with me it's gonna be some shit. So we're leaving. I'm getting you the fuck up out of here."

"Where are we going?"

"Far away from here, that's for sure." He slid me an envelope.

I opened it quickly. Inside was a deed to a house located in Colorado. I lit up with excitement then breathed a sigh of relief. "Can we leave today?" I asked. Despite Savior's coolness, I still felt we weren't safe from Chief, not for even a second. I knew he was going to be gunning for my black ass.

"Not today, but soon. I got one last transport to do, then we can go." He took one look at my worried face and kissed me. "Aye, don't worry. Now what did you want to tell me?" He stroked my cheek softly and stared at me, and the fear was there again.

The way he looked at me, so gentle, with his eyes shining every time they swung in my direction and his lips always curved like they were going to crack into a smile, I loved it. But what if I told him all the shit Chief had made me do, would he still look at me that way? Would he still want to be with me and make love to me?

I had been battling this fear ever since we went to Vegas and made love. But I couldn't hold on to these secrets any more. If he really loved me, he had to love all of me, accept me and all the shit I had done and went through, or else it wasn't real love.

I took a deep breath and told him everything, from jerking off Mr. Berry, to all the foul shit Chief had done to me, the strip dominoes and masturbation shit I did in front of his friends, taking drugs into a jail, what happened at the hotel, the threesome with another girl, how he threw me out in the street half-naked, and the latest incident from the night before. Each time I told him something else he had this crazy look on his face.

The last thing I told him was about the beating Chief gave me that led to the miscarriage. Just speaking of the miscarriage made my voice crack, and I ended up crying again.

After what seemed like five minutes of silence, Savior said, "Why you just now telling me this stuff, Harlem?"

"I was scared if I told you all the shit I had done, you would be ashamed of me and wouldn't want me, Savior. And I was scared that if I told you about the miscarriage, you would try to do something crazy to Chief."

He shook his head angrily then he blew out a blast of air. He whispered, "Muthafucka. You know what, Harlem, that shit is over with, but I ain't gonna lie. I wanna kill that fool for treating you that way."

"See, Savior, don't do anything crazy."

"About that miscarriage . . . is that why you tried to kill yourself?"

I nodded.

"Baby, I wish I had known." He rubbed my tummy as if there was still a baby in there.

I smiled letting him know it was okay.

"Damn, Harlem, what can I say to make this right? Nothing. I'm sorry you had to go through all of that shit. It wasn't your fault, and believe me when I say it's over now. I'm not going to let anybody else do any more foul shit to you."

I believed him. After a couple seconds of silence, I asked, "What do we do now?"

"We wait till I get the call."

The call came a couple days later. We were living it up being together. Only thing was, we had to lay low. Even though we were a little ways from Chief in some city called Chino Hills, Savior said it didn't take but a hot minute to hop on a freeway and find us. It had been a couple days, and the hiding-out shit was driving me crazy. I couldn't leave the house. Savior or his friend, Bam, went out and got whatever I needed, even some clothes, underwear, bras, and whatnot.

To pass the time, Savior and I had sex like three times a day, played his Xbox, and watched TV. I read a couple of the books Savior had lying around. I expected him to only have dumb chick and car magazines, but he had books by James Baldwin, Cornel West, Lisa Delpit, and Bell Hooks. We also talked all through the night and made plans on our future together and shit.

"Damn, I miss Lady," I whined, all hugged up on Savior as he was lying on his back on the couch and I lay face down on his chest.

He kissed my forehead. "I'll get you another dog."

"Savior, it won't be the same. I love Lady."

"I know, but you can't go back there. Which means you can't get her," he said gently.

I sighed and snuggled closer. "I know."

As Savior's cell phone went off, I bit my bottom lip nervously.

"Hello. What's up, Chief?"

Since they were both using a chirp phone, I could hear the whole conversation. My hands started shaking, and I felt my stomach knot up. But I kept quiet. I didn't want Chief to hear me.

"What up, man? We got a change in plans. I need you to head north, but you buying. I'm gonna let Solomon take care of the transport next week 'cause we got more important shit to deal with. Six houses been robbed for the stash, and one of those houses had the main stash."

"Shit!"

"Stuckey behind the shit," Chief said calmly. "But I'm not concerned with that faggot now. I won't have to deal with him much longer anyway. I'ma get this shit straightened and take care of him at the same time. So I need to get a re-up. That's why I'm sending you to a new connect in Oakland. We gonna use half of the product to take over Rickerson Village. Don't fuck up this time."

"I won't. How much you puttin' up?"

"Two hundred and fifty *G*'s, a hundred for the supply, fifty for you taking the drive, and another hundred to take out Stuckey."

I held my hand over my mouth to stop my gasp from being heard.

"Tate riding with you. You can pick up the dough from Solomon and swing by to get Tate on the way to Oakland. Call me when you make it out there. I'm expecting you back in two days."

"All right."

"Oh and another thang, Harlem ran away. If I wasn't so busy trying to get my operation under control and dealing with Stuckey, I would have put you on it, since you so good at tracking muthafuckas down. But money is first, and hoes are always last. And, nigga, you betta remember that, fucking with these hoes in LA. So when you get back from Oakland, I need you to find her dumb ass."

Savior winked at me. "Shit, with all the trouble she giving you, you want her back?"

"Yeah."

"Why?"

"So I can fuck the bitch one last time before I kill her."

I closed my eyes and gripped my hands over my heart to stop it from pounding so hard. I walked out of the room so I wouldn't have to hear any more of the phone call.

Chapter 30

All that night I couldn't stop thinking about what Chief had said. His words rang in my head over and over: "So I can fuck the bitch one last time before I kill her." And maybe, just fucking maybe, all of this shit was a set-up. Maybe Chief knew that I was here and was toying with us. He could have the trap ready and waiting for us to fall in.

I sat in the living room nibbling on my nails and waited for Savior to pull up. His friend Bam wasn't too far from me, and having him around was irking my nerves, even if it was for my protection. Once he saw Savior pull up and approach me, he retreated to the back yard.

Savior was smiling big at me, a couple of bags in hand. "Hey."

I didn't respond.

He stood in front of me, staring down at my face and holding the bags. "I went to Marie Callender's to get you some food. I know you sick of junk, so I got the chicken fried steak, potatoes, and steamed vegetables. They had all these desserts."

He disregarded the look on my face and continued talking.

"When we went to Medieval Times I know your greedy ass was crazy about that apple pie *a la* whatever, so I got you one. We still have ice cream and—"

"I don't want you to go on that transport, Savior."

"What? Come on now, don't start that shit. You know I gotta go."

"No, you don't!"

"Come on, baby. Matter of fact, change the conversation before this food gets cold. Get up and let's go eat."

"No! I'm not stupid." I slapped at the bags in his hand. "I know what you up to. You gonna try to steal that money. You ain't going on no real transport, are you?"

"Harlem"—He put the bags down and pulled me to my feet—"listen, I'm doing this for us. It's the last thing I'm doing for Chief, I promise. Then we outta here. We jettin', baby, I promise."

Since he avoided the question, I figured I must have been right on track. But I knew deep down whether or not he was doing the transport or stealing the money wasn't important, and that wasn't what was bothering me. I didn't give a damn what he did with Chief's money. The truth was, I didn't want him to have any more dealings with Chief. Period. It was too risky. I would have been scared either way.

Through my tears I blinked and yelled, "What if it's a set-up? What if he tries to kill you, or the people you going to see do it? Don't be stupid about this." My words were coming out broken up, because every time I uttered a word a sob came after it. "You are all I have left, Savior.

All . . . I . . . have. I can't lose you. Damn, Savior, don't you understand? I love you too much." The thought of him never coming back made my knees crumble, and I kept sobbing.

Savior swung an arm underneath my legs, and an arm around my waist. He then carried me into the bedroom.

Over and over I said, "You are all I have, Savior."

I made love to Savior that night like I never made love to him before. I kissed every crevice of his body, making him scream. I went down on him and sucked his dick so long and hard, he growled. I pleasured it until his sweet cream filled my mouth. Then I exchanged his for mine as I spread my legs and let him taste me until I whined and scratched at his arms while I came over and over again. I fucked him so hard, we were both panting. Then I let him ride me as rough as he wanted to until I came like I never came before, and it seemed like he did too. It was a scheme, though, to get him to not leave. I guess, I thought if I filled him up on lovin', he wouldn't.

In the morning when I felt his movement, I rolled over quickly and looked at him. He opened his eyes slowly. My eyes looked hopeful, I guess.

"Last night was good, Harlem, but I'm still going on the transport."

I sucked my teeth and turned away from him, giving him my back. He slipped closer to me and spooned me from behind, rubbing my waist. I tried to slip away, but he gripped an arm around me in a snug, gentle hold.

"I can't promise I'll be here when you come back," I said in a snappy voice.

"Girl, I'll whip your butt if you leave this house."

"Savior, you said you'd never lay a fuckin' hand on me!"

His low laughter rumbled in my right ear.

"I'm just messing with you. You right. I would never lay a hand on you. Any man who hits a woman is a fuckin' coward. I'm not that. And I love you too much."

I was getting real weak because tears were flowing from my damn eyes again. What was this man doing to me? "If you love me, then why don't you do what I say and keep your ass here?"

He sighed and released me. "I already told you what I have to do, Harlem. In this situation, you are just going to have to trust me."

I exhaled and stared at the ceiling. *It's not you I don't trust.*

My nerves were messing with me that whole day. I couldn't eat shit. I didn't bother trying to get any sleep either. I just sat on the couch and waited to hear boots hit the mat, telling me my man was home and not lying in a pool of blood somewhere, his head blown off.

By two in the morning I finally dozed off, but I was waking up every five minutes and checking to see if he'd made it back home. At one point I even put some clothes on and was gonna go out to find him, which was silly because I had no idea where he was and couldn't even drive. But, hell, sometimes love made you stupid.

Bam put a stop to my silliness. He blocked me from leaving the house by standing in front of the door. I sucked my teeth at him, rolled my eyes, and stomped into the bedroom, where I lay awake that whole night.

It wasn't till late that next night that Savior made it back home. And you better believe that before his arrival, that whole day I gave Bam hell. That morning when I found Bam eating cereal in the kitchen, I snatched it out of his hands, with tears in my eyes. "Savior is supposed to be back today. Today. How can you sit here and eat fuckin'

Fruity Pebbles when he could be lyin' dead some-fuckin'-where, Bam?"

He stayed calm, kept his usual poker face. I never knew what the hell he was really thinking.

"It's still early, Harlem. Give him time."

I huffed out an impatient breath, shoved the bowl back on the kitchen table, and slammed into the bedroom.

With every hour that passed I would stomp to wherever Bam was. "Is it still fuckin' early? He ain't here."

He simple nodded.

When it reached nightfall, I couldn't take any more. I attacked Bam as he sat on the couch watching TV, taking my frustrations out on him.

He sat there quietly as I swung my fist at him.

"Why the fuck won't you do something?" I yelled threw my tears.

He let me vent on his ass until my body got tired of fighting him, and sleep. I went into the room and took my emotional ass to bed.

My sleep was interrupted by someone kissing me on my mouth passionately. When I opened my eyes, Savior's face came into full view.

I smiled. "What time is it?"

"Eleven-thirty." He pecked me one more time and exclaimed. "Baby, I did it!"

I inhaled deeply and reached over and hugged him

"No more transports, Savior? No more dealings with Chief?"

"No more transports, no more Chief. Did you hear what I said, baby? We done. Now we can get the fuck up out of here. And since Chief don't expect me until two more days, by that time we'll be long gone. Our plane leaves tomorrow, and we can be out."

Yes! I didn't care what he did or how he did it. I was just glad this shit would be over in one more day.

The next morning Savior was watching the news, and I was curled up in his lap on the couch. I didn't get enough sleep the night before and was dozing off and on when someone knocked on the door. Since the worst was almost over for us, I wasn't tripping.

Savior was, though. He pulled out his gun, making me nervous, and cocked it. "Go in the room," he ordered, not looking at me.

I rose quickly and rushed out the room. Only, I didn't go into the bedroom like he ordered. Instead, I hid in the hallway, so I could get a view of the visitor.

When he yanked the door open and pointed the gun directly at them, my heart damn near jumped out my chest and onto the floor.

"What the fuck you want?" Savior demanded.

Chief's friend, Solomon, smirked as if Savior's gun was a joke. He raised his hands. "Relax, Sav. I didn't come here to kill you. You know Chief got more class than that. It's Sunday. There are rules to this shit, remember? Naw, you wouldn't. You are, after all, fucking the boss's woman. That was some low shit, Savior. I mean, I can understand why, she is fine and all—"

"Get to the fuckin' point before I forget the code and blow your ass off these steps." Savior held the gun sideways.

I watched Bam slip past me and hide on the other side of the door, his gun drawn.

"Well, first of all, did you really think you were going to be able to bail the fuck out with Chief's dough? That was some silly shit to do. The connect called us and told us you never showed up. It don't take that long to get to Oakland. In fact, Chief was being generous in giving you a two-day grace period. And to top that off you were supposed to roll with Tate, dumb ass. Leaving him hanging added even more suspicion. You sure ain't no natural criminal. How the hell you get on Chief's payroll? Nigga, you been trailed. You think you slick too, huh?" He laughed. "Chief also know about your other indiscretion. So therefore, nigga, I just came here to give you a message. Chief said y'all, meaning you and Harlem—he know she's here—y'all walk the streets, both of y'all dead men. Chief also want his money, and you ain't got too long to give it to him."

He looked over Savior's shoulders and spied me hiding in the hallway. My eyes widened. Then he winked at me, shoved a medium-sized box into Savior's hands, and left.

Savior didn't reply. He just slammed the door and locked it, while Bam continued to watch the bastard from the window.

I rushed back in the living room on legs that felt like jelly, my eyes as wide as golf balls. Shit, I was scared as hell now. "We can't leave now, Savior. The moment we step out the door we might be killed."

"Calm down, Harlem."

"Hell, I can't. I'm scared for our lives now." I sank down on the couch and stared off into space.

"Don't trip. We'll figure something out."

But I couldn't be too convinced.

Savior sat next to me and put the box on the table. When I reached for it, he placed a hand over mine silently.

"We might as well open it," I said, curious to see what was inside the box. "Shit, we know it's not a bomb 'cause we'd be dead by now."

It was probably a picture of me with a knife through it.

Or one of those letters with cut-out magazine words spelling out shit like, "You're dead, bitch."

I tore off the pink ribbon and lifted the lid. As soon as my eyes got a view of the contents in the box, my stomach lurched, and I threw up all over the floor. When I was done vomiting, I let out a horrific scream.

The box contained the limbs, head, tail, heart, and intestines of Lady.

Chapter 31

I counted the tiny cracks in the ceiling. My eyes were red and my throat was dry and strained from screaming. Despite how much I loved Savior, this morning was a wake-up call that he wasn't strong enough to take on Chief alone. The fact of the matter was, it had to be either Chief or us. One of us would have to be taken out. There was no way I wanted to walk the earth looking over my shoulders, wondering if and when he would find me. I'd rather be dead than live my life that way.

Savior stepped in the doorway and stared at me for a moment. I held his gaze briefly and smiled slightly to let him know I was partially okay then put my head down.

"If you wan—"

"Before you say anything, I been doing some thinking about this situation, and I think I know a better way to go about it, besides just up and leaving," I began. "And most of all, I don't want to spend the rest of my life in fear that one day Chief is going to find me or you. So, before we leave, there's somebody I want to go see."

"Who?"

"Stuckey. I want to go talk to him. You said they have beef. And when he was at Chief's, he didn't look too happy with whatever had went down between the two of them. Maybe he would be willing to help us take Chief out before he does us first. What other options do we have?"

Stuckey wasn't hard to find at all. He was in a little hobby shop located in Long Beach called The Spot, where they sold and taught people how to make model cars and airplanes. It seemed like a popular place 'cause it was filled with kids and adults. But it probably was a damn cover for a drug house. That's what they usually did. They put the drug money into businesses so they seemed legit and put it in other people's names, or they used it as a cover.

Chief himself owned three different liquor stores and a laundromat. Only, I could never fully understand, if you had money to buy businesses, why you didn't walk away from the drug game completely? It was greed, plain and simple, and I couldn't think of anybody greedier than Chief.

We found Stuckey in the office seated behind a desk, looking at some papers like he was a legit businessman, as opposed to what the fuck he really was—a drug dealer, gangster, and a murderer.

I'd told Savior to wait outside for me, that this was something I had to handle on my own. He didn't want to leave me in there with that man, but I insisted. He slipped me a small gun, which I stuck in the new purse he'd bought me to cheer me up. But I thought the smarter thing to do was put it in my bra. I made a note to do that later and planned to never ever go anywhere again without a gat.

On the way over we had dropped Bam at the airport. He was getting the hell out of Cali too, headed to Chicago. I couldn't blame him. The shit was getting too hot for all of us.

Stuckey looked me over, which was what most men did when they saw me, checking out my face and body, appraising me, whatever. I was used to it, but it was a different look in his eyes. It wasn't the same lust I was used to.

"What is it I can do for you, young lady?"

I relaxed back in the chair and stared at him for a long time. "A few things. For starters, you can tell me how you knew my mother, Aja."

"It's a touchy subject."

"Why?"

"I hoped the day would come that I'd have the opportunity to tell you that I was in love with your mother. And it's just possible that you, Harlem, are my daughter."

I got all up in his face. "Wait a minute! Hold the fuck up! My daddy is Earl Scott, and, yeah, he's a fucked-up junkie, but he's my daddy, not you." I sat back down.

He chuckled. "I know you hurt, but just listen. If your mom talked about me—"

"She didn't really, so you must not have been too damn important to her."

He ignored my smart comment and continued, "I know she talked about Aces, the club. That's where she met me. She was looking for a job, and frankly, I thought she was the finest woman I'd ever seen. I hired her as a singer and fell in love with her, and she knew it too. But I learned I wasn't the only man in love with her. She wasn't just fine, she had a spirit about her that you could just soak up, Harlem. You got it too. And when she sang them songs . . . Whew!" He closed his eyes. "It could've been a hundred guys in the room, and the woman could've been blind, but you would've sworn she was singing that song just for you. But your mama was also a flower child. I know she probably told you that. She didn't have inhibitions. She was a thrill-seeker. And I couldn't keep her in one place, no matter how much I tried. She wanted to be out and about and getting into shit she had no business getting her ass into."

"So? That don't make you my damn daddy."

"Listen, she was pregnant by me, four months to be exact. We were doing so good. She was doing her singing and entertaining, and me, Chisom, and Ramsey were running the chop shop. We were brothers. But there were always fucking issues with a nigga like Chisom. No amount of control was enough for him, no amount of money was enough. He wanted to run everything. When you got two business partners, shit, just don't go like that. And when you got other muthafuckas in the same line of work as you, you have to respect their shit and their territory like they respect yours. But Chisom never wanted to hear any of that. The nigga thought he ran New York. He didn't. None of us did, and though me and Ramsey were content with what we had, Chisom wasn't.

"And one day Chisom did something really stupid that cost us a lot. He called it being ambitious, I called it being greedy and stupid. He threatened one of them Italians across town. Told him who he was and that he was taking over that area, an area no nigga should ever enter. Them Italians never entered ours. Then, to show his ambition, he robbed him, and the Italian called him a 'nigger.' Now Chisom had a temper and a hard time walking away from shit, so he pistol-whipped that Italian and ran off, thinking it wasn't going to get back to him at that time of night. Without a witness, it probably wouldn't have. Since his dumb ass gave the dude his name and he already had a reputation, they knew exactly where to find him. At the club."

His eyes started to water.

"Anyway, when they came looking for Chisom, they found Ramsey instead. When he wouldn't tell them where Chisom was, they shot him execution-style in the parking lot. The guilt was fucking with Chisom, who blamed himself for Ramsey's death. As sure as the sun is shining, the shit was his fault. And my silence, I guess, was the confirmation he needed. It was then that Chisom started using off and on when the pain of Ramsey being gone hit him. He did it recreational only, and I think it was then that your mother flirted with it too. She had an ache in her heart sometimes. It came and went. And when she had it, she wanted me around. But I couldn't, because the club came first to me. She knew it, and she hated me for that. So when I couldn't be there, Chisom, it seemed, could. And he showed her that heroin could too. And I know deep down that Aja never thought it would take her to the places she went to. It hooked her, and so she wasn't the same. I was so blinded by the club and my grief over Ramsey, I couldn't see it.

"Chisom was always envious of me. But the way he did it was fucked-up. He introduced her to something he knew none of us should've ever used. He did it to lower her, humble her, so they'd have something in common. We never used our real names back then, only our middle names. Chisom's first name was Earl."

I gasped. The room was suddenly very quiet.

"You telling me that my—Earl—is your brother?"

He nodded. "And Ramsey is our little brother. And Earl and I were both in love with the same woman. So after Ramsey's death, we made plans to get the fuck out of Harlem. It was right after she found out she was pregnant with you. And she was a lot further along than she thought. She felt you would be the salvation she needed to get clean.

"We sold the club and had the money to get a good connect. But, let's just say, we didn't all travel together. Aja and my brother ran off with the money, and by the time I found them, she was strung the fuck out, and so was he. It wasn't no need for me to kill them. He was my brother and I still loved her. And they were dying on their feet, so I moved on."

I was trying to convince myself that his ass was lying, but the eyes I was staring into were the same as the eyes on my face. And the beauty mark in the corner of his mouth was identical to the one I had on my face. "That still don't explain how you are my father."

"My brother can't have kids, and it's the main reason he hated me. I was born with the looks and the ability to procreate and he was born with a high-ass IQ and the ability to influence. So I know, without a doubt, you're mine."

"Well, if you knew all this time you had a fuckin' daughter, why didn't you come get me?"

"I didn't know, Harlem. All this shit is new to me. Your mother told me you had died. And I never set foot in the projects so, Harlem, how was I supposed to know? And I been locked down for twelve years. But when Chief told me where he found you, it all made sense. And I even went a step further. I found out where Earl was, and that wasn't too hard. Shit, my brother got a rep in the projects. They say he's the one who goes around the projects stealing shit. That didn't surprise me.

"Anyway, I went to see his ass, and he admitted what I suspected . . . that you are my child. And, believe it or not, I did go looking for you. But you gotta understand, Chief and I are at war now. I can't walk up to the nigga's house and ask for you or snatch you away. Not now. But my plan was to do it when this shit is over. Me telling him now, that you are my seed, would have given him more ammunition against me, and not to mention what he could have possibly done to you, Harlem. But I still had niggas casing his place for the past two weeks. They claim they never caught sight of you, so my back was against the wall."

I sat back shocked. All this time the man that raised me didn't have a damn thing to do with my conception. What the fuck was wrong with my mama, passing a man off as my daddy? But Mr. Earl wasn't innocent in this shit either. *Mechanic, my ass.* "Just out of curiosity, where is my father—I mean uncle?"

"He's in rehab, trying to get his life together. He said he found God. He even sounds like a different person. And, yes, he told me what he did to you. The shit was horrible to hear. I'm not going to lie, I wanted to blast his ass away when he told me about that sick shit. I even pulled out my gat and pointed it at him. Something in me felt like he almost wanted me to pull the trigger. He begged for forgiveness, not just from me, but from you."

Fuck his forgiveness.

After a short silence, I said coldly, "You should have blasted him away."

He studied me for a moment. Then he said softly, "That's your anger talking."

"You should have blasted his ass away."

"It's fucked up what you had to go through. No one should have endured what you endured. But—"

"What the fuck you want me to say, Stuckey? I have no sympathy for his ass and probably never fucking will, despite the fact that 'he found God.' And if you wanna blame someone for all the years you missed out on being in my

life and seeing me grow up, blame his punk ass 'cause as
sure as the sun is shining, it's his fault."

"Seems to me that you will never be able to put this behind you until you have closure. Seeing him one last time
and telling him how you feel just might give you that. He's
over at that home on Cedar Avenue in Compton. Don't
wait eighteen years like I did. Go and see him to put this
out of your heart and mind, Harlem."

For a thug, Stuckey sure was philosophical.

"You'll be at peace, Harlem."

"I doubt it." I looked away and wiped the tears off my
face.

What he didn't understand was that Earl had mis-
treated me all of my life, like he hated the damn
sight of me. I made straight A's in school, he didn't give a
fuck. I never got a high-five or pat on the back from him. I
was even on the honor roll. You think he cared? I excelled
at everything I tried, and it didn't mean shit to him, because for some reason, he despised my ass.

Once I even brought it up to him. I was six years old. He
was sitting in the living room, and I came inside. I ran up
to him and pressed my palms against his cheeks. "Daddy,"
I said, "how come you don't do stuff with me like the
other daddies around here? The other kids' daddies ride
bikes with them, they take them up to the park to go play,
they get them ice cream off the ice cream truck." I went
on and on about what I had seen other fathers do for their
own kids. "Why we don't do none of that, Daddy?"

First he placed his hands on mine, making me smile.
Then, in the next instant, he applied pressure, making me
scream in surprise, and I started crying. He had this evil
look on his face when he told me, "Don't ever put your

fuckin' hands on me again, girl." Then he swatted my ass so hard, he left a mark.

I ran out the room crying and buried my head in my mama's lap. I never said more than two words to my daddy again. Stuckey would never understand any of that, because I didn't.

"I know I can't change the past, but I can start making up all the time we lost now. Whatever you need, Harlem."

I paused and clasped my hands together, raised them to my lips. "I do need your help, Stuckey."

"With money? You want to go away to college? What?"

"I need you to help me kill Chief."

He was speechless for a moment.

"Harlem, I have a hit on Chief. It just ain't possible for you to be there when the shit goes down."

"I want to see him die."

All Stuckey did was smile. "Now what would a young lady want to see that for? You supposed to be sugar and spice."

"Cut that bullshit out right now. You have no idea about the shit I been through in my life. Ain't shit about me sugar, and ain't shit about me spice. It was never an option for me. I didn't have no tea parties or dollhouses. I had two addicts for parents that were torn between two worlds, the real one you and me live in, and the one they entered when they were high. Either way, either world didn't have no room for me. I done seen my mom prostitute herself for dope, jerked men off for dope, stripped to pay off debts. And that ain't the worst of the shit I done had to do just to breathe. Stuckey, a part of my soul is gone and can't nothing get it back. Can't nothing replace it. And I am what I am. I had a fucked-up life, and I'm just playing the hand I was dealt."

He looked at me for a long time before saying, "If you like, I'll let you know when the nigga's heart stops. Matter of fact, you and Savior are welcome to stay at my crib until this shit blows over. I got security around the clock. It's safer for you to chill there than run the streets."

I jumped in his face. "How do you know about Savior and me?"

"*Baby*, everybody in the projects knows about that shit. You gotta be my daughter, pulling some cold shit like that over on a nigga like Chief, running off with his favorite soldier and stealing his dough. Girl, you got some balls *fo sho*. That's from my blood running through you."

I sat back down and wiped the sweat off my brow, sweat that wasn't from any damn heat, but from nervousness. Because Chief's evil-ass face flashed before me.

"Of course I would like you to stay, Harlem. Believe me when I say I loved your mother. I would have loved you just the same. But I didn't get the chance. But I'm here now. Maybe we could work on having a relationship. We could spend time together and do the types of things fathers and daughters do. I always wanted a daughter, Harlem. And it would have been a blessing to watch you grow up. Girl, you look like your mama spit you out."

I shook my head. "I gotta get up and out of Cali. I seen and went through too much horrible shit out here. I want a fresh start and as normal a life as I can get. And with a hustler for a daddy, I just don't think that's possible."

He nodded his understanding but looked disappointed. Even hurt.

"But I will take you up on the offer to stay in your house. And once you tell me the black-hearted muthafucka is dead, I wanna go spit on his fuckin' corpse."

He looked at me for a long time and smiled. "That's my daughter."

Savior and I stayed on the 60 freeway for what seemed like an hour. I told him everything Stuckey had just told me about my mother and how the man I grew up thinking was my daddy wasn't, and how a damn near stranger, Stuckey, was really my father.

All Savior could say throughout the conversation was, "Whoa!"

I shook my head. "I know, my mom was a real fuckin' trip, huh?" *Mama,* I thought, *you need your ass whipped for this one.*

"People make mistakes."

"Yeah. I know all about that. I was raised by two walking mistakes."

We exited the freeway, which was practically empty due to it being so late. Once off, we stopped at a red light. Savior took the opportunity to kiss me.

And I know I wasn't hearing things when T.I. blared in my ears, making my heart speed up rapidly. But it wasn't coming from our car. My hands gripped one of Savior's as I peered out the rearview mirror.

"Damn, baby! You got a tight-ass grip."

I didn't reply, just kept looking at the side mirror at the Excursion behind us that had Chief's driver inside of it.

"Harlem, you okay?"

My breathing had become shallow. I pointed behind me with a shaking finger. Savior looked out his side mirror. My lips trembled, and my knees began to shake.

"Damn," he muttered.

The SUV honked at us, but Savior ignored it and took off as soon as the light changed to green. As the truck trailed behind us, Savior increased his speed.

My eyes shot back to the mirror. They were close. Right on our heels.

He made a quick right. "Harlem, I'm gonna get us out of this shit."

I didn't respond. My stomach was twisting in knots, and I couldn't stop my body from trembling.

He punched it to sixty and shot past a stop sign, took a quick left, then a quick right, and drove down another street. I gripped the armrest on the car door as he skidded to a stop at a red light.

When it turned green, Savior sped off again and quickly turned down an alley. I craned my neck to see the Excursion pause at the alley opening as if it was going to let us go. Then the driver busted a U-turn and went the other way.

Savior paused for a minute, put the car in reverse, and backed up to go the opposite way.

I looked wildly behind me through the back window as he closed the distance and we were about to dip out of the alley. But just as we reached the end and Savior was about to make a quick right, the Excursion, along with a black car, were on us and we were caged the fuck in.

"Harlem, duck!" Savior shoved my head down as glass shattered into the car from the impact from a bat one of the dudes swung at it.

A fist swept through the window and punched Savior in his face. Then three guys dragged him from the car and threw him on the pissy-ass alley ground and commenced to whipping on him.

I screamed loudly and cursed them bastards for putting their hands on him.

Suddenly, Solomon's ugly-ass face filled the broken car window. "Come here, bitch."

"Fuck you!" I scooted my body as far toward the passenger side as possible and swung my foot at his head.

He ducked and leaned further in the car, grabbed my arm, and dragged my ass out. I grimaced as broken glass prickled my skin.

He held my arms behind me, making it impossible for me to move them, and he leaned my body backwards to keep me off balance, so I was on the balls of my feet and leaning against him.

"Let me go, you cross-eyed muthafucka."

He tongue-teased my right earlobe and whispered, "You know you talk a lot of shit. Maybe I'm gonna have to stuff your mouth with my dick, just to shut you up."

I threw my head back and tried to spit on him.

He used his other hand to push my face away and laughed.

"You put your shit in my mouth, you gonna end up with a stump for a dick."

"Relax, boo. We'll have time for that later. Chief wanted you to see this."

I sobbed and shook my head as Solomon forced me to watch the three men continue to beat on Savior. One held him up, while another continued to pound his flesh with his fist, making Savior groan. The third one joined in the attack, swinging his bat at Savior, hitting him in his back and side. Blood was running down Savior's face as he still tried to fight back, but he couldn't. The dude holding the bat swung it again and hit Savior in the mouth, making me scream at the top of my lungs and struggle against Solomon. Blood sprayed from Savior's mouth, and he dropped to the ground.

They continued to hit and stomp his body until he stopped moving and his blood was splattered all over the ground at their feet.

"Savior! Savior!" I sobbed over and over again. A pain

rose in my chest, seeing him lying there like that and I couldn't do anything to help him.

The three men hopped in the Excursion, but Solomon didn't move an inch. His feet remained rooted in the spot we were both in.

One of the dudes in the passenger seat next to Chief's driver yelled, "What the fuck you waiting for? Let's go!"

"Ahhh . . . fellas, I'm about to make a quick detour."

When Solomon rubbed his dick against the crack of my ass, I knew just what *detour* he meant.

I screamed for help as loud as I could, but it didn't stop him from dragging me to his car, throwing me in the back seat, and trying to pull my pants and panties down. I used all the power I possessed to get his ass off of me. I scratched his face, kicked him in the nuts, bit one of his fingers, but still, some way he managed to get my pants down to my ankles.

He planted his knees into my thighs so I couldn't escape and held my hands over my head in one of his hands. Then, with the other, he unzipped his pants and yanked out his raggedy, little dick.

"I been waitin' to do his shit for the longest, but Savior's ass beat me to it." He stuck a finger in my pussy, making me close my eyes and squirm. "Let me get this shit wet and ready for me." He wiggled his finger around inside of me.

I cried again and kept yelling.

Just as he was about to stick his shit into me, he was plucked off of me and pushed aside by Chief's driver.

"Man, what the fuck are you doing?" Solomon yelled, pulling away from him and stomping his feet on the concrete like a damn kid.

The driver said simply, "You know what the orders were."

It was the first time I heard him speak. And his words

were like music to my ears. Because those words saved me from getting raped by Solomon.

"Man, I was just trying to get me a little piece. He's going to kill the bitch anyway. What fuckin' harm would it have done?"

When Solomon caught sight of the look of murder in the driver's eyes, he backed up slightly and said, "Okay, big man, it's your call."

Without another word, Chief's driver leaned over me and yanked my pants up around my waist and pulled me from out of the car. He held me in a tight grip and swept past Solomon. He didn't release me until me made it to the truck, where he shoved me in the back seat near one of the three guys that had whipped on Savior.

I stared out the window at Savior's body. He was coughing and spitting up blood, and I started crying all over again as they, without the least bit of concern, drove right by him, leaving him to die out there. Even Solomon sped away in the opposite direction in the black car. I kept sobbing and loudly sniffing and calling out Savior's name.

One of the dudes said, "Shut that bitch up."

Then one of them reached over and punched me in the mouth, knocking me out cold.

Okay. This is one of them situations where you don't wanna wake up, but with my head being kicked repeatedly, I really had no choice.

"Wake up, bitch," I heard from a soft, singsong voice.

When I did, the person was none other than Chief. There ain't no adjective that exists that would describe the expression on his face. I wanted to kick my own ass for not putting my gat in my bra. The moment I opened my eyes, his fist slammed directly into my forehead, giving me a big-ass coconut.

"Get up!"

I looked around. I wasn't in the car no more. I was back at Chief's house, in the entertainment room.

With a grip on my hair, he hung me in the air and delivered punch after punch to my abdomen. He set me back on the ground and slapped me across the face so hard, I flew in the opposite direction.

With all the strength I had, I tried to crawl on my knees.

He strolled over to me and kicked me back down. "I should have left your ass in the projects and turned a profit off your pussy." Then he kicked me over and over again in my stomach, till I was lying flat on the ground. "You ran away from me, Harlem? After all the shit I did for you? And you fucked Savior, my favorite solider. How fucking disrespectful!"

Chief lifted my head and repeatedly bashed it into the concrete until the ground sliced through my flesh and created a deep gash on my forehead. "Turn around and look at me, bitch."

He pushed me flat on my back, opened my mouth wide, coughed up a big glob of mucus and spat in directly in my mouth. I was in too much pain to use the muscles in my jaw to spit the substance out. But since my mouth was wide open, it slid out right along with the blood.

"Stay there, bitch."

Bitch, bitch, bitch, bitch, bitch.

His cell phone started ringing. He answered it. "Chief."

After a moment, Chief replied, " Oh, your punk ass finally cleaned your bruises and returning calls, huh? Listen, muthafucka, and listen well. Yeah I got the bitch, and you got my muthafuckin' money. Bring my shit now, or this bitch is going to die. Savior, I'm not playing with you. I'm at home. A home that, after today, you ain't welcome at, nigga, since you wanna take my money and betray me for some pussy." He kicked me again when he said the word *pussy.*

He slammed the phone closed and grabbed my hair again, pulling me to my feet. He punched me in my stomach, and I slid to the ground.

All his crew stood around and watched, some laughed at me getting my ass kicked, others shook their heads in shame.

I knew there was no way Savior, if he did come, could win this battle. There were too many of them. One guy followed Chief's every move, and another was posted up at the door. One was standing on the staircase.

I wondered where Solomon had escaped to. He probably thought one of the dudes would snitch on him and tell Chief how he tried to fuck me. And I guess the driver had done his job of getting me there, so he was gone too.

When Chief lifted me to my feet in a chokehold, one of them said, "Chief, don't kill her before Savior gets here. What revenge is that? Remember the plan?"

Chief nodded and threw me against a wall like I was a shirt. I hit it with a bang and slid to the floor.

"Before the night is over, I'm gonna kill you, Harlem. And you can yell as loud as you want to. Ain't no cops going to come save you. They on my payroll. And even if they wasn't, they wouldn't give a fuck about a ho from the projects whose kin to two dope fiends anyway. So If I wanna cut your slutty ass up in little pieces, I will. Or if I choose to set your ass on fire, bitch, I can."

I scooted as close to the corner near the edge of the couch. I was so scared I couldn't stop pissing myself nor stop my teeth from chattering. I believed every word he just said.

Chief left me alone after that. But I knew it would be short-lived. I was dying tonight.

He relaxed in a chair with a cigar in his hand. There was a bottle of Moet resting on the table next to him. He sipped from the bottle between taking puffs from his cigar.

I laid low in the spot I was in, on my side, sore as hell, wiping the blood that was trickling on my face away, hoping they would forget about me. I wasn't so lucky.

"Aye, nigga," Chief gestured toward one of the dudes. "Check this shit out, dawg." He grabbed what looked like a remote, flicked it, and the TV's in the room came on. Chief chuckled out loud. "Now, niggas, this is some must-see fuckin' TV. I'ma bootleg this shit and call it *Harlem Gone Wild*."

I peeked up and saw something very familiar on the screen. It was a shot of the entertainment room and me on the couch with my fingers in my pussy.

"Look at that nasty bitch, y'all."

The dudes stood in their spots and watched my two fingers disappear into my pussy and slide back out again.

"I can't wait until Savior sees this shit, man. I should have known you wasn't shit. Man, look at her ho ass—She enjoyin' that shit. Y'all see that? Look how she playing with herself in front of all them niggas."

The three dudes chuckled.

I was silent. That muthafucka Chief was crazy.

"I can't wait for him to see what kind of trampy ho he was trying to run away with. Aye, y'all check this shit out right here."

The screen then showed the infamous threesome between me, Chief, and that broad.

I squeezed my eyes shut as my naked body was displayed

on all the flat screens. How much further was he gonna humiliate me? The pain in my stomach subsided, so I rolled over completely on it and buried my face in both my hands. I didn't need to see any more of that shit. But I knew the tape wasn't even halfway done.

They had just watched the scene where the girl had kissed and rubbed all over me. There was still the scene where Chief had fucked me from behind while she lay under me and played with my clit while licking my titties. And the coochie-bumping scene, the shower scene. And the fucking Chief and I had done in the shower.

Chief was real at ease watching it. He was obviously not embarrassed by the fact that his naked ass was up on all of the three flat screens.

After the tape ended, he said, "We should have invited some hoes up here. Naw, what am I talking about? We got a ho here, a real fine one too, matter a fact, y'all." Chief rose from his chair and came toward me.

"No, Chief," I pleaded, holding my hands out.

He ignored me and began tearing my clothes off. "Harlem, didn't Savior tell you I said I wanted to fuck you one last time before I killed you? I wasn't joking."

Since I was going to die anyway I figured why not go out in a hail of fucking bullets. I fought him with the little strength I had left. I tried to kick him in his dick, which he already had hanging out the crotch of his pants.

He turned to his boys who were crowding around us. "Y'all can get some too. But if I were you I might use a hat, y'all. The bitch may have something. She out there like that."

He turned his back to me, and I managed to pull away and was crawling in the opposite direction. He grabbed me and straddled my body with his.

I yanked his hair and managed to scratch him in the face.

He got so pissed, he punched me in the side of my head. "Bitch, stop playing."

After that, I don't know if Chief got some or not. I really couldn't tell, because the punch knocked my ass right out.

It was déjà vu when my eyes opened back up. Only, I wasn't in my blow-up mattress in the projects.

My clothes were yanked off of me, and the next thing I saw was Chief unwrapping a condom and sliding it over his dick. I guess he was serious about not trusting my pussy now. He got back on top of me, and it was like old times. He placed his hand in my face and forced his dick into my pussy. "Hold her legs," he commanded.

One nigga grabbed one of my legs.

As he pounded his dick into my pussy, I looked the other way, non-responsive.

"Moan, bitch."

I wouldn't.

"Moan!"

Fuck you!

"Bitch, you gettin' kind of hard to please. I know how to take care of that."

He bit one of my nipples until my skin opened up and I started bleeding. I screamed in agony then.

"Yeah, bitch, that's what I thought."

Chief moaned and closed his eyes as he continued to fuck my dry pussy like it was the best feeling in the world as I lay there limp. He speeded up his pumping and all of a sudden said, "Aye, y'all get a good look at this." He pulled out his dick, slid off he condom, pumped his dick, and let the cum spill all over me like he did the night of my party.

"*Skeet, skeet, skeet,*" he said as it covered me.

I closed my eyes. How can I describe how it felt? I was pretty much numb. But the party was far from being over.

When I felt myself going out of it, I was awakened by Chief, who took a Hennessy bottle and poured it all over my face, washing the cum away.

"You know what we never got to do, Harlem?" Chief stared down in my face.

Weakly I shook my head. All the other dudes were hovering over me, waiting to get their turn.

"I never got to get in that ass. Well, tonight's the night."

No!

He flipped my body around so my ass was up in the air and I was on my knees. I heard him fumbling behind me. He was putting a new condom on. Then he gripped my hips in his hands and rammed his dick into my ass.

My mouth shot open, but the pain was so intense, I couldn't even scream. There was no easing his way in. He slammed his shit into me. He slid it out and struck my asshole again. I gasped as I felt my skin ripping.

"How it feel, Harlem? You gettin' better dick from Savior? Huh? So now after all this time you too good for mine? Shit, maybe your pussy is but your ass." He laughed and thrust himself forward. "Your ass *not.*"

I gave no reply.

Chief's boy, breathing heavily, pushed the camera all up in my face.

My eyes rolled in the back of my head, and I lost focus again. Everything looked like a blur. But when he started pumping into me faster and harder than before, my focus came back into view.

I gripped the edge of the bar, and my head was knocking back and forth from all the thrusts. My ass felt like it was being stabbed by a sharp object, the pain pulsating through me.

And Chief couldn't get enough of it. His hands pressed so hard into my butt cheeks, I could feel his nails breaking my skin.

Still, I didn't say nothing. Just waited until this shit was over. And for the second time in my life, I was craving death.

I watched Chief rise, put his dick back in his pants, and zip them. "Okay. I'm done. Who want dibs on this pussy and ass, man?"

I lay on my side and felt a mixture of cum and blood seep out of my ass. My thighs were sore from them being up in the air, and I still had three more niggas to go before this was over.

Chief told the dude who had helped him hold my leg, "Since you been doin' all the work, you can go next."

I watched the dude take a condom from Chief and approach me. He had an excited look in his eyes, like fucking me was a dream come true. Like sticking his dick in my pussy was like going to Disneyland.

He smirked down at me and started to unbuckle his belt.

Chief sat back down at his table and started downing his bottle of Moet. "Damn, Harlem, you sure know how to work a nigga!"

The dude made another step toward me and kneeled between my legs, his dick poking out and wrapped in a condom.

I closed my eyes, too weak and tired to fight him. And it wouldn't have made a difference anyway. These niggas were getting my pussy. I would just have to block it out of my mind. Just pretend I was asleep and having a nightmare.

He slid my legs open wide and pressed his dick against my hairline about to enter me. His eyes were closed as if he already knew what it was going to feel like. They remained closed, which is why he had a hard time finding my hole.

But when a window busted and some niggas came busting in the room, his eyes popped open instantly, and he left me lying on the floor naked.

I slipped my pants on and did the best I could with my ripped shirt. Then, quickly, I scooted completely behind the bar and peeked over to get a view of the dudes. There were two of them, and they had guns, just like all Chief's men had guns.

And everybody faced each other with guns drawn and pointing all over the place.

Chapter 32

"What the fuck is this, niggas? Y'all know who the fuck I am? I know y'all not trying to rob me!" Chief stood from the chair and pulled out his gat.

The other one hadn't even bothered to get his fly closed. He was looking wild-eyed at the intruders and pointing his gun at anything that flinched.

"Like *you* robbed me."

All the heads shot toward the voice at the door.

I breathed a sigh of relief as Stuckey stood in a doorway for a second, then walked in slowly, aiming his gat at Chief and stood next to the dudes who were facing Chief and his men.

When Chief shook his head and lowered his gun, all his niggas lowered theirs as well.

Stuckey indicated to his boys to lower theirs.

"Stuckey, what the fuck you want now?"

"I hired somebody to kill you in exactly four hours, but I thought the shit is a waste of dough when I can do the shit myself. And I don't give a fuck who is here. I warned you what I was gonna do if your monkey ass got too ambitious and tried to take over Rickerson Village, and you ignored that warning. So it's on now. You got two things I want, Chief—my streets and my seed."

Chief narrowed his eyes to slits. "Nigga, what? Your seed?" He turned around and looked at the men behind him. "What the fuck he talkin' about?" He turned back around. "You want a blunt, Stuckey? 'Cause prison made your ass fuckin' coo-coo, man."

"Harlem is my daughter, nigga, and you been fucking her and abusing her, you sick muthafucka. Savior told me you kidnapped her too. I'm getting her back, and you gonna die."

Chief shook his head and laughed in disbelief. "Ain't this some soap opera shit!" He spun around in a circle, his arms wide, before turning back to face Stuckey. "Harlem is your daughter?

"Yeah, muthafucka, and you betta turn her ova."

"Well, I'll tell you what, man, I ain't turning her ass over. Your daughter got some good-ass pussy." Chief cupped his balls and shook them. "And she about to make a whole lot of money for me—"

Bam!

My daddy fired his shit! It made a loud popping sound that exploded in my ears so loud I screamed. Smoke instantly filled the room. Another bullet pierced one of the flat screens, making it explode. Within seconds shots were fired all over the room. All the TV screens busted and exploded, the walls were covered in bullets, tables and chairs were toppling over, and shit was flying. The niggas acted like they were on a mission, and kept shooting at one another.

I squinted and saw Chief fire a shot that went through a

window and shattered the glass. A guy from Chief's crew screamed as a bullet came out of nowhere and pierced him in his chest. Blood colored his shirt as he flew backwards.

Chief's crew started firing more rapidly, but the bullets continued to spray all over the place, on the huge stereo system with the expensive speakers along the walls, and the DJ stand. Bullets penetrated the wall above, bringing down clouds of plaster all over me.

I screamed again over the horrifying blasts and curled my body into a ball as I shielded my head with my arms. A body fell heavily beside me, dead, and I scooted back from it, trying to avoid the growing pool of dark red blood spreading toward me across the floor.

As gun smoke filled my lungs, I tried to cough into my hands, but I wanted to keep my arms over my head, praying a bullet wouldn't hit me or flying glass cut me in the face. The bottles of alcohol on top of the counter flew every which way, flopped over, rolled off, and exploded in small pieces when they hit the floor, liquor spewing out and splattering everywhere.

I was in a panic. Should I try to run and get out of there? I wiped plaster from my eyes and took another quick peek. A nigga was struggling to stand after several bullets from Stuckey's boys ripped his body. Blood gurgled from his mouth, and he dropped to the ground before he could fire another shot.

Out of the corner of my eye, I saw a bullet managed to strike Chief in his leg and shoulder. Despite my terror, that shit was encouraging. I clenched my fists and prayed another bullet would hit him. In his moment of weakness I picked up the somewhat intact bottle and threw it in his direction. I missed. I ducked back down, so he wouldn't see I was the one who threw it. I wanted to do more, but I was scared he'd catch me.

One of Stuckey's boys went down when a shot hit him in his head. He was leaning back against the DJ stand, fighting the hell out of death as blood escaped from his mouth. He struggled to rise, only to slide back down and stay slumped over.

I gripped my arms tighter around my head, blocking out all the flying shit. My ass was hurting, and my titty was sore from where Chief had bitten me. And while the shooting had only been on for not half a minute, I felt like I was gonna go fucking crazy from the horror taking place on the other side of the counter. The noise was loud, and both my ears were ringing.

There was a brief lull in the firing and I looked up again, just in time to see one of Stuckey's boys take out Chief's third man. He would have been the last one standing, until the one lying on the ground raised his gun and struck him in his chest. The bullet ricocheted through him and hit Stuckey in his shoulder, making his body spin around and his voice howl. It weakened him, and he crouched down on one knee as blood poured from the wound.

Chief saw it and took the opportunity to fire at least six more times at Stuckey, but only hit him once. But the one shot was fatal. I watched horrified as Stuckey dropped to the floor on his other knee. Then he slumped on his side and stayed motionless.

And for a moment, the only person that was standing was Chief. Which scared the shit out of me. How could he be the last muthafucka standing? I crouched again behind the bar, my heart beating wildly. The puddle of blood from the dead body had reached me, and when I lost my balance on the balls of my feet, I stuck a hand down in the red liquid to keep from falling, my other hand covering my mouth for fear that Chief might hear my crying.

Just then, a rapid series of bullets was fired from the doorway and got closer as the shooter entered. I stood up in a half-crouch but I couldn't make out who came in. The room was dark to begin with, and many of the lights had been shot out as well.

Not far from me, Chief jerked left and right as bullets hit him, and the remaining windows that weren't broken were broke now as glass continued to cascade on the floor.

I screamed again and felt my ears ringing, knowing, just knowing, one of those bullets was for me. I ducked completely down again and didn't raise my head again for fear the shooter would see me and blast my ass away.

Then it was real quiet.

All of the men in the room lay dead. It was the craziest shit I had ever seen. Chief was dead. Stuckey was dead. I looked, horrified, at the dead man lying on the floor next to me covered in broken glass and splintered wood, alcohol dripping from the counter.

Plaster continued to sprinkle over us, and in the angled light, I could see it covering the body and the pool of blood. When I took a deep breath, I inhaled the plaster and nearly coughed. I covered my mouth, still wondering if I was the next to be killed.

"Harlem? Oh shit, Harlem!"

I knew that voice. I lifted my head and smiled with joy. I tried to stand, but once I got to my feet, I fell right back down. "Savior! I'm over here."

The smoke in the room had me coughing again, and I could barely see him through the haze.

Savior stepped over the dead bodies and limped his way

over to me, grimacing in pain with each step he took. He looked pissed when he saw how bad I looked.

I wanted to freak out too. I had just seen seven men murdered. "Let's get out of here, Savior."

He helped me to my feet, and I limped alongside him. He took small and slow steps so I could keep up with him. We went around the bodies, avoiding the blood that was all over the floor.

When we made it halfway to the door, I heard my name called and a chill ran up my back. We turned just in time to see Chief raise his gun and aim it at me.

Savior pushed me out of the way and claimed the bullet with his body.

I screamed as it ripped into him and he fell to the floor. "Savior!"

Chief aimed his gun at me again.

I froze when he cocked it.

He fired, but it made a clicking sound—the chamber was empty.

I quickly inspected Savior's wound. It was nowhere vital, just in his shoulder, but he was bleeding pretty badly. His heart was still beating, but he couldn't move. I kissed him on his mouth.

He mumbled, "I'm okay. But you gonna have to save us this time, Harlem. Get that muthafucka."

He slipped something heavy in my hands—a knife— and in that moment I knew enough was enough.

Disregarding my tears and the soreness in my body, I tucked the knife in the waistband of my pants and, with fear running in my chest, I rose up to face Chief, who was struggling to stand because of the shot that wounded him in one leg and another shot that had mangled his right arm. He had holes in his side and shoulder too where Savior's shots had hit him, but he acted like they were nothing more than flesh wounds.

As I faced him defiantly, he took one look at me and laughed. "Oh, you wanna fight me, Harlem? Is that it? Okay, you crazy bitch, I'll tell you what—I'll do this shit without a weapon." He tossed his gun aside.

Coldly, I said, "Come on, Chief." I stood up as upright as I could in order to at least reach his neck.

He staggered toward me and chuckled.

I stepped in and swung my fist, hitting him in his jaw.

He just laughed and slapped me across my face, causing me to almost fall.

I ignored the sting that rushed to my face and kept my balance.

"What you gonna do now, Harlem?"

Adrenaline pumping through me and making me forget about the pain I was feeling, I sidestepped his next swing, refusing to give up, leapt and connected with his nose. "This is what, you punk muthafucka!"

He howled and swung wildly at me.

"This is for all the fucking times you put your damn hands on me!" I kicked him in his fucking nuts.

He screamed and lashed out again, this time catching my shoulder and smacking me to the ground. Shaking his head, he turned his back on me for a moment, rubbing his eye with one hand and holding his nuts in the other.

I jumped up quickly and moved backwards on the tip of my toes so I wasn't getting too close to him and he couldn't reach out and grab me again. When the back of my legs bumped into something sturdy, I bent back and reached with one hand, keeping my eyes on him and feeling around. It was a heavy vase. I grabbed it and swung it with all my might, connecting with the back of his head with a loud thud.

"That's for making me go on them damn drug runs!"

He grunted, hunched over in pain. "Bitch."

I had to be quick as fuck on my feet because I knew Chief could crush me with one hand.

After shaking his head for a couple of seconds he lurched after me, but he could only see out of one eye, the other one was bleeding and leaking a fluid. He kept trying to wipe it all away, and there was blood flowing out the back of his head.

I probably didn't look much better myself. Every part of my body was in pain. I had several bruises, and my asshole was still bleeding. But I wasn't going to stop until the nigga was dead.

Despite the ache in my joints, and the combination of sweat and blood dripping down my face, I climbed up on a table to reach his height, and before he could swing on me, I bashed his other eye and socked him in the chest, knocking the wind out of him. "That's for throwing me out in the street!"

I jumped on him and continued to punch him in the face with my fist, causing his skin to tear and bleed. "This is for throwing me in the pool and leaving me in there to drown!"

When I tried to jump down, he grabbed my forearms then quickly grabbed my throat with both his hands. "You had your fun, bitch, but now I'm going to kill you for betraying me." His hands squeezed tighter, and he started choking me.

I twisted my body and struggled, hoping he would get weak and drop me. When it didn't work and his hold became stronger, I head butted Chief in his nose over and over until I saw blood pour from it. He still wouldn't release me, so I took my middle finger and as hard as I could, dug my nail into the bullet wound on his arm.

He yelled at that and released his hold on me.

I fell down painfully onto my back and was surprised to see him lunging at me again, with murder in his eyes.

I reached in my waistband for the knife Savior had handed me. "And this is just because I can't stand your evil, black-hearted ass!" I aimed it high, hiding it slightly.

As soon as he rushed toward me, I drove it with as much force as I could into his chest. Then as he froze, I leaned back, slid it out, and slammed it back into his chest as deep as it would go, till all I saw was the handle, the whole while screaming.

As blood poured out like red wine from the gaping hole, he collapsed on his knees, blood oozing from his lips. His eyes got glassy, and he fell backwards, powerless to stop my attack.

As he lay there shaking, I kneeled over him and continued to stab him all over chest as far in as I could, still screaming in rage. His head was twitching back and forth, but nothing else on his body was moving.

Then all of a sudden the twitching stopped. Chief was dead. Hell, I killed him. Me. Lil' ol' Harlem.

My heart was pounding in my chest as I checked to make sure nothing was moving on his ass. As I stared at his lifeless body laying in that pool of blood that continued to ooze out of his body. He didn't look so powerful or scary anymore.

Then, for the first time since the shootout, I looked down at my dead father. I wished things could have been different. I wish that I had really gotten the chance to know him. Maybe have a relationship, even. We were both put in a position that prevented that. But like I had learned, you can't change the past. You can only hope and work toward a better future. And that's what I was on my way to.

I stumbled over to Savior. "Come on, baby." I helped him to his feet.

Funny how crisis situations could give a woman so much strength.

Once he was up and my body supported half of his, we walked out of that place, Chief no longer a threat to us.

Epilogue

I held onto Savior as we entered the concourse at Colorado Springs Airport. We had just checked in our bags. We always traveled light because wherever we went we always wanted to bring back souvenirs. So when we sat and reminisced over those moments we had something to look at.

"Baby," I said, pulling my hand away, "I have to pee before we get on the plane. The last place I wanna be is on the toilet when the plane is in the air."

He grabbed it back. "I'm going in with you."

I laughed. "Savior, stop playing."

"I'm not. I don't want to let you out of my sight ever again."

I laughed. He was always this way when we went somewhere, and I didn't mind one bit.

Those words brought me back to all that had gone down this past year. Losing my mother, being brutalized by a man who I thought was my father, being victimized by

Chief, losing the man who was my real father, almost losing Savior twice, and having to take a man's life. In the
midst off all I had been through, Savior said the thing he
admired about me the most was my spirit. He said my
spirit wasn't like any other he'd ever seen, and that I had
way too much damn courage and way too much forgiveness in me. But he said having way too much was not a bad
thing at all.

Well, I needed way too much of both of those for my
final move in Cali. I had decided to make a trip to Cedar
Avenue in Compton to see my father before we headed to
Colorado.

I went to the front desk of the establishment and waited
patiently as the nurse talked into the phone. Behind her I
could see a room through glass windows. The people inside were watching TV, playing ping-pong, or reading. I
scanned the rec room for sight of my father. None of the
faces in there looked familiar to me. I thought maybe he
was in his room, or outside.

"Can I help you, young lady?"

I smiled. "Yes. I'm looking for Earl Scott."

The nurse narrowed her eyes at me. "And you are?"

I held on to Savior's hand tightly. "His dau—um, his
niece. Harlem Scott."

She stared at me for a long moment. "You weren't noti-
fied about Mr. Scott's departure?"

"Departure?"

The corners of her cheeks rose in a half-smile, and she
looked down briefly before saying. "You really don't know,
do you, dear? Mr. Scott left for home about a week ago.
Shortly after, because the hospital didn't know who to
contact, they contacted us and said that he was taken to
the hospital. He had overdosed and went into cardiac ar-
rest. The last time we checked, he was still there.

"We have an open-door policy. He is allowed to leave on his own recognizance and is allowed to come back when he's ready. We really liked your father. In the time he was here, he made such great progress. But the addiction he had was just too strong for him to fight it. He said nice things about you too."

She scribbled an address down on a piece of paper and handed it to me. "This is the location of the hospital. He's on the fifth floor in intensive care. The last time I checked he still hadn't pulled out, but with God there's always hope."

"Thank you, ma'am." I took the paper from her and walked away with tears in my eyes, Savior rubbing my back all the way to the car.

I guess it was too much to hope Earl would finally get his life together.

"Take me to the hospital." I handed Savior the paper with the address.

I felt like I was being stabbed with pain when I saw the man all my life I thought was my father in that hospital bed hooked up to all those machines. If it wasn't for Savor holding my body halfway up, I would have collapsed on the floor. See, it was one of them things where as much as I hated him, I loved him all the more, 'cause he and my mama were all I'd ever known. The only family I ever had.

"Harlem, you gonna be okay?"

I wiped tears away and nodded. "Yeah. You can wait for me outside, Savior."

He released me and slipped out the door, leaving me alone.

I turned back to Earl. He wasn't moving an inch. His eyes were closed, and I didn't know whether the machine was making his heart pump or if it was doing the shit on it's own.

Some people say even if a person is brain-dead they can hear you. Some people even say sometimes a loved one's voice can bring someone out of a coma. I didn't know if I really bought the shit, but I tried.

The sound of the machine's beeping put my nerves on edge as I approached the bed slowly and peered down at his face. Nothing.

"It's me. It's Harlem. To be honest this is the last place I ever expected you to be. I met Stuckey, and he told me what the deal is. He said you were trying to get your life together. And now you're here." I grabbed one of his hands in mine. "And I know it seems like you messed up, but it's not too late for you to try again. It ain't ever too late. Stuckey said you felt bad about what happened in the projects. When you . . ." I paused, unable to get the words out.

"If you still stressing over what you did to me, don't worry about it. It's over." I sobbed on the words. "It took a lot for me to get to this point, but I forgive you. I realized I can't be at peace with you and even myself if I don't get past this, and this is my way of doing that. You can have your redemption. And I hope you come out of this. I hope everything works out for you."

I backed away from the bed, from Earl and the heart monitor with the slow beat, and sat in a chair and began to cry. I cried until no sound came out, until my knees balled up in my chest, and I let out a sob. I needed to get this out.

Ten minutes later, I kissed his cheek and walked out of the hospital. He never moved an inch.

Shortly after that, I found out some crazy news. It turns out we didn't need a damn dime from Chief.

We had just came back home from the hospital when someone came knocking on Savior's door for me, a man in a suit who I didn't recognize. I was about to pull my gat out of my bra, but he seemed harmless.

The man said, "Are you Harlem Scott?"

I nodded.

He handed me a paper with an address on it. "You need to be there on the thirtieth at twelve noon for the reading of the will of Blake Stuckey Scott."

Needless to say, I was about to be surprised as fuck.

It turned out that Stuckey had left me all his money. And I'm not talking no chump change. I'm talking about one million, two hundred fifty thousand dollars, and twenty-five cents. Not to mention the property he had left. And the shit was all mine!

How could I have known I would have such good luck? Maybe God did love me after all. Although I talked shit, deep down I always knew he loved me.

I was surprised he didn't leave anything to his brother. But it wouldn't have mattered if he did. I found out, shortly after the reading of the will, that the man I grew up thinking was my biological father, Earl, had died in that hospital of the drug overdose. And even though I know now that he wasn't really my father, it still hurt and probably always will. But I was happy I had made my peace with him.

Then Savior and I took a drive to Ontario to visit Gladys and let her know Chief was gone for good. I even gave her the deed to Stuckey's business, hoping she could do something with it. I would never forget her for risking her life for me. I would be forever grateful.

She hugged me so hard, I couldn't breathe, and kissed

my face so many times, there was slobber all over it, but I didn't mind. Gladys will always be all right by me. She said she was going to turn the business into a soul food restaurant and that Savior and I could eat there for free.

I just laughed. "Gladys, you crazy as hell."

We sold Stuckey's house and got some extra dough for it. Savior and I decided to relocate anyway, despite Chief being gone. There was nothing more in LA to see or do. No matter how pretty Cali was, and no matter how much people talked about it being the place to be, the land of the wealthy and of movie stars, it would always be tainted to me. I had much too much history there, which I wanted to put behind me.

We were able to get a lawyer and get that stupid shit expunged from his records, and we went ahead and moved to Colorado, although I would have preferred Rome.

We didn't rush into anything stupid like marriage or having kids. Although I wanted to have a child, I figured if Savior was my true soul mate, like I felt in my heart he was, those things would happen later on. Right now, I wanted to live my life.

I started college like I'd always dreamed, majoring in social work, just like that girl I'd met at my birthday party when I was with Chief. I still wanted to be a social worker and help out as many kids as I could.

And, yes, I enrolled in nearly all the clubs on campus. I was a social butterfly, dancing at the step shows, marching for children's rights, and sitting in on ciphers.

Savior enrolled in school too. He was considering trying out for the baseball team at school, or maybe even coaching.

I told him both were good ideas, because I knew he could do whatever he wanted to do. We both could. There was nothing holding us back now.

Every day with Savior was a pure blessing. Of course, we had our problems. Everybody did. Sometimes he didn't put his clothes away, or cap the toothpaste, or he left the fucking toilet seat up so I always damn near fell in. But these things weren't half as bad as the shit I had to deal with when I lived with Chief.

Savior never raised his voice at me, called me out, or hit me, and when we made love, it was so gentle, I always ended up purring when we were done. He treated me better than I ever thought I could be treated or deserved to be treated.

He told me, "Get used to it."

Eventually I began to see my worth. It was a lot higher than I thought it was.

Savior made me realize all that shit that happened to me, all the shit Chief forced me to do hadn't tainted me in any way. In fact, all it did was make me stronger, to never sweat the small stuff.

When girls at my school stressed about gaining weight or being too fat, I laughed. 'Cause Savior loved the hell out of me and an extra pound or two wasn't gonna change that, or who I was on the inside. It just gave me more cushion.

When the girls worried about failing a class, I would just shake my head. I knew I could always retake it.

One day a girl asked me, "Damn, Harlem, does anything ever stress you out?"

I shook my head. "No, girl. I've had enough stress to last me a lifetime. Life is way too short to worry. I'm living my life."

She sucked her teeth. "Um-hmm. What have you ever had to worry about? Having to balance time between school, all them damn clubs you in, and that fine-ass boyfriend of yours?"

"Something like that."

I kept the real deal to myself. The only people I talked about my issues with were my therapist and Savior. That girl could think whatever she wanted to.

Savior and I tried to live a normal life. We've craved it. We vacationed often, and we'd been back to Vegas to gamble. We'd been to Florida, Texas, and even cold-ass Alaska. Going to all those places made us more knowledgeable about the world, more cultured.

I wished a lot more kids were able to get out of the projects like I did. It would show them there's a whole 'nother world outside those gates.

On this trip, we were going to Rome and staying for a whole month. And I was gonna kill Savior if he didn't crush grapes with me like I'd always dreamed of doing at one of those vineyards.

I still thought about my mom. The one thing I always wanted to ask her before she died was, "Did I make you proud?"

And I wanted to let her know that no matter what she did or how much she failed, I would always love her and see her as the same mama. I guess I'll never know if she was proud of me.

Sometimes, when the house was real quiet and I was alone, if I listened carefully I'd hear her voice. She wasn't fussin 'cause she didn't get no fix, or hassling my daddy for one neither. Nor was she crying. She'd be singing in that beautiful voice of hers:

Just call me angel of the morning
Just touch my cheek before you leave me, baby

The voice was a sign that she was right there with me. And despite all the pain I had been through, the ache her death brought me, all of this happened for a reason. It gave me strength to endure anything that came my way, and a love that nothing can break. And I guess that made everything okay.

about the author

Karen Williams is a native of Long Beach, California. She has a B.A. in Literature and Communications and works as a corrections officer. *Harlem on Lock* is her debut title.

My Little Secret
BY ANNA J.

Coming in September 2008

Ask Yourself

Ask yourself a question . . . have you ever had a session of love making, do you want me? Have you ever been to heaven?
—Raheem DeVaughn

February 9th, 2007

She feels like melted chocolate on my fingertips. The same color from the top of her head to the very tips of her feet. Her nipples are two shades darker than the rest of her, and they make her skin the perfect backdrop against her round breasts. Firm and sweet like two ripe peaches dipped in baker's chocolate. They are a little more than a handful and greatly appreciated. Touching her makes me feel like I've finally found peace on earth, and there is no feeling in the world greater than that.

Right now her eyes are closed and her bottom lip is

tightly tucked between her teeth. From my view point between her wide-spread legs I can see the beginnings of yet another orgasm playing across her angelic face. These are the moments that make it all worthwhile. Her perfectly arched eyebrows go into a deep frown, and her eyelids flutter slightly. When her head falls back I know she's about to explode.

I move up on my knees so that we are pelvis to pelvis. Both of us are dripping wet from the humidity and the situation. Her legs are up on my shoulders, and her hands are cupping my breasts. I can't tell where her skin begins or where mine ends. As I look down at her, and watch her face go through way too many emotions I smile a little bit. She always did love the dick, and since we've been together she's never had to go without it. Especially since the one I have never goes down.

I'm pushing her tool into her soft folds inch by inch as if it were really a part of me, and her body is alive. I say "her tool" because it belongs to her, and I just enjoy using it on her. Her hip-length dreads seem to wrap us in a cocoon of coconut oil and sweat, body heat and moisture, soft moans and tear drops, pleasure and pain until we seemingly burst into an inferno of hot-like-fire ecstasy. Our chocolate skin is searing to the touch and we melt into each other becoming one. I can't tell where hers begins . . . I can't tell where mine ends.

She smiles . . . her eyes are still closed and she's still shaking from the intensity. I take this opportunity to taste her lips, and to lick the salty sweetness from the side of her neck. My hands begin to explore, and my tongue encircles her dark nipples. She arches her back when my full lips close around her nipple and I begin to suck softly as if she's feeding me life from within her soul.

Her hands find their way to my head and become tangled in my soft locks, identical to hers but not as long. I push into her deep, and grind softly against her clit in search of her "j-spot" because it belongs to me, Jada. She speaks my name so soft that I barely heard her. I know she wants me to take what she so willingly gave me, and I want to hear her beg for it.

I start to pull back slowly, and I can feel her body tightening up trying to keep me from moving. One of many soft moans is heard over the low hum of the clock radio that sits next to our bed. I hear slight snatches of Raheem DeVaughn singing about being in heaven, and I'm almost certain he wrote that song for me and my lady.

I open her lips up so that I can have full view of her sensitive pearl. Her body quakes with anticipation from the feel of my warm breath touching it, my mouth just mere inches away. I blow cool air on her stiff clit causing her to tense up briefly, her hands taking hold of my head trying to pull me closer. At this point my mouth is so close to her all I would have to do is twitch my lips to make contact, but I don't . . . I want her to beg for it.

My index finger is making small circles against my own clit, my honey sticky between my legs. The ultimate pleasure is giving pleasure, and I've experienced that on both accounts. My baby can't wait anymore, and her soft pants are turning into low moans. I stick my tongue out, and her clit gladly kisses me back.

Her body responds by releasing a syrupy sweet slickness that I lap up until it's all gone, fucking her with my tongue the way she likes it. I hold her legs up and out to intensify her orgasm because I know she can't handle it that way.

"Does your husband do you like this?" I ask between licks. Before she could answer I wrap my full lips around her clit and suck her into my mouth, swirling my tongue around her hardened bud, causing her body to shake.

Snatching a second toy from the side of the bed, I take one hand to part her lips, and I ease her favorite toy (The Rabbit) inside of her. Wishing that the strap-on I was wearing was a real dick so that I could feel her pulsate, I turn the toy on low at first wanting her to receive the ultimate pleasure. In the dark room the glow in the dark toy is lit brightly, the light disappearing inside of her when I push it all the way in.

The head of the curved toy turns in a slow circle while the pearl beads jump around on the inside, hitting up against her smooth walls during insertion. When I push the toy in she pushes her pelvis up to receive it, my mouth latched on to her clit like a vice. She moans louder, and I kick the toy up a notch to medium, much to her delight. Removing my mouth from her clit I rotate between flicking my wet tongue across it to heat it, and blowing my breath on it to cool it bringing her to yet another screaming orgasm, followed by strings of *"I love you"* and *"Please don't stop."*

Torturing her body slowly, I continue to stimulate her clit while pushing her toy in and out of her on a constant rhythm. When she lifts her legs to her chest I take the opportunity to let the ears on the rabbit toy that we are using do their job on her clit while my tongue find their way to her chocolate ass. I bite one cheek at a time replacing it with wet kisses, afterwards sliding my tongue in between to taste her there. Her body squirming underneath me lets me know I've hit the jackpot, and I fuck her with my tongue there also.

She's moaning, telling me in a loud whisper that she can't take it anymore. That's my cue to turn the toy up high. The buzzing from the toy matches that of the radio, and with her moans and my pants mixed in we sound like a well-rehearsed orchestra singing a symphony of passion.

I allow her to buck against my face while I keep up with the rhythm of the toy, her juice oozing out the sides and forming a puddle under her ass. I'm loving it.

She moans and shakes until the feeling in the pit of her stomach resides and she is able to breathe at a normal rate. My lips taste salty/sweet from kissing her body while she tries to get her head together, rubbing the sides of my body up and down in a lazy motion.

Valentine's Day is fast approaching and I have a wonderful evening planned for the two of us. She already promised me that her husband wouldn't be an issue because he'll be out of town that weekend, and besides all that they haven't celebrated Cupid's day since the year after they were married so I didn't even think twice about it. After seven years it should be over for them anyway.

"It's your turn now," she says to me in a husky lust filled voice, and I can't wait for her to take control.

The ultimate pleasure is giving pleasure . . . and man does it feel good both ways. She starts by rubbing her oil-slicked hands over the front of my body, taking extra time around my sensitive nipples before bringing her hands down across my flat stomach. I've since then removed the strap-on dildo, and am completely naked under her hands.

I can still feel her sweat on my skin, and I can still taste her on my lips. Closing my eyes I enjoy the sensual massage that I'm being treated to. After two years of us making love it's still good and gets better every time.

She likes to take her time covering every inch of my body, and I enjoy letting her. She skips past my love box, and starts at my feet, massaging my legs from the toes up. When she gets to my pleasure point her fingertips graze the smooth, hairless skin there, quickly teasing me before she heads back down and does the same thing with my other limb. My legs are spread apart and lying flat on the bed with her in between, relaxing my body with ease. A cool breeze from the cracked window blows across the room every so often, caressing my erect nipples, making them harder than before until her hands warm them back up again.

She knows when I can't take anymore and she rubs and caresses me until I am begging her to kiss my lips. I can see her smile through half-closed eyelids, and she does what I requested. Dipping her head down between my legs, she kisses my lips just as I asked, using her tongue to part them so that she can taste my clit. My body goes into mini-convulsions on contact, and I am fighting a battle to not cum that I never win.

"Valentine's Day belongs to us right?" I ask her again between moans. I need her to be here. V-Day is for lovers, and her and her husband haven't been that in ages. I deserve it . . . I deserve her. I just don't want this to be a repeat of Christmas or New Years Eve.

"Yes, it's yours," she says between kisses on my thigh and sticking her tongue inside of me. Two of her fingers have found their way inside of my tight walls, and my pelvic area automatically bounces up and down on her hand as my orgasm approaches.

"Tell me you love me," I say to her as my breathing becomes raspy. Fire is spreading across my legs and working its way up to the pit of my stomach. I need her to tell me before I explode.

"I love you," she says and at the moment she places her tongue in my slit, I release my honey all over her tongue.

It feels like I am on the Tea Cup ride at the amusement park as my orgasm jerks my body uncontrollably and it feels like the room is spinning. She is sucking and slurping my clit while the weight of her body holds the bottom half of me captive. I'm practically screaming and begging her to stop, and just when I think I'm about to check out of here she lets my clit go.

I take a few more minutes to get my head together, allowing her to pull me into her and rub my back. Moments like this make it all worthwhile. We lay like that for a while longer listening to each other breathe, and much to my dismay she slides my head from where it was resting on her arm and gets up out of the bed.

I don't say a word. I just lie on the bed and watch her get dressed. I swear everything she does is so graceful, like there's a rhythm riding behind it. Pretty soon she is dressed and standing beside the bed looking down at me. She smiles and I smile back, not worried because she promised me our lover's day, and that's only a week away.

"So, Valentine's Day belongs to me, right?" I ask her again just to be certain.

"Yes, it belongs to you."

We kiss one last time, and I can still taste my honey on her lips. She already knows the routine, locking the bottom lock behind her. Just thinking about her makes me so horny, and I pick up her favorite toy to finish the job. Five more days, and it'll be on again.

NOW AVAILABLE FROM

COMING SOON FROM

Q-BORO
BOOKS

FEBRUARY 2008
1-933967-31-5

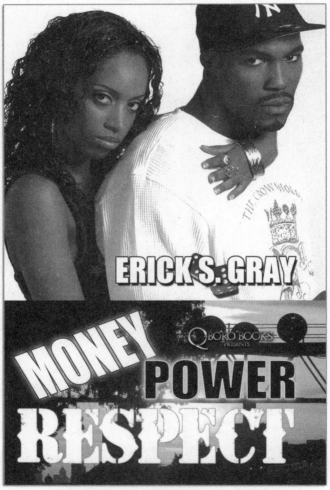